Arms of Love

Also by Kelly Long

Arms of Love

Kelly Long

THOMAS NELSON
Since 1798

NASHVILLE   DALLAS   MEXICO CITY   RIO DE JANEIRO

Published in Nashville, Tennessee, by Thomas Nelson. Thomas Nelson is a registered trademark of Thomas Nelson, Inc.

Thomas Nelson, Inc., titles may be purchased in bulk for educational, business, fund-raising, or sales promotional use. For information, please e-mail SpecialMarkets@ThomasNelson.com.

Scripture quotations are from the King James Version of the Bible, and from the NEW AMERICAN STANDARD BIBLE®, © The Lockman Foundation 1960, 1962, 1963, 1968, 1971, 1972, 1973, 1975, 1977, 1995. Used by permission.

Library of Congress Cataloging-in-Publication Data

Long, Kelly.
  Arms of love / Kelly Long.
    p. cm. — (Arms of love; 1)
  ISBN 978-1-4016-8496-9 (trade paper)
  1. Amish—Fiction. I. Title.
  PS3612.O497A89 2012
  813'.6—dc23   2011051153

Printed in the United States of America

12 13 14 15 16 QG 5 4 3 2

For Dad and Gil

And for Ward

Glossary

ach – oh

broomaing – roaring

bruder – brother

buwe – boy

daed – dad

danki – thank you

Derr Herr – the Lord

dobbelstein – fine checked fabric

dochder – daughter

Englisch – not Amish

fater – father

fees wesha – foot washing

freeda – peace

gens – geese

glaws – glass

gorda – garden

Gott – God

grossmuder – grandmother

gut – good

hartz – heart

hausfrau – housewife

herr – sir

kesselhous – baking house

kinner – children

knepp – traditional Amish fare

kraut – cabbage

kumme – come

mamm – mother

mawd – maid

mei – my

messer – knife

milch – milk

narrish – crazy

nee – no

reebs – beets

schnitz – traditional Amish fare

schwester – sister

sei se gut – please

sohn – son

tzellar – cellar

wunderbarr – wonderful

ya – yes

Author's Note

Post-traumatic stress disorder can affect veterans, police officers, and anyone who has seen or been involved in a potentially violent event or trauma. Sometimes survivors, especially children, will block out the event from their minds but can still experience nightmares, stress, and anger. It may take years before a survivor can confront or admit the event and its effects in life.

This book is respectfully dedicated to all of those who struggle with PTSD, especially my father-in-law, who was a "tunnel rat" in Vietnam, and my brother, who served valiantly for seven years as a police officer, lost his partner on duty, and still fights for recovery and peace . . .

Chapter 1

March 1777
Lancaster, Pennsylvania

I am going to die with the birth of this child, Adam."

Twenty-one-year-old Adam Wyse stared at the older woman, his mother's best friend and the mother of the girl he loved. He had little doings with the ways of women and understood the bearing of offspring better in terms of the horses he raised. But there was something calm and certain about the statement Mary Yoder had made, and he sought to turn her from such premonitions.

"You are anxious, 'tis all, as any . . . woman would be near her time." He had almost said *mare*. He cast about the room in hopes that inspiration would come to him. Instead, the bright sun of spring beguiled through the windowpanes. He longed to be outside, holding hands with Lena.

"Adam. This is not the fancy of some nervous horse; I have given birth to three other *kinner* with no problem. But this time—well, the Lord has revealed it to my heart, and I must make preparations now, especially with Samuel absent."

The past three weeks had been a hard time for the Yoder family.

Samuel Yoder had been hauled off to jail after refusing to give up his last cow to the Patriots' cause of revolution, and there was no telling when he would be released.

Adam chafed a bit under Mary's scrutiny and tried to look anywhere but at the mound of bedclothes covering her abdomen. "Would you like me to send Lena to you?"

"*Nee*. I would like you to make a dying woman a promise."

"Mary . . ."

"A promise, Adam. But some questions first, if you will?"

He nodded, resigned. "Of course, but I—"

"*Gut*. Tell me, have you kissed my daughter?"

"What?"

"You heard me well."

"*Nee* . . . Of course not."

Mary laughed. "But not for lack of wanting, eh?"

He felt himself flush like some green lad, knowing he had held himself off like a wolf on a leash for want of kissing Lena in the past, convicted by her youth and delicacy.

"I wanted," he said, unable to keep the roughness from his tone.

She reached to pat his hand. "As is normal. But I am glad that your relationship has not progressed that far—it will make things easier later."

"Later?" he asked, but she was on to another question.

"I know how your *fater* abuses you, Adam. I have seen the scars on your back. Why have you not left his home?"

"I—" He broke off in confusion. He'd never been confronted by the truth of his private life in so forceful a manner, even by Lena. It was not so simple a question to answer. His father did see fit to discipline him harshly, careful not to "spare the rod," but he hadn't actually beaten Adam in several years. It was more torturous games of the mind now.

"Well?"

He swallowed hard. "I stay because . . . because I am bound there. I cannot easily go out into the world without my father's blessing, and—well, perhaps I deserve what I get from him."

Mary snorted. "You deserve to be hurt, Adam? And your *mamm* standing by, helplessly? She can do nothing. She is a victim too, as is Isaac." She covered his hand with her own.

He thumbed the contours of her fingers and shook his head, thinking of his older brother. "Not Isaac . . . He gets away from it somehow. He has escaped."

"*Nee,* 'tis not true. He's lost himself in his own world, in his books and studies and animals, but he won't walk away free. No one who lives in that house will ever be free."

Adam felt unexpected tears burn at the back of his eyes. He swallowed hard. "*Ya,* there's truth in that."

"I believe that no one should have to live under such oppression of the spirit."

He smiled then. "You sound like a Patriot."

He was surprised when a thoughtful look crossed her face. "Well, maybe I am."

"What?" No Amish person would ever admit to supporting the cause of the Revolution—except for a few men, mostly young, who had done so outright by enlisting . . . as Adam himself had secretly considered. But to hear a woman, a neighbor he had known all his life, speak in such a way was confusing, especially with her husband jailed.

"*Ach,* do not worry, Adam. I am not being unfaithful about Samuel's plight. But there is in me something that believes there are things worth fighting for. Do you agree?"

He thought about the bondage his mother was in to his father. "*Ya,* some things."

"Is my *dochder* one of those things, Adam?"

He met her eyes, confused. "Lena? I know 'twill sound forthright, but she loves me true, and I her."

"*Ya* . . . this is so."

"Then why would I have to fight for her?"

Mary withdrew her hand from his to rub absently at her belly. "Because of the promise I mentioned before."

"I will do whatever you ask."

She looked at him, her eyes the bright turquoise blue of Lena's own. "Will you, Adam?"

"If it is within my power, and with the Lord's grace, *ya*."

She smiled faintly. "Grace? *Ya*, that you will need . . . for I ask you to promise, Adam Wyse, to give up Lena's love, to give her up, until you are free from your *fater's* rule and are ready to build a new and free life for the two of you. I cannot die knowing that you would take her to your home as our custom decrees."

"Of course I would take her to my home; it is our way. But *Fater* would never harm her."

"And what of your *kinner*, Adam? Can you be so sure? What of your sons? And, Adam, it hurts me to speak thus, but do you trust yourself? What if you gave into a rage like your father's?"

"Mary, I would never—"

"Perhaps I overstep . . . but I would still have your promise."

Inwardly Adam reeled as though he had been struck; he could not fathom the request. "I can build a new home—away from my father's house—farther out into the community."

"If this were your intent, you would have done so by now."

He bowed his head and felt a thickness in his throat. "You ask too much."

"With the Lord's grace, Adam . . . remember? You said that."

"But I . . ." He stopped. He would not give in to the sob that beckoned from the depths of his heart. Give up Lena? How would he even go about it? He could not imagine breathing without her, let alone living out a life until he could do what Mary asked.

"My time is short, Adam. Do you promise?"

He stared at her. Was she mad? He was a man of his word, but Mary was near her time and probably not thinking clearly. He could promise and give her the comfort she wanted, and then they could resolve things later.

He took her hand. "I do so promise, Mary Yoder."

She sighed, a restless, broken sound. "*Gut. Danki*, Adam. You will see . . . Your arms will be full of love again before long."

He nodded, watched as she drifted off to sleep, and then left the quiet room, deep in thought.

<hr>

"What did *Mamm* want?"

Lena Yoder looked up into the face of her beloved and couldn't help but think how beautiful he was. His dark hair hung heavy to his shoulders, and the strong bones of his face were the perfect frame for his strange golden eyes.

He looked down at her now as they stood in the early garden and gently ran the back of his hand across her cheek. She shivered in delight, longing to lean into his touch.

"She wanted to talk, 'tis all."

Lena ignored the prick of conscience that saw something hesitant in those golden depths. "She loves you, Adam."

"And I her . . . and her *kinner*."

"I am sure that John and Abby will be glad to know that," she teased, giving him a bright smile.

But he didn't smile in return. Instead he drew close to her, bending so that his breath brushed her ear. Her heart stopped when she thought he might kiss her . . . but he merely stood close, tantalizingly close, and then drew away.

She felt heat rise into her cheeks and looked up at him, but he was gazing at the afternoon sun, now dipping behind the endless rows of ancient trees.

"It grows late. I had best start for home."

Lena felt a pang of disappointment, but she knew he had work to attend to. She slipped her hand into his as they walked toward Tim, his big dappled horse.

"I'll come tomorrow, Lena . . . to make sure that all is secure."

She nodded as he mounted. Then he stared down at her, his eyes intent. "Be safe, my love," he said.

"Of course." She smiled. But something cold and unfamiliar, like a splinter of ice, pierced through her as she watched him ride away, and she shivered despite herself.

Chapter 2

Adam tossed restlessly against the coarse linens of his wide bed and flung his arm up to shield his face.

It was the same engulfing blackness as always, as if he were wombed in the dark, unable to breathe. And then the red haze came, like some eerie dawn breaking over shrouded and jagged edges, until he gasped with the burn of the bloodlike sun and its shadow. He tried to beat against it, through it, flailing his fists in useless movement that only seemed to elongate the shine of the hazy red. And then it was winter and all snow, but for the sun, which still burned, turning his hands and arms and neck crimson as he tried to swipe himself clean with strokes of his shaking hands. But his efforts were futile, and then he was falling into nothingness, his soul left somewhere behind with a child's cry. His face stung; his fingers were numb; and then, strangely, he was in Lena's arms, pressed secure against her shoulder, sobbing for want of something and nothing and everything . . .

Adam woke with a strangled cry and tried to gain control of his racing heart and raw breathing. He stared around the shadows of his room and shivered in a cold sweat. Then he lay back down, searching the recesses of his mind for the nameless fear. But nothing came save the familiar feeling that he had been ravaged, his spirit burdened with a load he could not name. And then, as he always did, he began to pray.

———— ✦ ————

Lena pushed the spade into the damp earth and found the ground still frozen beneath its surface. She took a deep breath and piled her slight weight on the edge of the tool; her rough-soled shoe slipped and she fell. Facedown. For a long while, and despite the chill, she lay there breathing in the comforting smells of mud, melting snow, and the slightest promise of new grass. She only lifted her dirt-stained face when the feeble cry of an infant lingered in the early morning air, and she knew that she must rise. *I must rise. I promised.*

She placed her palms flat against the earth and was pushing up when the reverberation of hoofbeats shook the ground. She jumped up then, scraping at her face with the hem of her apron, the better to see. She abandoned the spade in an attempt to cross the slippery dirt to the house, but the horse and rider were upon her before she'd gone three steps. She stared up at Adam and worked to blink back tears.

He slid down and looped Tim's reins over the wood post before gently catching her close in his arms.

"What are you about?" he asked softly as he lifted a hand to skim some of the mud from her cheek.

"*Ach*, Adam . . . I dig my *mamm's* grave. She died this morning giving birth. There was so much blood . . . I didn't know what to do." Lena sobbed and moved toward him, expecting to find refuge in his arms, but he stared at the farmhouse, his body tense. "Adam? I am sorry . . . I know you loved her too."

———— ✦ ————

Adam bit back the words of comfort that came to his lips and brushed past Lena to retrieve the spade. He struck the ground with force.

"Adam . . . what . . . you don't have to do that," she said, scrambling to reach him.

"I know. Is it a boy or a girl?"

A lesser man might have felt disarmed by the pain that darkened her already shadowed eyes, but Adam steeled himself. He longed to hold her to him, to feel her delicate frame yield to his willing strength. But he had made a promise before *Gott* and Lena's mother, and he had no choice but to keep it. His world felt as though it had slid from him, and he tried to concentrate on the dirt before him.

"It is a girl," Lena said, breaking into his thoughts.

He looked at her, gripping the handle of the spade with all his strength to keep from taking her in his arms.

"Go and tend the babe, and send John to me."

She swiped at her splattered face with a shaking hand. "I don't think that a ten-year-old boy should dig his mother's grave, Adam, do you?"

Her question, protecting her brother from the duty of death, edged at something in his mind, but he couldn't capture the thought. He rested his foot on the spade. "Yet you would do it yourself." He paused, then spoke in a soothing tone, deciding he could at least comfort her with his voice. "I mean no harm to the boy; I thought to send him to the woods for firewood. It would be better if he were not about."

Lena nodded and walked up the steps to the front door of the farmhouse. Her small back was straight, her kerchief still white in places over the fall of her shoulders, where the golden mass of her hair had worked loose from beneath her head covering and straw hat. Adam tore his gaze away and stared at the ground, feeling an eerie sense of being outside of himself before he snapped back to the moment. He would do better with a pickax.

He heard Lena's melodic voice echo from within and then the

sounds of the infant's cries diminish. The door opened with a creak, and he looked up to see ten-year-old John, pale and thin, edging out onto the porch, his fingers pressed into a crevice of the limestone wall. The boy appeared to be of a sober and studious bent of mind, but there were times when Adam wondered what really went on behind those intense blue eyes.

"Take the horse, *sohn*, and go fetch some wood for the fire. Ride into the forest on this side of the river. Neither British nor Patriots camp there."

"You would trust me with the horse?"

Adam smiled, trying to remember what it was to be ten and failing entirely. "*Ya*—you have tended him while I have visited, haven't you? It's a sad morning today. Some time alone in *Gott's* woods would help you, I think."

"They took our horse, Benjamin, when they came for *Fater*."

Adam nodded. "I have heard. General Washington's army must have need."

"You still have your horse." There was a slight irony in the boy's statement.

"So I do."

John wet his lips and looked with longing at the steed. "I would like to ride."

"Then ride."

The boy stared at Adam and straightened his back, so that for a second he seemed remarkably like his sister and older than his years. "I will walk."

Adam shrugged, tossing a spade full of dirt. "As you wish."

John lifted a birch basket from a corner and unlooped a small hatchet from a peg in the stone wall. He walked off in the direction Adam had indicated without another word.

Adam smiled to himself. They were a strong family, the whole lot of them. Then the renewed cry of the infant reminded him that it was a parentless family for now, and that Lena would have a far greater load than she could possibly carry. Although he regretted her loss, he allowed himself to imagine the privilege of helping with her burdens. Then he shook his head. That was impossible now; he had given his word. And he turned his attention back to the ever-deepening grave.

Lena fancied she could hear the earth turning over from Adam's digging outside, then realized it was only the beating of her heart. Abigail, her eight-year-old sister, was still in her nightgown, blond hair hanging to her waist in a tangled mass. *Mamm* would have seen to it by now . . .

Lena rubbed her fingers against her temple as she tried to think where to begin. Her spontaneous rocking from foot to foot would not soothe the new babe for long, but she had no idea where a wet nurse might be found. She could give the infant goat's milk, of course, but her *mamm* had asked specifically for a wet nurse before she died, murmuring about too many infants not surviving without the touch of a woman.

And then there was the body to be washed, but no one to bless the burial. She could send for Deacon Wyse, Adam's father, but what she knew about the man made her reluctant to ask. She suppressed a sob. This wasn't the time to mourn. And *ach*, how to break the news to her father . . . His health hung in the balance as it was; to carry news to him in jail of the loss of his beloved wife might be more than he could bear. In truth she had not been to see him in the three weeks since he had been taken because her mother had seemed to weaken each day after he was gone, finally becoming bedridden with the pregnancy. Lena told herself that she should have known things would go badly for the delivery; she should have tried to send for a midwife. But she hadn't been sure when the baby would come . . .

"Where is *Mamm*, Lena?"

Lena turned back to her sister and knew that she could not reveal that she felt near to madness under the burden that *Derr Herr* saw fit for her to carry. But of course, she and Adam could marry now perhaps, and he would lift some of the load.

"Abby, come here. See our new baby. *Mamm* named her Faith."

Abigail skipped over for a quick look, then turned to the other room. "Is *Mamm* sleeping? I won't wake her, Lena. May I go in?"

"*Nee!*" Lena broke off at the stricken look on the child's face. "I mean to say . . . *nee, mei schwester.* You cannot." The infant kicked weakly in her arms and let out another mewling cry. "Abby, *Mamm* died this morning, after giving birth to Faith."

The little girl's lip quivered. "I don't believe you. *Mamm? Mamm!*"

Only the front door opening in her path waylaid Abigail from entering the room where her mother lay. Adam caught the little girl up in his arms and made soothing sounds in his throat as she beat her fists against his broad shoulders.

After a few moments the child cried herself still, and Adam let her slide to the floor. She immediately came to press herself into Lena's skirts. "I'm sorry," she sniffed. "I will be a big girl like *Fater* told me."

Lena smiled gratefully at Adam, but he looked away. She patted her sister's head while she balanced the baby in one arm. "It's all right, Abby. John and I will take care of you. And we will all take care of Faith."

Adam cleared his throat. "I'll send for my mother to come and help you this morning once I've finished outside. And you have need of a wet nurse, *ya?*"

Lena couldn't control the flush that burned her cheeks. At another time they might have laughed together at speaking so casually of such a thing, but she sensed a strange distance in him. She told herself that she had not realized how attached he was to her mother. He must be as stricken with grief as she was.

"*Danki*, Adam," she said.

He turned on his muddy heel. "I will also send my *gut bruder* to your aid this day, Lena. I think his studies make him more than able to bless the burial, while I tend to the other . . . unsavory things."

"I thank you," she said, and he nodded, closing the door with a brisk snap.

Adam tried to let the rhythmic motion of the horse beneath him bring some solace to his soul. His conversation with Mary Yoder burned through his brain as he tried to recall every word they had spoken. Then, like some hot brand held against his skin, the thought came that he could forget about the promise and go on as before. But then he prayed, and his mind cleared a bit. If Mary Yoder knew that she must give up one world to gain another—heaven at that—and leave behind a new babe and her other *kinner*, then surely he should be able to do the same—give up Lena for a time, to gain a better world in the future. His breath came rapid and shallow, and he felt as though he'd been running a long distance. He knew that he would try to honor his promise, no matter how much it hurt.

Despite his ease in speaking of the matter to Lena, Adam felt no such confidence in his ability to find a woman from whom the infant could nurse. He racked his brain as he rounded Timothy on the turn to his family's farm, which lay a mile from the Yoder home. Perhaps his mother should attend to the issue . . . but then, there was Mary Yoder to bury.

He pushed away his thoughts and dismounted, entering through the front door of the stout limestone farmhouse and slipping off his hat and cloak. His father had gone from the table to work the horses, but

Isaac still sat, his dark head bent, studying the Bible. A bevy of odd cats were curled around his brother's feet—strays that were more feral than house cats. But that was Isaac—always bringing home a strange animal.

The *Martyrs Mirror*, that heavy tome so valued for its descriptions of persecutions of Christians in the Old World, lay open on the table. Although Adam was familiar with the valuable book, he had little wish to dwell on the specific details of the deaths of thousands of martyred Anabaptists, as his *bruder* was wont to do.

Adam's mother placed a warning finger to her lips, and he obeyed with a faint frown. He rounded the wooden plank table and ignored the rumble in his stomach that reminded him he had missed the early morning meal. He took a heel of crusty bread from a platter and slipped an arm around his mother's waist. At nearly forty, Ellen Wyse was still as slender as a girl and had managed to keep her cheerful outlook upon life despite her husband's whims of mood. Adam bent his head and whispered of the Yoders' loss.

Mary Yoder had been both friend and neighbor, and the news was enough for his mother to interrupt her studying son. "Isaac, Mary Yoder died this morning in childbirth."

Adam watched the slow awareness flood his brother's dark eyes; it was the same ponderous consideration he gave to anything before he spoke, and it annoyed Adam to no end. He knew it was deliberate, this slow delivery of speech, so that others would be forced to hang on his words. But perhaps a man who believed he might someday become a bishop should speak with weighty accord.

"A sad loss, to be sure," Isaac said. "But always, as *Derr Herr* wills . . . It is a mercy that the child survived." He reached down to scratch a one-eared tomcat.

"*Ya*," their mother agreed, bowing her head.

Adam rolled his eyes at his brother's expression of the obvious.

"*Ya*, and the babe hungers. I will ride into town to seek a wet nurse if you will go and help Lena tend to things, *Mamm*. And I know you would be a comfort to her, Isaac." He was surprised at the sting of jealousy that accompanied his words, as he realized that soon enough Lena would accept his brother's help more than his own, if he continued to push her away.

His mother lifted a basket from the floor. "I'll take some fresh gingerbread and the new churning of butter over with me. The younger *kinner* will be hungry as well. How is Lena?"

Adam shrugged, avoiding his *mamm's* questioning gaze. "Strong, I guess, but broken too. She may display different feelings to another woman."

Isaac closed his Bible and rose. "Lena is strong, but even she will be bowed by this load. Perhaps it would be proper for me to offer her spiritual counsel at this time. I am sure it would please her father."

Adam clapped his hat on his head and scowled. "Why not bury her mother first?"

"To be certain." Isaac blinked. "It would be unseemly to—"

"I'll meet you both there as soon as I can." Adam crossed the tongue-and-groove kitchen floor and escaped before his brother could finish. He'd had more than enough food for thought this morning, and the idea of sleepy-eyed Isaac "counseling" Lena burned the back of his brain like liquid fire. He mounted the horse and turned toward Lancaster, intent on making short work of the three-mile distance to the bustling town.

Ruth Stone swallowed a sob as she clutched her babe tighter and watched her cottage home burn to the ground. It was her fault, she told herself. She had let the chimney get blocked. Ever since Henry had been killed in the fighting a few weeks past, she had found it hard to concentrate. And now she had nothing but a few meager possessions and her child. She had nowhere to go, no one to lean on. She turned from the ashen remains of her home and started to walk—heading anywhere and nowhere . . .

———— ✦ ————

Once Adam had gained Lancaster, he realized how absurd a chore he'd set himself up for. Wet nurses certainly did not promote themselves, and he felt like he was sinning every time he stole a glance at a matronly bosom. What in the world was he to do?

Finally he slid off the horse and approached a simply dressed young woman with a small toddler in tow. He stood in front of her, and the busy crowds swarmed around them. She looked up and took in his strength, and he saw the look of apprehension that crossed her brow. The child began to whine, and Adam knew he had to make haste.

"Uh, miss . . . missus . . . I see that you have a healthy-looking son there—great lungs on him. I have a friend who is in need of someone to nurse her babe . . . and I wondered if—"

The woman pushed past him, her face flushed with anger. He knew she probably would have slapped him had he not had the foresight to take a step back.

"Crazy Amish," he heard her mutter as she made haste to put the crowd between them.

Adam sighed. Maybe he was crazy . . . He glanced over at the poplin-covered bosom of a well-endowed older woman and got jabbed by a parasol for his troubles. Perhaps he would have better chances on the outlying farms. He quickly remounted Tim and with a shudder left the town behind.

———— ◆ ————

Ruth Stone stumbled with listless abandon along the rutted dirt road, not caring where her bare and blistered feet led. She knew she must look a sight, her graying red hair escaping the confines of her ruffled cap and her apron splattered with mud from the puddles she had trodden through. She carried a small wrapped bundle in her arms and another on her back, and she barely glanced up when the horse and rider pulled abreast of her. She no longer feared the British nor the Patriots, who would seek their freedom at any cost.

"Woman? Are you well?"

The man's voice was deep, quiet, and resonant. It penetrated some of the distance in her mind, and she focused bleary eyes up at him.

"Nay, I surely am not."

He smiled, a flash of well-kept teeth in a tanned face and strange light from his unusual golden eyes. "Your tone says you have spirit yet. What is your situation?"

She snorted. "My situation? My work, if you mean? I have none. The Lord has seen fit to take hearth, home, and husband all in the space of two weeks. I have nothing but my babe here. I simply seek to walk until I can go no farther."

He nodded. "My sympathies for your burden, but there are others in need this day as well."

"That is none of my concern."

"But it could be. A girl is left this morning without a mother to tend for three younger children . . . one a babe newly born. The child shall surely die without someone to nurse it."

She gave him a wry look. "Are you wondering if I still have milk, young man?"

He had the grace to blush, and something about his dark hair reminded her of her own husband when he was younger.

"Well, aye, that I do. My Mary here is but three weeks old." She indicated the bundle in her arms.

"Did you say *Mary*?" He had an odd expression on his face.

"Aye . . . Mary. Named after her grandmother."

"That's . . . good."

She studied his simple clothing more closely. "You're one of them, ain't you?"

"Them?"

"The peace-seekers. Quaker? Or Amish?"

"Amish, *ya*." He smiled. "The Quakers wear fancier shoes."

"Hmm . . . and this girl is Amish, the one with the babe?"

"Yes."

Ruth closed her eyes for a moment. "My Henry enlisted right off to fight for freedom from the king. He died two weeks ago in a skirmish; they buried him where he fell."

"I am truly sorry."

"Sorry? Yet you do not fight." She watched something harsh and tight cross his handsome face.

"No, I cannot."

She drew herself up with a sudden decision. "Haul us up there then, Amish man. No sense in another dying in this infernal world."

"I thank you."

There was a flash of relief in his eyes before his easy calm settled back into place, and she decided that here was a deep pool of a man, one who didn't show himself too readily. Her suspicions were confirmed as they rode along and he began to speak.

"It would be best if you were to arrive at the young woman's farm on your own, as if you'd walked there by chance. I can drop you off, say, a quarter of a mile back or so."

Ruth clutched one careworn hand tighter about his lean waist and readjusted her bundle of scant belongings and then the babe. "And be there a reason why you'd like to practice such deception? I thought your kind was against sin."

He laughed. "Aren't we all called to be 'against sin'?"

"Maybe some take it more seriously than others."

"Perhaps."

"So will you be telling me the truth of the matter or not?" she pressed, feeling she had little to lose if she raised his ire.

"She will hate me."

"The little Amish girlie? Because you found her a wet nurse?"

He chuckled again. "*Ya . . . Nee.*"

"You hurt her? Because I don't stand for seeing a woman hurt."

He sobered at once. "Nor do I."

"What is it, then?" She watched the tanned line of his throat as he half turned in profile, considering.

"She will soon believe that I love something more than her."

Ruth drew a breath, feeling interested against her will. "And will she be right?"

He shook his dark head. "I used to think I knew."

"Well, what is it then that rivals your love?"

He nudged the horse with one knee and murmured so low that she had to strain to catch the word on the breeze.

"Freedom."

Chapter 3

L ena lifted her head from prayer and felt caked mud move with the stretch of her neck. Then she scrubbed her face and hands with a wet rag, trying to remove the grime. She glanced to the bentwood rocker where she'd settled John with his newborn sister. Abigail pushed the chair from behind with gentle hands, and Lena's head rang with the momentary silence of the babe. She'd hoped that Adam's mother would have arrived by now, but perhaps Adam had gone in search of a wet nurse first, before going home. It could be no easy chore for a man to find such a person, and Adam could be long delayed. She appreciated his willingness to take on such a task and thought what a wonderful husband he would be to her. Then she dragged her thoughts back to the moment and pivoted toward the bedroom door. Somehow she must prepare her mother for burial. She steeled herself with the thought of the women who had tended to the body of the Lord. Surely she could draw on their same strength of purpose.

A hearty knock broke into her thoughts and sent Faith squalling once more. Lena ran to open the door, expecting to see Ellen Wyse. Instead she blinked at the apparition of a tall, disheveled woman in ill-fitting clothing. Someone needing food, no doubt, but Lena had nothing to offer this morn. She shook her head and was about to close the door without a word when the other woman held up a big, work-reddened hand.

"Your babe's hungry. I can help you. I have milk from my own baby girl here." She bent forward and uncovered a cherubic sleeping face under a thatch of red hair.

Lena glanced at the woman's ample bosom, then wondered wildly if this was Adam Wyse's idea of a wet nurse. Yet hadn't she just been in prayer for the needs of her family? She opened the door wider.

"I'm Lena Yoder, but I have no coin to pay you."

"Ruth Stone, and my babe here's Mary."

"Ma-Mary?" Lena stuttered.

The woman gave her a curious look. "Aye. Not a strange name, by my reckoning."

Lena nodded. "*Nee* . . . it was my mother's name. She died early this morn."

"Then payment is not what is needed here. Mebbe I was meant to help."

The woman brushed past her and went to where the children were huddled. She laid down her baby in the nearby wooden cradle and dropped her other bundle to the floor. John stared up at her, and Lena saw him draw the babe closer against his thin chest. It was only at her slight nod that he relinquished his hold to the outstretched arms of the strange woman. Faith quieted again, but then began a frantic mewling as she turned her head toward the woman in a rooting reflex. Ruth Stone then scooped up her own child and balanced both babes with competent ease.

"Let me have the chair, young man."

John rose in haste as the woman fumbled with her bodice, and Abigail scampered to Lena's side. In a moment the air hung with blissful, layered silence.

"'Tis hungry she is, the poor wee one. My own babe doesn't nurse as well. I guess she can tell when things are worryin' me."

Lena felt a rush of sympathy amid her confusion. "I am sorry for your worries. May the Lord bless you for your kindness."

"Ha! The Lord owes me a blessing or two for sure, but what I have I gladly give to this mite. What do you call her?"

Abigail piped up. "Faith. *Mamm* named her that this morn—before she died. It's strange, I think, that your babe has the same name as my *mamm*. It is strange, isn't it, Lena?"

The last words came out in a brave squeak, and Lena reached to slip an arm around her sister's shoulders.

"A sign from the Lord, Abby. Again, we thank you, Ruth Stone."

Ruth nodded. "Faith is a right good name too—if faith there be."

"Of course there be faith," John cried. "What else is there?"

The woman rocked meditatively as the satisfied smacking sounds of the babe increased. "Love, maybe . . ."

This time Lena wanted to cry aloud. Love! *Ach*, yes! She dreamed of it as being more than a quickening of the heart, a memory of laughing golden eyes, the brush of dark hair soft against her cheek. She wanted a love that surpassed the realities of the war, and after seeing the fragility of life this morn, she knew more than ever that she could not have that love at the risk of knowing she might lose it . . . lose him . . . perhaps to the call of the war. And death seemed so possible to her now—anything might happen to Adam, and she knew she wouldn't be able to go on without him. Still, a small Voice inside her reminded her of her faith, of that power of *Gott* that could conquer all pain and loss . . .

She marshaled her thoughts but knew that time would never abate her desire for him. She was like the tinder to his flame, and she never wanted to be free of that burn . . .

She patted her sister, preparing to go to the bedroom once more, when another knock sounded on the front door. John opened it to reveal Ellen and Isaac Wyse.

Lena felt a moment's dismay at her muddied appearance, then dismissed the thought with a labored tiredness until she felt Isaac's eyes sweep her dirty dress.

"*Sei se gut*, come in," she murmured and received Ellen's warm embrace with gratitude. Isaac merely shook her hand. That was proper, she supposed, on the heels of the wistful thought that the strength of a man's touch about her shoulders might be welcome. She recalled the fast light of sympathy that had shown in Adam's face earlier that morning and wondered that he had not touched her . . .

A satisfied burp reminded her of the two babes and the strange *Englisch* woman who sat in the room's best chair near the fireplace.

"Uh . . . this is Ruth . . ." She sought for the surname, but it eluded her.

"Stone," the older woman said comfortably. She had put Mary back in the cradle and turned Faith to be patted against her shoulder. "I find I can help out here a bit with the feeding and all, as I've got my own babe to nurse."

Lena flushed and told herself that she imagined that Isaac's nostrils flared in disgust. After all, feeding a babe was a natural and *Gott*-given part of life.

"Lena," Ellen said softly. "Shall I help you with your mother? Perhaps Ruth will talk with the *kinner*, or Isaac can take them outside."

"I must prepare my thoughts, *Mamm*. For the burial. I cannot think with the *kinner*—" Isaac broke off at Lena's surprised stare and cleared his throat. "I mean . . . I would like some time to reflect . . ."

Lena felt a surge of gratitude. Surely it was a blessing to have a man to oversee the burial, and one with Isaac's mind was all the more fitting.

Ruth Stone spoke up. "The young ones can gather about and hear a story, if they'd like."

Lena murmured her thanks and hustled Abigail and John forward, despite the boy's stiffened shoulders. She knew he'd come to think of himself less and less as a child since Father had been imprisoned, but she had no time to worry about that now. She must see to her mother.

Once they were settled, she watched Isaac slip outdoors and then allowed Ellen to go and open the door she had so been dreading to enter all morn.

Chapter 4

Adam wanted to return to the Yoder farm and aid in the burial, but he could not bring himself to see Lena and not comfort her, touch her . . .

"Easier company among the Redcoat prisoners," he muttered aloud to his horse as he rode into Lancaster. In truth, Adam had taken up a cautious acquaintance with a British officer who was kept an idle prisoner of war in Lancaster. The town was held by the Patriots, and it was the unusual custom of Lancaster that a British officer, although the enemy, need only give his word as a gentleman that he would not leave the city limits, and he was free to go about his business. Adam had even heard that the agreement was stretched upon occasion by the city fathers to allow for picnics outside the town, held by the more charming and unconcerned ladies of society. Major Dale Ellis, though, was a family man as far as Adam understood, and a possible friend.

And friendship had been hard to come by at times lately, especially among certain men of the Amish who had taken up arms with the colonists, leaving their faith and families behind. Yet it seemed to Adam that they were forging a new way of life by fighting, a life of freedom—and an idea began to take shape in his mind.

As he entered the bustling town, he noticed many eyeing Timothy's sleek and healthy form. Horses were prized possessions, even among the British ranks, but the Wyse family's ability to pay had protected Tim—at least for the present. As a dissident peace-seeker, Amish Joseph Wyse had signed allegiance to Britain as all the others had done upon their arrival to William Penn's Woods. But oaths to the Old Country meant little since the Declaration of Independence, and many viewed the Amish as cowards for not taking up arms. Adam hated the connotation; there was no cowardice in yielding. He knew yielding and how difficult it was to bend but not break in the process. Then he thought anew of his promise to Mary Yoder, and his throat tightened.

He dismounted and looped Timothy's reins over the post outside the town granary, which was serving dual purpose as a jail and trading place. The regular jail was bursting at the seams with prisoners of war, but to house the pacifists with the Hessians and the enlisted soldiers of Britain seemed incongruous somehow. And while the local militia-turned-army regiment claimed it had no place in the numerous acts of violence against the peacekeeping peoples, they went along with the so-called fair imprisonment of those who would not enlist . . . Lena Yoder's father, for one. Despite the fact that the older man had paid the tax fines levied against him, the tribunal had still found fault when he wouldn't surrender his last cow for the militia. He'd been hauled away along with his stock and imprisoned for three weeks. And now his wife was dead.

"I say, do you have a fascination with prisons, or is it a prisoner himself who draws you here?"

Adam turned round to see Major Dale Ellis in a rumpled, but still elegant, blue frock coat, his usual white wig gone and his blond hair caught back in a queue. Adam's puzzlement must have shown on his face, because Dale waved a hand at him and smiled.

"There's nothing that says I need wear uniform while a 'guest' of

Lancaster. Anyway, the bloody thing was starting to reek, and I found lice in the wig."

Adam grinned. "And I hear the latest saying hereabout is 'Any fool with a musket can kill a Redcoat.'"

"That is so. Would you care to join me for a cool tankard? I've just had word from the infernally slow mails that my wife gave birth to our third son back in Somerset . . . three months ago."

The slight irony in the man's tone made Adam think of how fast a babe must seem to grow, especially to a father who yearned to be with the child.

"My congratulations, and my condolences for missing so much of the first of his life. But as the Lord would have it, perhaps he may have greater need of you later on."

"Spoken like a father."

Adam shook his dark head and thrust aside the tantalizing image of Lena carrying his child, her soft belly rounded against the press of her skirt, her cheeks flushed with good health and rosy awareness following his purposeful kisses . . .

"Perhaps soon then, by the look on your face," Dale said with a laugh.

Adam dragged his mind back to the present with embarrassment.

"Well, being a father is something I didn't know if I could ever truly become," the British officer went on. "I had a sire who thought the only way to reach a boy was through a beating; it took a long time to realize that I didn't have to become what he was."

Adam looked at Dale in sudden confusion and wary alertness. It was almost as if the man could see into his own past. He thrust aside the familiar feelings of anxiety that came whenever he tried to recall the tense moments of his latter childhood, when he was seemingly unable to please the man who'd given him life. And it had been sudden too, this displeasure of his father's. He could remember other times when he was younger that there had been smiles and encouragement from the man. He swallowed and shook his head a bit to clear it.

"You look thoughtful today, Adam Wyse . . . Considering joining the cause?"

Dale smiled, but his words struck Adam to the core, and he looked away.

"Did I say something to offend you? I know the Amish do not fight."

Adam snapped his gaze back to the other man's. "The Amish fight. They struggle to keep their ways, and to keep their sons from running off to enlist. They do fight."

Dale shook his head. "Again, forgive me. It was only a joke; I didn't mean to offend. I say, there's seriousness in the very air of this place. This country is like a woman. She labors over war to give birth to a new way, a new freedom. And I have never enjoyed watching my wife labor."

Adam drank in the words he heard . . . He thought of Mary's death during labor, the promise, a new way of life . . . It suddenly seemed as though his world was in turmoil, with a strange possibility of freedom at the eye of the storm.

"About that tankard, then, my good man?" Dale asked.

"Another time," Adam replied abruptly, realizing the attention that they were drawing among the passersby—a pacifist and a British major, red coat or not. At any other point he wouldn't have cared, but today . . .

"As you wish."

Adam heard the disappointment in the other man's voice and chose to ignore it. Their conversation had unsettled him, and at this point in his plans, he needed all of his wits about him. He composed himself as Dale walked away, then approached the shadowy entrance to the makeshift prison. He passed the coin and the round loaf of bread from beneath his cloak to the guard, as he'd done daily.

"Remember . . . no word as to who brings food for Samuel Yoder," he instructed, as he hoped for the hundredth time that no word of his doings would ever reach Lena's father's ears. For some reason Samuel Yoder did not especially favor Adam, and he wouldn't appreciate his daily bread coming from someone he did not like. Adam had gone over the situation a thousand times in his mind, wondering why Samuel was against him but still allowed his presence in the Yoder home. Yet Adam was used to strange behavior from the men in his life and decided that he must simply be an annoying person in some way. But how much more would Samuel dislike him when he kept his promise to Mary . . . ?

In truth, he wouldn't care much for himself at that point. He thrust the thought aside.

The guard grunted, interrupting Adam's grim thoughts. "Heard yer prisoner's got a pretty piece of a daughter. Rather it be her than you what comes to feed 'im."

Adam's eyes darkened, but then he smiled. "I'd have to agree. But perhaps this will interest you more at the moment." He reached beneath his cloak again and produced a leather bag, tossing its weight briefly in the air. There was no mistaking the clink of the coins within.

The guard cast him a wary but attentive eye. "'Ere now . . . what's this?"

Adam smiled. "Much. And more if you'd like. Let us say that I have discovered the need for Samuel Yoder to be somewhere else."

The guard blinked and leaned closer. "Hades, ye mean?"

"No, my treacherous friend. Not dead—gone. Escaped, if you prefer."

The guard snorted and stepped back. "And me court-martialed in the exchange, no doubt. Get on with ye. I don't care how much money ye've got, you bloody coward."

Adam sighed. He should have known better than to expect that the dolt of a guard would fall in line with his plans.

"Fine. But there is one thing that I'm guessing you do not have and might well value, even on the off chance that you were found responsible for the escape."

The guard scratched his pockmarked cheek with the tip of his musket, then spat on the ground. "What might that be?"

Adam leaned forward and whispered, "My horse."

He saw the light in the other man's eyes and knew he'd won, even at the cost of Tim's company and the berating he'd probably get from his father.

The guard cast a quick look around. "How'd you arrange it, then?"

Adam considered as he spoke, his hesitation only heightening the tension. "I'll have a brief conversation now with Samuel Yoder."

"I thought ye wanted to keep things all secret like?"

"Not to tell him about the food. Just about our little plan . . . and to unlock his cell. Then I'll create a diversion in the street that you—a loyal, upstanding citizen—must see to for a moment, as it's happening right in front of your post."

"Huh?"

"Just give me the key and five minutes with the man. Take the horse. His name's Tim. Go easy on the bit, though, or he'll take you flying."

The guard squinted in thought. "I'll go in with ye and slip open the door; ye ain't keepin' the key."

"Good man." Adam nodded. He should have thought of that himself.

"I will never have a child." The vow escaped from Lena's lips before she could think to stop.

Ellen Wyse glanced across the deathbed. "It's normal to feel that way, I should imagine."

Lena stared at her for a moment as they bundled together the last of the bloody sheets. Normal? What could possibly be normal about this moment? The shrouding of her mother's body, veiling one world from the next . . . the stark stillness and the reality of death striking against her consciousness like shards of stone. No . . . nothing could ever be normal again. And death pervaded, seemed to prevail even, in the times in which they lived.

Lena bit her lip at this last irreverent thought, as she considered the *Martyrs Mirror* and all of those who had perished by horrible means. At least her mother had been home, in her own bed, and had lived to name her new daughter.

Lena looked up as she realized that Ellen had spoken. "*Sei se gut*, I am sorry. What did you say?"

Ellen fingered the simple hem of a pillowcase, looking slightly abashed. "It's nothing really, my dear . . . just a hope I've cherished for a long time that you and Adam might . . . Well, being a *grossmuder* would be a great blessing."

Lena felt herself flush to the roots of her bundled hair. Despite the strangeness of the setting and the covered face of her mother, Lena knew that life must go on. That it *would* go on, with or without her contribution to the generations. And yet, despite her vow of moments before, she could not help but think what a child of Adam's making would look like. Her blush deepened when she envisioned the gold of his eyes lapping with the blue of her own . . .

But there was the ever-present shadow of the war, and she wondered if some Penn Dutch surnames would soon pass into obscurity because of the surprising number of Amish boys willing to join the Patriots in their fight against the British. Ellen spoke as if there was still hope beyond the war and death. Lena knew that her own faith had a long way to grow before she felt the same.

She bent to snatch up a cloth from the floor and added it to the pile to be washed. She did not know how to respond without bursting out that she, too, despite her fear, would love to carry Adam's babe.

Ellen cleared her throat. "Forgive me, Lena. To speak of life in the face of your loss was unthinking. I—I loved your mother dearly. She was my only friend hereabouts, with the next nearest farm nearly five miles way. I doubt that I shall ever find the friendship of a woman of such strength and character as your *mamm.*"

Lena smiled then. "There is nothing to forgive. I—I too pray that *Gott* will bless Adam and me with many *kinner* in the years to come. I spoke without thought earlier. And I deeply value your words of praise for my *mamm.* I know it is not our way to praise one so highly, even in death."

Ellen stretched her hand across the deathbed and Lena took it, feeling an accord of strength. "Lena, what women say behind private doors is sometimes as much blessed, I think, as the words of the bishop himself."

Lena looked at her with mild shock. "Truly?"

"*Ya.* It is given to women to often minister to the dead, and how can we mourn without praising as well?"

Lena nodded, tears filling her eyes at this simple wisdom. "*Ach,*" she whispered, "you bring balm to my soul. Thank you."

Ellen squeezed her hand. "The Lord has a plan and a blessing in all of this for you, Lena. I am sure of it."

Lena could only nod at this declaration of peace and pray that it would be so.

Chapter 5

A dam followed the guard into the dim interior of the building. He could hear the hustle and bustle of granary business being conducted above, but the bowels of the building echoed with coughing and muted groans. Lancaster was a curious mixture of Loyalists, Patriots, pacifists, and, of course, prisoners of war. The makeshift jail was dark and damp, though Adam had heard that conditions in the Reading jail were worse. It seemed that the Patriots had no stomach for the peace-keeping sects, and jail was the least of what might happen to one whose faith did not support the bearing of arms.

He felt his way along thick stones, having to bend at places to match the guard's shorter stature, then came to a small, iron-barred space in which a single candle gave off smoky light.

Lena's father sat in a straight-backed chair next to a table, the only two articles of furniture in the room, and dozed with a troubled frown on his grizzled face. Adam had the sudden urge to bolt, wondering for the third time that morning whether he should be the one to bring the news of Mary Yoder's death. Yet he knew how difficult it would be for Lena to do, and he hoped to spare her the pain.

The guard unlocked the door, then brushed past Adam, disappearing back into the dark passage without a word. Adam cleared his throat, and the older man stirred, drawing the tattered gray blanket closer about his thin frame.

"Eh? Who is it?"

A rat ran across Adam's foot as he stepped from the shadows to press against the bars. "Adam Wyse."

Samuel Yoder jerked wide-awake then.

"And what is your business, Adam Wyse?" The older man's voice was hoarse, and his overly patient tone seemed to Adam to be thinly veiled contempt.

"I must speak quickly; I bring sad news."

"Go on with it then," Samuel said coldly.

Adam sighed, pressing his head against the chill iron bars. "Do you know that there was a time when I would have given anything for your approval? Can you tell me why you are against me?"

"Because there is a darkness about you, Adam Wyse. Be it your past, or who you are now . . . I cannot discern, but it is not what I would choose firstly for my daughter's life. Now, if you please, your news?"

Adam sighed. So much for receiving a clear-cut answer from the man. Then he remembered his mission.

"Your wife . . . Mary died this morn giving birth to another daughter."

"As the Lord wills."

The reply was what Adam expected, but the sight of the older man's head bowed in sorrowful acceptance was almost more than he could watch. He fisted his hands on the bars, longing to touch, to clasp hands and pray. He thought of past church meetings, before the war began, when his people had felt freer to gather together. He supposed he'd been less of a cynic then, believing more in the will of the Lord and less in his own personal power. He sought to retrieve that place in his mind and spirit at times, but it seemed chained away from him, held just out of reach.

Samuel raised his head. "Go on with you. You've told your tale."

"I would help you—help Lena, if I can."

"She needs no help of yours!" Anger flashed from the bleary eyes of the prisoner as he rose up from the chair.

"Quiet," Adam hissed. "*Sei se gut.*" He pushed on the door so that it gave a bit of a telling squeak. "I've settled with the guard. In a few minutes you'll hear a commotion from the streets. It'll be enough time for you to slip away and go back home."

Samuel stared at him, then laughed aloud before breaking off into a cough. He shuffled closer to his chair and sat back down.

"And you think that no army is bound to look for me there? It will only bring more trouble for Lena. Your plan is not thought out, nor is it righteous. I stay here until properly released."

Adam wanted to grind his teeth at both the sensibility of the words and the refusal of the man to even try. "You could at least see her, reassure her . . . then go into hiding."

Samuel closed his eyes, and Adam gripped his hands against the bars. "I merely seek to do what I can."

The old man looked up and shook his head sadly. "You seek to do what you desire, Adam Wyse. That is what moves you—not *Gott.* Following one's own desires brings nothing but evil for those who try to keep to the way of the Lord."

"Is it not the way of the Lord to bring freedom—be it to you, here and now, or to those who would worship freely and may have to fight to keep that right?"

"Freedom? At what cost, Adam? So that our people can be persecuted once more, hunted down, dragged to prison, left to die alone as they once were in the Palatinate? Make no mistake, this war of revolution brings more division, more of a sword to our people than one could imagine. And you, above all, as I can see in the darkness surrounding you, should recognize this. So again I ask you, at what cost?"

"I don't know."

"Then you had better find out before you do unthinking harm. Now go, and send the guard back to lock the door."

"Have you no message to give to Lena? To John and Abigail?"

"It is all as the Lord wills. Lena will find her way. I am sure of this."

Adam's temper broke. "*Ya*, and I wonder how sure you are of your wife finding her way to death alone this morning with only a terrified young girl to tend her?"

"May *Gott* forgive your words, as I do."

Adam suppressed a snarl and tore himself away. It took a full minute for him to compose himself before blinking out into the light and meeting the crooked smile of the guard, who'd probably made it a point to overhear every word.

"Done with your business, then? I'm still keeping the horse. Had a friend take him to stable in case ye might change yer mind."

Adam swung to the empty hitching post and resisted the urge to throttle the guard. He stepped into the mud to start the long walk home when a shadow fell across his path. He lifted his head to meet the cold gray eyes of his father.

"On foot, *sohn*? Now why is that?"

Joseph Wyse stared level into his second son's golden eyes. He couldn't repress a certain fatherly pride that the boy was his height exactly: just over six feet, and much better built. But he knew, in truth, that physical strength did not matter, not in the relationship that the two shared. It was mental strength, the power of the will that bound them, and Joseph was determined to keep the tipped balance of power that lay between him and the boy. He also wanted nothing to interfere with his rising role as a deacon among the scattered Amish farms.

"Again, *sohn*. I ask you about the horse."

"Tim's gone, sir." Adam's strong throat worked in the sunshine against the white of his collar.

Joseph considered. Adam must have tried to barter the horse for Samuel Yoder's freedom and lost. He pushed aside a sudden memory of his own father's fury when he'd lost a milk cow to a wolf pack. The beating had broken his ribs and left him unable to walk for nearly a week.

He pushed aside the familiar tormenting thoughts and cleared his throat. "So how fares the prisoner?"

He watched Adam flinch, just slightly, but it was enough to bring him a simmering satisfaction. So long as the boy feared him, all was as it should be.

"*Fater* . . . I-I'll take any punishment you think deserving for the loss of Tim. I was only trying to help the Yoder family."

"*Any* punishment?"

Adam dropped his gaze to the muddy ground, then nodded. "*Ya, Fater.*"

Joseph never would have had the courage to suggest such a thing to his own father. He reached out to clasp his son's shoulder and relished the startled play of muscle beneath his fingertips. Adam looked back up, and Joseph slid his hand away, smiling.

"Let us consider it for what it was, Adam. I know your feelings run deep for Lena Yoder. And what is one horse to us, even in this fair country's debacle of affairs? Forget it. I'll make excuse to your mother and brother."

Adam's golden eyes shone with a mixture of confusion and happiness. "*Danki, Fater.*"

"*Gut.* Now I'll leave you to walk home with your thoughts." Joseph smiled again, knowing the length and dangers of the long walk home. "A *gut* day, my *sohn.*" He mounted the seat of the small Conestoga wagon and turned the horses with ease, sparing nary so much as a backward glance for his son.

Chapter 6

Lena winced as Isaac flung the last shovelful of dirt onto the dark mound.

He wiped his sweating brow and exhaled as he rested a foot on the shovel.

"That's done, then," he said. "Now we can get on with the service. Adam might have at least stayed for the burial."

But Lena closed her eyes against his casual words. She knew Isaac was practical and stalwart in his faith. Perhaps she should have more of his attitude in approaching life . . . and death. It was the Lord's will, and her mother had taught her much about acceptance in faith. But the fact that Adam had dug the grave with little remark and Isaac fretted over filling it in made a pitiful comparison.

She thrust aside the unworthy thought. Isaac's strength lay in his mind and not in his body—not that Adam himself didn't possess keen intelligence. *Nee*, she must learn to accept Isaac as her future brother-in-law. She sighed between her teeth, not wanting to dwell on thoughts of Adam at the moment of her mother's burial.

Isaac began to speak in High German, in sober tones. Lena bowed her head and stretched out her cold hands to encircle John and Abigail. Ruth Stone was inside the house, rocking the babies. Isaac's voice wore on until he concluded with an Amish proverb that set Lena's teeth on edge: "Blessed are the laps that are full of *kinner*. Blessed was Mary Yoder."

The idle and irreverent thought that her mother's lap was now full of dirt skimmed Lena's consciousness, to be banished with haste. She nodded her thanks to Isaac, who clearly expected some word for the service performed. She moved forward to press his arm.

"*Danki*, Isaac. That was beautiful."

He nodded. "*Mamm*, if you could see to the *kinner*, I would have a word with Lena alone."

Lena heard his words through a sudden, swamping tunnel of dismay. She knew he meant to offer spiritual counsel, but somehow, on the heels of the burial, she could not think of such a thing. Yet she was used to pleasing others, keeping peace. She stifled a sigh as Ellen stepped forward and led Abigail and John back inside the house.

"Shall we walk a bit?" Isaac asked.

Lena nodded, trying to concentrate on the sodden landscape, the lichen on a rotting log, the post at the end of the fence that needed straightening. There was still, after her father's twenty years of work, a fair meeting of forest and apple farm, a need to hold back the trees and wildlife that encroached like an inexorable tide. She became aware that Isaac had repeated himself, and she murmured an apology.

"I said," he went on stiffly, "that I am here to offer you counsel and compassion, should you so desire. I know that my brother is not always of a heavenly bent of mind, so I thought that I would seek to give what I can."

She stopped, her leather shoe catching in some bracken, and for a moment she could hear Adam, his voice hoarse with emotion, praying aloud for her safety and a good night's sleep, as he was often wont to do. How unfair was it that his own brother did not see this side of him?

"Isaac, I thank you for the offer of your counsel, but I have no need of it at present. I must do as my *hartz* convicts and trust *Derr Herr* to help us manage. He will provide for us—as will Adam." She focused on believing the words she spoke, offering both petition and praise to the Lord through the silence in her heart.

Isaac snorted. "Does it not occur to you, Lena, that it is I, through the Lord, of course, who am your provision of spiritual refuge?"

"*Nee*," she said. "Forgive me, Isaac, but I don't understand."

He frowned. "Your mother is gone, your father imprisoned. The bishop is far afield. Surely you see your need for spiritual counsel."

She laid a soft hand on his arm. "Again, Isaac, please forgive me. But my spirit is too distraught within me to speak of such things at this moment." She went on gently. "And Adam is my spiritual bedrock, Isaac."

"Your thoughts are not clear," he said, clasping his hands behind his back and nodding in understanding. "I will press my offer at a later date."

"And my reply will be the same."

Isaac smiled. "You are stubborn, like my brother. But you will be my sister-in-law. My offer stands should you ever desire my help."

"Of course," she breathed, feeling a wave of relief and thinking that time might ease his rather pompous overture. But he was right in saying that her thoughts were not clear at the moment. How could they be?

Isaac offered a stiff arm to her and escorted her to the house. A few minutes later, she saw him and his mother off with a brisk wave as they departed in their heavy Conestoga wagon, the only sure means of travel in the mud and ruts of spring. Lena wished she had as sure a means of navigation for her own mind and heart over the days to come.

Adam's heart sank as Joseph Wyse drove off without a backward glance. Surely his father had considered the long miles back on foot and the fact that his gun was gone with his horse. And no gun meant no protection from the wild animals that still prowled the land.

Adam stood in the street until the last turn of the wagon wheels disappeared in solemn revolution over an empty rise in the road ahead, then put one foot in front of the other. It was always the same . . . some hope for peace between them, then a cruel twist of happenings and the returning flood of fear. What was he to do? He'd prayed, tried to speak of it, begged, and always, his father was the same—boiling with provocation and challenge.

He wondered why his father seemed to garner such hate toward him and why he, in turn, would give anything for a scrap of praise from the man despite his harsh ways. Adam had been seventeen the last time his father whipped him. He no longer remembered the infraction, but he knew Joseph had had a hard time stopping with that particular beating. Adam's back had taken weeks to heal, and even now, the whitened scars on his shoulders could still ache with residual pain.

Actually, Adam preferred the whippings to the subtle cruelties his father had progressed to—like leaving him the long, empty walk or mocking him for the affection he'd held for a dog that had died the year before. And then there was Lena . . . He shuddered when he thought of the power his father held over him in knowing his love for the girl. It was a vulnerability, like an open wound, but he was too transparent in his affections to hide anything from the cold gray eyes that seemed to study him with the targeted precision of a long rifle. And now, with the promise he had made to Mary Yoder, his father would gain even more power over him, unless . . . unless he did something different.

He listened to the sound of his own footsteps as he jumped from rock to rock to avoid the mud. Then he thought of Tim, and his eyes stung. He told himself that he was foolish to cry over a horse when the country was at war. He was grateful that Lena was not present to see his pain, as she had been that cold winter day when he was seventeen . . . The memory of that time flooded back as he walked.

— ◆ —

"Rebellion . . . in all its forms . . . will cease from this house!"

The hiss of the lash punctuated his father's words as Adam clung to the thick wooden post where he was bound. He tried to let the wood absorb some of the force from his father's arm and concentrated on the count . . . *Sixteen strokes. Four more to go.*

Out of habit, he was careful to make no sound, knowing that it would just provoke his father and make his mother feel worse. He wondered dizzily what would happen if his father ever forgot to stop, and he tried to concentrate on the blinding white of the snow across the open yard.

"Tend your brother."

Adam heard the whip drop to the ground and exhaled, though the breath cost him. He felt his hands cut loose, and he pressed against the post, trying to force himself to stand. He could not steady his legs and waited until the blessed feel of icy water hit his back.

"Why do you persist with *Fater*, Adam?" Isaac caught him around the waist and turned him with gentle hands.

"Cannot—help myself." He tried to smile, his eyes closed for a moment against the swamping intensity of the pain.

"I don't know why you stay. Though I—I'd miss you if you weren't here."

"*Danki.* But I have my reasons. Is *Mamm* gone?"

Isaac nodded. "*Ya.* Lean against me if you can."

Joseph Wyse was precise with the whip, so accurate that he could take the head off a dandelion at twenty paces. He confined lashings to the shoulders and upper back, not letting the beatings maim but rather linger long with burning pain. He always saw fit to have the family present when Adam was disciplined, but he refused to allow Ellen to tend the boy's wounds. It was either Isaac or the hired girl, Betty, who saw to him.

Adam much preferred his older brother's clumsy hands to Betty's deliberate touch. The girl always wanted to steal a kiss after she dressed his wounds with bear's grease. His head usually throbbed with her ministrations, which were simply a veiled excuse for getting near him.

They'd reached one of the smaller barns, and Isaac stopped to let him rest, though the cold made Adam's teeth chatter in his painful, shirtless state. Suddenly their mother called from the wide back porch.

"Isaac! Your *fater* wants you . . . now."

Adam heard the worry in her tone and knew it wasn't for her elder son, but because she longed to tend to him.

"I'll open the door for you and send Betty. I tell you, there are times when *Fater* does this that I would take hold of him and—" Isaac eased his supporting arm away and handed Adam his shirt.

"*Ach*, well, *gut* on that . . . ," Adam muttered, forcing himself to concentrate on standing. He leaned against the open barn door and watched Isaac amble away.

It wasn't like Isaac to show such emotion. His older brother moved with confidence around their father, never the receiver of the lash, perhaps because of his studious and holy bent of mind. Isaac was also endlessly obedient, not raising so much as a dark eyebrow in question of Joseph Wyse's whims—until a moment ago.

Adam's temperament was different, despite his desire for his father's approval. He was impulsive and quick-tempered at times, so it was inevitable that trouble oft befell him. But he was no coward, seeking escape from the discipline his father saw fit to bestow upon him. Joseph Wyse was a respected leader among the local Amish; how he treated his second son was apparently of little consequence to that position.

Adam limped into the barn, not having the strength to swing the door closed behind him. *Betty will see to it.* He breathed in the mixed smells of hay and cows. His father kept only a few *milch* cows for the family's needs; horses were what made and maintained the Wyse home and hearth.

He reached and grabbed up a candle, then shuffled back to the coals of the small, self-contained smithy and waited until the light flared. He heard a sound behind him and turned, the flame held high, and peered into the gloomy stacks of hay.

"Betty?" he called, not in the mood to play a game. His pulse began to race. He was never sure why, but he was nervous when he was alone sometimes, as though he expected danger and had to be prepared for anything.

The hired girl didn't answer, and Adam went back to the work-bench, laying his shirt on the dark wood and setting the candle down in its holder. "Betty. Just come, please, and tend my wounds. I want nothing else from you."

"What else would you want from her?"

The female voice was clear, melodious, and caused him to swing back around with such force that he gasped aloud in pain.

Through the light and shadows of the open barn door, Lena Yoder rose up like some beauteous apparition from between the haystacks.

"Lena?" he asked, appalled that she might have witnessed his punishment.

"*Ya*," she whispered, moving out from the hay and coming close to him.

Her plain cloak did nothing to hide the beauty of the young girl who was his friend and neighbor. Even through the haze of pain, he couldn't help but admire the golden strands of hair that peeked from beneath her round, flat-crowned beaver skin hat, which was tied neatly beneath her chin. Her lithe form seemed to sway as she moved, and when she got closer to the fall of candlelight, he could see that her turquoise blue eyes were wide with sympathy. He thought with shame that he'd rather take ten strokes more than have her look on him with pity.

"What are you doing here?" he asked, his voice coming out rougher than he'd intended.

"*Mamm* sent me with some extra eggs. I heard your father's voice raised in ire, so I slipped into the barn."

"You—saw, then?"

"I had no idea that your *fater* . . . that he . . . Is this the first time?"

Adam wanted to laugh. "*Nee*, but it's nothing."

She reached out a small hand and touched his bare arm. He shuddered and she immediately withdrew. "I'm so sorry. Your back must burn like fire."

Truthfully, Adam had not thought of his back for a *gut* full minute. He was only aware of Lena's scent, like wild roses, and her nearness. He'd fantasized about the girl more times than he cared to recount. She was well within marrying age in their society; still, she was so young. He caught an iron grasp on his emotions and was turning back to the workbench when her voice came again, thrumming across his mind and sensibilities.

"*Ach*, Adam, let me help you."

Let her help? He couldn't imagine what it would be like to have her delicate fingers against him. He wet his lips and shook his head.

"*Nee*, Lena, you'd best go home. I'll be fine." He wanted to kick himself for uttering the lie, but the situation didn't warrant any more trouble.

"So, 'tis Betty you want to tend you." Her young voice rose a bit.

He blinked. "Betty?"

"*Ya*, and you never answered my first question, Adam Wyse. What else would you want from her?"

He heard the wounded pride in her voice and longed to soothe it, but her question had him treading deep water. He wasn't sure that Lena even knew what she was asking. "Nothing," he murmured, risking a brush of his knuckles against the hands she held clasped in front of her belly. "I want nothing from Betty."

Something flared then in the depths of her eyes that sent his stomach churning; it was the beginning of instinctual knowledge, an understanding of the power that a *mawd* might hold over a man. She stepped closer and looked up into his face, letting one hand rest against the front of his rib cage.

"Then do you want something from me?" she murmured, and Adam felt a roaring in his ears. His own breath magnified, his own heartbeat grew louder. Her pink lips parted, and he felt himself move, almost as if he were watching from a distance, and bent his head. She stretched on tiptoe, light as thistle against him, and then he caught himself—one exquisite breath from her mouth.

"Lena," he gasped. "I—cannot."

She smiled then, he felt more than saw, as she inched the lapse between them. If she put her mouth to his, he knew he could not have stopped kissing her in return had it meant another hundred strokes of the lash. He kept a furious grip on the workbench behind him and let his eyes drift shut.

"Adam? 'Ere now, where are ye?"

Lena pulled away as the strident voice of Betty shattered the moment. "Dearest Adam," Lena whispered. "Remember—a first kiss will be forever . . ."

He shook himself from the heated memory now as he landed a foot in a splay of mud. "*Ya*, right . . . ," he muttered aloud, shaking his shoe. "Forever."

Chapter 7

⌣

"Please, Deacon Wyse—will you come and bless Dan's grave?"

Joseph stared down into the anxious blue eyes of the young Amish boy who had his little sister in tow. They had hailed him from alongside the road while he managed the wagon.

"You're the Kings' *kinner, ya?*" he asked, trying to recall if Dan was a family name.

"*Ya.* I'm Abram, and this is Martha. But, *ach,* if you'd come quick . . . We want the burial done right, and *Mamm* doesn't know we come to find you."

Joseph sighed inwardly. The Kings lived on the opposite side of Lancaster, away from his home, and perhaps they had been meant by fate's hand to detain him. He was not sure that he could have borne to see Adam walking alone along the dangerous road and pass him by. As always, his feelings wavered like a giant pendulum in regard to his second son, who looked so much like his own father—with those unusual, all-seeing golden eyes.

He swallowed when he considered Adam's offer of "any punishment." The last time he'd whipped the boy had been years ago, and it had shaken him to his core. He hadn't wanted to stop, hadn't wanted the lash to cease hissing against the still starkness of the fallen snow.

But he had stopped, gone inside, then went to the bedroom and dropped to his knees, sobbing aloud for what he'd done to his boy.

"*Sei se gut*, will you come?" Martha piped up, breaking into his thoughts, and he nodded. The child smiled, though her face was tearstained, and she moved forward to slip a hand into his. He was jolted by the gesture, by the feel of the tiny fingers curled so trustingly into his palm, and he hauled her up beside him on the seat. Then he turned to look down at the boy. "How old are you, *sohn?*" he asked.

"Eleven this March." The boy had followed his sister onto the seat with ease.

Suddenly Joseph remembered Adam at this youngster's age. He grunted as he took the reins of the wagon with one hand. "A fine age. A fine age to be alive."

He ignored the curious look Abram gave him and had to concentrate hard on the road as Martha again placed her hand on his, leaning her slight weight against him. How long had it been since he'd ridden with one of his boys thus? Or with Ellen even? The road became blurry for a few moments.

They arrived at the King farm and the children scrambled down, leaving Joseph to follow, deep in thought. He saw a small mound of dirt, freshly turned, near the back porch of the house, and decided that Dan had been a child. The thought made him sick to his stomach for some reason. But when he came upon the open grave, it was to find the still, small form of a golden puppy, curled up as if asleep.

"It's a dog," he couldn't help but exclaim.

Frau King had come off the porch and heard him speak. "*Ya.* 'Tis sorry I am to trouble you, Deacon Wyse, for such a small matter. I didn't know *mei kinner* had gone to find you."

"It is fine," he soothed, though his insides churned. "All of *Derr Herr's* creatures are valuable."

"That's what I told Abram," Martha whispered.

Joseph braced himself for the onslaught of emotion as the child once more trustingly touched his arm, one finger in her mouth.

"He said it don't matter, but it do."

It don't matter . . . It does not matter . . . The words began to beat a swirling tattoo in Joseph's brain, and he had to blink to stop the refrain. Why was he so upset over a dog, over a child's mere touch?

"*Ya*, it matters," he heard himself respond. "Now let us pray in silence for *Gott's* grace in giving life to—Dan."

Joseph removed his hat and bent his head, trying to detach himself from the panicky feeling in his chest. The death of the wee dog seemed to overpower him, oppressing his senses, 'til he thought he might not be able to draw another breath. He raised his head abruptly and jammed his hat on.

"A *gut* day to you, and a better tomorrow," he said as he brushed by Martha, nearly gasping in relief to be out of sight range of the dog's shiny-coated body. He got up onto the wagon seat and nodded to *Frau King* while avoiding looking down at the children. He hauled on the reins and turned the horses without looking back.

Ruth laid the babes in the carved wooden cradle near the tiled fireplace and sat down to look about the room. The "keeping room," the little Amish girlie, Abigail, called it. A sitting room is what Ruth might have said in her own home. She pushed aside memories of the rather small but comfortable house she'd had in the countryside and tried to concentrate on the austere but functional room of the Amish farm. Trying to garner peace from the simplicity of everything being in its place, she closed her eyes, exhausted. A shadow crossed her face, and Ruth looked up in surprise.

"I've brought you a meal," Lena whispered. "I know you were feeding Faith and Mary earlier and couldn't come to sup. Will you eat something, please?"

Ruth blinked her bleary eyes and looked at the plate before her. When was the last time someone had offered to nourish her? Not even Henry, Lord bless him, had been one for such fussing.

She reached up and took the plate with hesitant hands while the Amish girl bent to arrange a linen napkin comfortably about her. Ruth stared at the steaming yams and crusty rolls drizzled with honey, and breathed deeply of the fragrant stew.

Lena slid into a chair near her. "One thing my *mamm* taught me was how to cook. I hope you like it."

Ruth noticed how the young girl worked to steady her voice, and nodded her head. "It's a piece of beauty, miss. I'm not sure I've ever been served like this."

Lena nodded and smiled as Ruth began to eat. The older woman felt she should say something, but she wasn't even sure she could begin to piece together her day aright—it had all happened so fast.

"I like you," Lena said with sudden candor, and Ruth watched a pretty flush mount the young cheeks. "I mean that I want to thank you for helping today. I wish you might choose to stay for a bit, both you and Mary, as long as you want. But as I've told you, I have no coin."

Ruth chewed reflectively. "Came here ten years ago as an indentured servant; met Henry the same way. We worked off our debts for some years and then built a life for ourselves. I don't want to be no hired woman."

Lena sat forward earnestly. "*Ach*, but I did not mean it like that. I need help . . . We all do. There's no telling when or if my father will be released from prison."

"What did he do?" Ruth swallowed the smoothness of the honey and thought it bliss.

Lena reached to rub her temple beneath her hair covering. "I guess I have not had time to explain much in this day. You know we are Amish? My father paid the extra taxes and we gave food to Patriots and British alike, but the local regiment came and meant to require one half of all of our stock and provisions. My mother was poorly, and my father had seen too much of this commandeering. He protested, and they took almost all of the stock and hauled him off to prison. That was about three weeks ago. We'd been managing, but then *Mamm* became sick . . . I should have walked into town to find a midwife."

"No sense fretting about what's done, what's gone. I need to learn that for myself, I guess. But ain't there a midwife among your people hereabouts?"

Lena shook her head. "One who travels by mule. It takes her nearly two months to circulate to all of the Amish spread about. If there's a woman due, she'll wait. There was no telling where she was."

Ruth finished her plate and could not resist running a finger around the remnants of the stew. "That was fine eating, dearie. But things will be finer still if you let go of troubling yourself about what you might have done."

"You are right. We—we believe in the Lord's will. I should remember that."

Ruth snorted. "The Lord's a mite favorable toward some, it seems, and not so to others."

"Will you tell me about your husband?"

Ruth gripped the edges of the pewter plate. "Not much to tell. Loved to laugh, but had a real stubborn streak in him too. He enlisted right off. There was a skirmish somewhere a couple of weeks past. A rider come to the house and told me Henry was gone. That's all . . . until the house fire. I guess I got addlepated over Henry and forgot to tend the fire right. My fault."

Lena stretched across the small space to put her hand on the other woman's knee. "I am so very sorry. Your loss must be even greater than my own. I—I imagine that you lost everything in the fire."

Ruth's throat constricted at the simple touch. "Pretty much everything's gone, though my babe was spared. I came here with nothing but a change of clothes, a few coins I grabbed, and one page of the Bible I tore out 'afore everything burned."

"Just a page? What does it say?"

"Don't know. Tore it out as a keepsake, like."

Ruth was surprised at the girl's excitement. She herself felt as if one page from the Good Book was about all there was coming to her from God, all that would ever come. Yet even now, the soft breaths of the two babes beside her soothed her heart. She heaved herself out of the chair and crossed the room to the heavy dresser where her bundle lay. She undid the knots on the twine, and the smell of smoke rose to her nostrils, bringing stinging tears to her eyes.

She crossed back to Lena and held out the tattered page with its ragged end. "Read and see what it says. My eyes are bothering me a bit."

Lena tilted closer to the fire. "It's from Ezekiel," she murmured. "A difficult book to be sure, but I know one verse here from memory. The Lord says, 'For, behold, I am for you, and I will turn unto you, and ye shall be tilled and sown.'"

"Ha!" Ruth gave a laugh, feeling like she couldn't comprehend the full meaning of the words. "Well, I sure have been ploughed under, if that's what it says then."

Lena turned to her with steady eyes, blue like the sea. "*Ach*, I know it sounds hard. Even for me to listen to since I learned it as a child. But we turn the soil when we farm, to make room for new growth . . . and the Lord promises the seeds of that growing. But more than that, Ruth, He says that He is for us. He's on our side."

Ruth considered for a sad moment before shaking her head. "*Our* side? For us, dearie? Who does that mean in a war, then? I know you've been trained to believe, but I ain't. I told you, it's a keepsake, 'tis all."

She reached out for the page and Lena handed it back with visible reluctance.

Ruth cleared her throat. "I expect you'll be wanting us to move on, then?"

The girl looked at her in surprise. "Whatever for? Because we believe differently? *Nee.* I think the Lord brought you and Mary to us, and us to you. I want to help you, Ruth, and will be glad if you will stay as my friend."

Ruth nodded, feeling like she'd just been graced by the touch of a faerie's words. "A friend. Well, then, that I will be to you, dearie. A true friend."

Lena squeezed her hand, and Ruth allowed her rough fingers to encircle the slender palm, willing to try to do all she could to keep her promise of friendship to the slip of a girl.

<hr />

"There's a man out at the grave."

Lena looked up in surprise as she entered the room half an hour later. She had finally found time to bathe and to change into her other black dress and a clean kerchief and apron. She'd also dampened her hair and added a new prayer covering.

Ruth turned from the dusky window, and Lena reflected that since her father had been imprisoned, she and her mother had been more nervous of strangers about the place. But perhaps Isaac had returned to express further regrets.

"Do you want me to go and be rid of him?" Ruth asked, hands on ample hips.

"*Nee*, I will go. Perhaps 'tis a wanderer in need of food."

Lena slipped outside, drawing her cloak close about her as she stepped off the porch and into the twilight.

The broad-shouldered, long-legged stance of the shadowy visitor was unmistakable, and she nearly stumbled in her anxiousness to get to his side.

"*Ach*, Adam. I missed you so today. I—I thought you might come back for the burial."

She heard him draw a deep breath.

"*Nee*. I—I had some things to attend to in town."

"Oh." She shivered a bit, longing for him to pull her close, but he made no move. Again she reasoned that he must be as distressed as she over her mother's death. And perhaps he did not know how to share his grief. She curled a tentative hand into his large palm and felt him stiffen. She drew away, hurt and confused.

He cleared his throat. "Lena . . . I must tell you something. I have been thinking of enlisting in the fight."

The words spilled from him in a rush, and she struggled to make sense of what he'd said. Surely she had misheard.

"What do you mean?" she asked softly, looking up at his profile, chiseled hard in the moonlight.

"The Patriots have need of *gut* farriers and horsemen. I—I could make money, more than I do from *Fater*, and build a new life."

She scrambled to keep up with the strange conversation. "A new life? But our life together has yet to begin, Adam."

"I meant that I could build a new life for myself, Lena." His tone was sober, deadly serious, and she put a hand to her heart.

"What are you saying? My *mamm* died today, and you . . . and you . . ." She broke off, unable to suppress the sob that came from her throat.

He turned to her then, catching her arms in a tight grip. "Lena, listen to me. Your father has never liked me, never trusted me. Maybe he is right—maybe there is something about me, about my life right now, that is not good for you."

"*Nee*, 'tis not true. You've never let Father's opinions affect you before; why should you now? And you are a *gut* man, Adam . . . a *gut* and faithful man."

"Stop!" he snapped, dropping her arms. "I came here to tell you that what we had between us is over."

"But . . . I have loved you since I was a mere child," she returned dully, trying to absorb the stabbing hollowness of what he said.

"I know that," he whispered.

She faced him, stretching to see his expression in the pale light. "You have . . . fallen in love with another, perhaps?"

He shook his head, his jaw tensing as if her question struck him with physical pain. "*Nee*, Lena. 'Tis not that. I simply feel the call to build a life for myself that rings with freedom."

"And what is more free than the air of the field? Or the turn of a leaf? Or the cry of a babe at dawn?"

He closed his eyes against her words, and for a moment she thought she had reached him through this strange fog. Then he stared down at her once more, the moonlight highlighting the gold intensity of his eyes, and what she saw there, she saw to be truth.

<hr />

Adam was stricken with pain so deep, he knew he'd rather take a hundred beatings from his father's hand than do this to Lena. Part of him questioned Mary Yoder. Could she have known that what she asked would hurt her daughter so? It would be so easy, even now, to stretch out his arms and gather Lena to him, to dampen her mouth with kisses and to whisper promises of hope in the shell-like softness of her ear. But he could not . . . not if he meant to keep his word.

He had not intended the break to be so soon nor so profound. He had told himself that he would put it off until Lena had time to recover from her mother's death. But the reality of her need for someone to watch over her and protect her was a pressing issue, and he knew that marriage would be all too easy a way to dismiss what hope he had given to her mother.

Lena moved slightly, to rest against a nearby fence rail, as if for support. He wanted to tell her the truth, but he could not. Not when he'd discovered that enlisting might help him build a free life the fastest.

"And what of your faith?" she asked in ragged tones, surprising him as always with the way she understood the darkest of his thoughts.

"There are some things worth fighting for," he said, wondering if it were really true.

"You would give up being Amish? Deny what others endured and were martyred for . . . our way of life?"

He couldn't answer; he didn't know the answer. And more than this, he realized that if he did enlist, did manage to build a new life, he would have to ask Lena to give up being Amish one day—if she would still have him.

And then her voice softened and she spoke in careful tones. "Adam . . . I will accept it if you say that you no longer want . . . want me. But you know I have seen you act—differently—before. Could—could this be one of those times . . . when you are not quite yourself?"

He flushed with embarrassment. He knew exactly what she spoke of—the flashbacks to something namelessly horrible, the nightmares . . .

"Do you remember the time we were together in the field, and you slept?" she asked.

He remembered all too well . . .

It was high summer, the fields dark green, and patches of violets lay thick upon the ground. They were seated beneath one of the old oaks on her father's land, having walked far from the house. He had fallen asleep, lulled by the soft comfort of her shoulder, though he always worried about touching her, never wanting to trespass against propriety, even though he wished that he could. Then he began to dream, and the nightmare came in the daylight, and he'd awakened with a low moan. Lena was looking at him, gently wiping the damp hair from his forehead.

He had snapped fully awake then, rolling from her and knocking a stray elbow against her arm. He'd stared at her blankly until he shook himself. "Don't ever let me do that again," he'd ground out.

She smiled in confusion as she rubbed her arm. "Do what?"

"Fall asleep." His eyes scanned the green fields as if searching for something.

"I can stand a few nightmares, Adam. Everybody has them at one time or another."

He shook his head and stared at her hard. "I mean it, Lena."

She blew out a breath in frustration. "Well, then, how exactly are we going to sleep togeth—"

She'd broken off, blushing, and he'd shivered, torn between fear and desire.

He looked at her fully, and a deep sadness drew over him. "Together? As man and wife? I—I do not know."

He'd crawled closer to her and bent with tenderness to stroke her arm where she rubbed it. "I know I cannot risk hurting you in my sleep, as I did just now."

"It is nothing," she choked, and he knew she feared the soberness of his attitude, the strangeness of his behavior.

Now he blinked away the confusing memories and stared at her in the moonlight. "*Nee*, Lena. I am sound of mind. I mean what I say."

She nodded, and he watched her delicate neck bend as if yoked to comprehension. Then she raised her chin and looked him in the eye, and he could not help but admire her spirit.

"I do not understand fully, Adam, but I will accept what you say. *Gott* is for me . . . and for you. I will pray for you, for I can't turn off my feelings like damming a spring. But I will go on, and the *kinner* and I will be well."

She pulled away from the fence post and brushed past him, her cloak touching his arm and sending tiny sensations of longing through his chest. He turned to watch her go and told himself that he was mad to have spoken to her as he did. But then *Gott's* voice came to him, a heart echo of soothing over the tumult in his chest. *Faithful servant. All will be well . . . but wait . . . wait.*

He had no choice but to hope in the comforting words, though he felt far from anything faithful or good. He heard the farmhouse door snap closed and shut his eyes against the sound as tears pressed and fell at the foot of Mary Yoder's fresh grave.

Chapter 8

I t grows late." Ellen Wyse spoke from where she stood near the dining
table. Her hand stroked Adam's pewter plate with nervous fingers.

Joseph turned from his contemplation of the flames in the fireplace and looked at his wife. She was, in truth, a beauty still. He knew
he had chosen well in marriage—not that he'd had any instruction in
the matter of choosing. His parents had been . . .

He dragged his mind back to his wife, away from the gnashing
images of his younger life. It mattered little that Ellen had only managed to produce two healthy sons; the small family graveyard bore
testament to the other three she had lost in attempting to perform her
duty. He could ask for nothing more.

"Serve the meal, Ellen," he said, ignoring her obvious worry and
moving to his seat at the head of the table.

Isaac soon joined them, and Joseph saw him glance toward his
brother's plate.

"Adam's late again. I wonder where he eats half of the time."

Ellen bore the kettle of fragrant squirrel stew to the center of the
table and stepped away to catch up the basket of biscuits from a tall
wooden shelf. She took her place, then glanced wryly at Isaac. "Likely
he does not eat at all."

Joseph's hand came down with a rap against the wood of the table. "Then he does not eat. Stop fussing, Ellen."

He watched her delicate neck bend in submission before bowing his head for silent grace. The moment was broken by the opening of the front door.

Adam entered, looking chilled and disheveled.

"Forgive me, *Fater, Mamm,* for my lateness." He moved to take his seat, his eyes sweeping the table.

Joseph lifted a single finger, and Adam gave him a wary look. "You have missed the blessing of the food your mother has worked to prepare. You need not participate in this meal, Adam."

"But, Joseph," Ellen spoke up. "The long walk . . . He must be hungry."

He gave her a quelling glance, and Ellen dropped her head.

Adam rose to his full height. "I find that I am not hungry after all, *Mamm.* In truth, I do not think I can stomach another morsel."

Joseph fingered the edge of his pewter *messer* at this unusually level and challenging response to his command. Something was wrong with Adam. The boy looked surprised himself at his own words. Jospeh felt a surge of fear in the recesses of his mind.

"Why do I think that you speak of more than mere food, my *sohn?*" he asked, keeping his voice quiet. The candlelight played on the edge of his knife.

Adam swung an intense gaze in his direction, and Joseph had to force himself to remain calm.

"What do we talk of here, *Fater?*" Isaac asked, breaking the tension of the moment.

Joseph lowered his *messer* and lifted a biscuit. He broke off a piece and crumbled it between his fingers. "Nothing to trouble you, Isaac. I'm sure Adam is simply tired." He glanced back to the golden eyes of his son and saw the confusion there, the return of the boy's usual vulnerability. He felt a surge of relief in his belly and cursed the weakness within him that feared his own son and the truth.

"*Ya, Fater.* I am tired, 'tis all. Please forgive me. May I go to bed?"

Joseph gave a brief wave of dismissal but did not begin to eat again until Adam's footsteps had faded up the oaken staircase. It was clear that the boy had experienced something to produce his unusual flare of restlessness and attempt at noncompliance. He needed to be watched more closely.

━━◆━━

Adam looked up at the knock on his door. It was far into night and the candle burned low on his bedside table.

"*Kumme* in," he said, hoping it was not his father. But then, *Fater* never knocked.

To his surprise, it was Isaac, looking rumpled, with his white shirt untucked, his brown hair tousled, and a raccoon in his arms.

Adam leaned up on one elbow on the bed.

"New pet?"

"He has a bite on his hindquarters. I thought I would keep him awhile until the wound heals."

Adam nodded. His brother's love of animals was something that had existed for as long as he could remember. Along with his books, Isaac seemed to lose himself in the comfort of tending smaller creatures.

"Is that why you seek me out at this hour? To show me a raccoon?"

Isaac smiled. "*Nee.* I saw your light, and it disturbed me." He reached beneath his shirt and produced two crusty rolls of bread. "Here. I thought you might be hungry."

Adam sat up and wolfed down the rolls, not caring for a moment what would happen if their sire heard the doorway conversation. When he was done, he eyed his elder brother speculatively. "I thank you, Isaac.

'Twas good. But you've seen me go hungry before and seen my light burn in the wee hours. Why bother now?"

Isaac shrugged. "I fed the coon; I could do no less for you."

"Ah."

"And I thought that perhaps something besides *Fater* troubled you. Do you want to talk about it?"

There was just enough diffidence in his brother's tone to make Adam want to pour his heart out. If Isaac had been sympathetic, curious, or simply nosy, he would not have talked. But he longed to share the truth of his loss of Lena with someone.

"I gave up my relationship with Lena."

"What?" Isaac's question was a low roar, and Adam looked at him irritably.

"Come in here and shut the door before *Fater* is up."

Isaac shut the door and turned to lean against it, stroking the raccoon in his arms. For once, Adam noted, his brother's dark eyes were anything but sleepy; there was an interested speculation there that was enough to give him pause.

"Why would you give her up?" Isaac asked. "I will admit that she is stubborn and willful, but she is by far the most beauteous lass about."

"How do you know she is stubborn? And I thought future Amish bishops should not care about such earthly things as physical beauty."

"I tried to offer her spiritual counsel, but she refused it. She said that you were her spiritual bedrock."

Adam ducked his head as if he'd been struck a physical blow. "Go on."

"As for her beauty—'tis a gift from *Gott*, is it not? I would have to be blind not to admit that I have thought upon her on occasion with some—chaste—interest."

Adam looked him in the eye and had the unnatural feeling of

wanting to strangle someone. Was Isaac suggesting that *he* would want to court Lena? And how would that play into his promise to Mary, who could not have possibly foreseen a potentially meddlesome older brother.

"*Ya*, well—keep that interest chaste, *bruder*."

"But you said you have given her up. Surely I will not be the only man who might seek to have a role in her life. She needs a man badly at this time."

Adam gritted his teeth. What could he say? He couldn't have it both ways—be apart from her and then still want her as far as the rest of the world was concerned. It was an impossible dilemma. He flung himself backward on his bed and drew a bare arm across his face.

"*Danki* for the bread," he said in a tone of dismissal.

"Adam, I—"

"Good night."

He heard the door close gently but stayed awake 'til dawn, wrestling with the haunting thought of Lena's heart falling prey to another.

———— ◆ ————

Lena rolled over in the bed and remembered the previous night. She felt bruised from the inside out . . . raw and hurting. She sat up with caution, and from long habit made sure not to elbow Abigail in the process. She gazed down with bittersweet pleasure at her *schwester's* sweet, freckled face in the play of morning's light and knew that she had overslept. She should have been up as *Mamm* would have been, long before daybreak. She swallowed hard at the thought of the terrible previous day of death, new life, and Adam's horrible visit, but she was determined to move onward. She slid upward with care, her plain white linen gown caught round her legs beneath the wool coverlet. She felt her ruffled nightcap askew, so that her long blond hair brushed the tops of her hands as she pressed against the straw-filled mattress.

An image of what it might feel like to have Adam kissing her came to her in a sudden rush, and she clenched the mattress. It was as if her mouth stung with sensation from the very idea of his kiss. But she was being foolish. She knew Adam well enough to understand that he meant what he said, and he had meant it last night. It felt like her arm had been cut off abruptly, leaving a jagged and painful injury that would require long recovery.

Yet even now a moment of concern wrung her heart when she thought of his sometimes-odd behavior, and she slowly unclasped her hand and smoothed the mattress cover.

She wondered if moments like last night, when Adam did not seem to be fully in control of himself, had frightened him in regard to her, made him worry that he might hurt her in some way without thinking. But no. Surely it was his interest in the war, something she had not sensed in great depth about him before, that stood between them.

She bowed her head to begin her morning prayers with Adam on her heart when her thoughts were interrupted by John slipping into the room without knocking. He was fully dressed for the day, but his hair, brushing his shoulders as the Amish men's did, was slightly askew.

"I cannot abide her," he announced, and Lena felt Abigail stir against the pillow.

"Shhh," Lena said, then went on in a whisper. "What is the difficulty?"

"That woman, Ruth Stone," John hissed back fiercely, his hands pressed against the wood of the oaken door. "She orders me about as if, well, as if she were *Mamm*. And she ain't."

"Is not," Lena corrected absently. She slipped from the bed and went to her brother, laying a firm hand on his shoulder. It amazed her that he was so tall for ten years; he barely had to lift his head to meet her gaze. "John, you are the man of this house while *Fater* is gone. There is no one who doubts that. But *Derr Herr* has sent Ruth to us to feed baby Faith and help us out. And I need the help. I do not know how *Mamm* did it all, to tell the truth."

"She has already had me to the smokehouse, out for firewood and water, and now she wants me to milk the single miserable goat that the scum who took *Fater* left behind."

Lena's eyes widened in shock at the boy's language. It was one thing to disagree with the taking up of arms, but quite another to describe human lives, created by the hand of *Gott*, as "scum."

"John, where have you learned such words? And why would you choose to use them?" She had never known her *bruder* to be anything but reticent. Had their mother's death unleashed some hidden anger in the boy?

He shook off her hand. "'Tis true, Lena. They are scum, and you know it." He blew out a breath of disgust. "Tories, Brits, and now a Continental army formed from a miserable local militia. Have you seen their flag? A piked soldier holding back a lion." He snorted. "Better that they chose a half-loaded musket and a stolen cow!"

"Why are you shouting, John?" Abigail asked sleepily from the bed.

Lena rolled her eyes, then glared at her brother. "See, you've woken Abby. And I would like to remind you that there have been any number of Amish boys who've left home and our way of life to join that army and fight for free— Well, to fight."

John met her eyes. "Too bad you have not always been so understanding when it comes to the war . . . and to Adam."

"What are you talking about?"

"You heard me," he said. "I was outside last night when Adam came over. I heard what was said."

Lena felt her eyes sting with furious tears. "You are old enough to know that it is wrong, John Yoder, to listen to others' conversation. Besides, I thought you came in here to complain of Ruth Stone."

"I'm sorry, Lena. Forgive me. I shouldn't have said all that." John was back to his normal self, but his angry, adultlike comments had made Lena uneasy as well as hurt.

He put his hand on the door latch. "I'll go milk the goat and try to praise *Gott* for Ruth Stone." He was gone before Lena could speak, closing the door behind him.

Lena just stood, staring at the closed door, unsure of what had occurred except that her normally placid brother, the one she had considered a child still, was having some very manly thoughts. She could not resist the clutch of fear at her heart that he might try to join the fight somehow. Boys as young as ten had been known to run off, never to be heard from again. She pushed aside his insinuations about her attitude toward the war . . . and Adam.

"Is John angry, Lena?" Abigail asked.

Lena pivoted on her bare feet and stared at her innocent, tousled-haired sister. She thought of her *mamm* and went back to the bed, catching the child close for a hug.

"*Nee*, Abby. He is . . . becoming a man."

Abigail giggled, and Lena suppressed a troubled sigh.

Chapter 9

I t had been two days since the night at Lena's, and Adam's mind still
burned with the memory despite the cool spring breeze that lifted
his long hair from the back of his neck. The days had seemed an eternity. She was not only his love but his best friend, and the loneliness he
now felt cut him to the core.

His face was flushed from the heat of the smithy where he was
shaping new shoes for the chestnut mare in the far pasture. He had
left the barn doors wide-open and relished the scents and sounds of
spring. He hated winter, with its unrelenting cold and the rigors of the
snow—the bleakness of this thought made him wonder how Samuel
Yoder would eat this day in prison. Adam could, of course, walk the
coin and bread into town, but there were dangers in being afoot. He
considered the situation with a prayerful bent and was about to strike
the shoe with the anvil again when the sound of rapidly approaching
hoofbeats caused him to look up.

He gazed in amazement at the laughing apparition of Major Dale
Ellis, blond hair askew, blue frock coat and lace collar intact, as he came
to a rushing halt in front of the barn. Dale was mounted on a fine bay
gelding and led Tim, saddled but riderless, directly behind him.

Adam put down his tools. Dale laughed again and let go of the lead, leaving Tim to come directly to Adam's hands.

"I believe, sir, that I return something which rightfully belongs here, on this no doubt fine farm."

Adam said the first thing that came to mind. "You are not permitted to go beyond the city limits of Lancaster—you could be hanged."

Dale waved an airy hand. "Aye, I know. Death and dismemberment and all that hoptrop—just what one of your earthy Patriots would love to dish out to an Officer of the Realm."

"I do not understand." Adam stepped out into the sunshine and offered a jug of water up to the other man.

Dale took a swig and wiped his hand over his mouth. "I will make my telling quick, so as not to meet some dire end. I won Tim here from some miscreant militia man who was too far into his cups early this morn . . . much too far to be betting what he did at cards. And since I as a prisoner can own no horse, I thought I'd return him. I've seen you about with him and figured that foul guard took advantage somehow." Dale jumped down and moved to water his own mount at a nearby trough.

Adam smiled. "Perhaps, but let me give you coin for your trouble. And I do mean trouble, if anyone finds out. This is no ladies' picnic, after all, for the town fathers to turn a blind eye to. And where, might I ask, did your own fine horse come from?"

"The same unfortunate card game, I fear," Dale muttered, shaking his head, then remounting in an expert manner. "I don't know what I will do with this horse—dedicate it to the cause, I suppose. And, my fine Amish fellow, friends do not exchange coins over gifts. That is, if I have your friendship during my rather boring imprisonment?" The question hung between them while Dale's eyes bored into Adam's intently.

Adam hesitated for only a second before extending his hand and grasping the other man's firmly. "I will call you a friend," he said.

Dale let go of his hand and smiled. "Good. Then I will tell you why I am here in truth. There is a famed, or infamous, I should say, Tory hunter in Lancaster. A Major George, to be precise. He has the authority of the Pennsylvania State Court behind him. It was announced just this morn that there was to be a trial, such as it may be, and set for high noon. I made it my business to secure the list of those being tried. Samuel Yoder is to stand. I thought you might want to be present."

Adam swallowed hard and thought of the four Amish men said to be dragged in and tortured in a nearby town by the Patriots, their very countrymen, for being dissident peace-keepers. Who but *Derr Herr* could know what fate awaited Samuel Yoder? Adam knew he must tell Lena and must get himself there before the tribunal began. Even if they could do nothing, it would still be better to learn of the man's fate firsthand rather than through a rider and late tidings.

He looked up into the keen blue eyes of the other man and realized all that he had risked in bringing the information. "Truly," Adam said, "you have my thanks and my loyalty . . . whatever you should need in time."

Dale gave a faint smile. "You may live to regret that, my friend." He turned his mount in a fine cloud of dust and rode off with a flourish, tipping his head to Joseph Wyse, who was just then walking toward the barn.

Adam knew instinctively that he could not explain Dale's errand to his father. Joseph would try to persuade him against going into town. He braced himself for his father's words.

"Who was that? And why is Tim back?"

"'Twas no one, sir. A friend returning a debt, you might say."

His father frowned and stared hard at him. "*Ach* . . . well, I've no time to discuss things this morning, Adam. I have a buyer coming to look at that mare. I will need you to give her a good grooming."

Adam swallowed. "I cannot, sir. I've business in town I must attend to at once." He tried to keep his voice level; it was a rare occurrence for him to act in direct defiance of his father's immediate wishes.

A muscle tensed in his parent's chiseled cheek for just a moment before he swung on his boot heel and roared toward an adjacent barn. "Isaac!"

Adam took the opportunity to slip away.

He passed the open door of the *kesselhous*, and the delicious smell of fresh baking bread wafted out. His *mamm* waved floury hands at him from the dim interior, and despite his hurry, he could not resist stopping for a moment to see her.

"Do you need something, Adam?" she asked, her smile bright as always.

He smiled back and shook his head, moving to give her a quick hug. Then he snatched a pinch of dough from one of the pieces in the kneading tray and moved on.

Once inside the main house, he took the stairs two at a time and hurried down the narrow hall to his room. He caught up his wide-brimmed straw hat and went to his plain-hewn dresser to open the top drawer. He had coin; his father had paid him a man's wage since he'd turned eighteen and had continued to work on the farm. He had managed to save most of it, but he had no idea how coins of the realm would help or hinder the whims of this Major George. Then, as he grasped the drawer edge, the thought came to him, something cool and solid like resting a hand against limestone on a summer's day: he needed to stop and pray.

The whirlwind of anxious hurry, fear, and a noticeable tightness in his throat began to subside as he leaned against the dresser top and let his mind drift to thoughts of *Derr Herr*. There were many times in his life when all he could seem to do was to think thoughts of praise when he was praying—to focus on the simple wonder of the created world. To give thanks for the wind, the grass, the call of a morning bird. In truth, he often felt silently simple-minded when the family worshipped together because he could not seem to focus on higher inner words or petitions as he felt the others around him seemed to do. And when the time came for larger group worship, with Amish coming from far away to gather as they once had in the Old Country, he experienced even more discouragement and frustration with himself as a spiritual man.

He knew the hymns, of course, sung without instruments, in the deep monotones that both soothed and reminded him that he came from a heritage of martyrs' lamentations mingled with hard-won strains of praise. But then, this thought of the past only led him to the present to reflect more upon the war for freedom and on the reason his people had come to Penn's Woods, to find freedom in the face of religious extermination . . . And then his mind would be off at full gallop until he could discipline himself back to the moment at hand, to the simplest of prayers. He drew a deep breath.

"Dear *Gott* in heaven, my *Fater* . . . my true *Fater* . . ." The thought was upon him before he could extinguish it, and he bowed his head lower. "*Danki* for this day, for my family, for Lena. I pray for her *fater*, for the words that come from his lips if he is accused, and for anything that I might do to help but not hinder. I lift up to You this Major George, this earthly judge, that You would guide his thoughts and actions. Let all be done according to Your will, O Lord . . . and please, please ease the burden of this promise I have made. Bless Lena, *Gott*. Keep her safe and please teach me to allow You to battle and give me the desire to follow the ways of my people. Amen."

He slid the drawer closed, feeling more centered, then took a step deeper into the room. His hand hovered for a moment over his long rifle, mounted neatly on the white wall. The gun was not something he'd normally carry, except to hunt, because of the length of the barrel. But something made him take it all the same. He grabbed up the needed ammunition in a pouch and headed out.

He avoided his mother's eyes when he approached, knowing she would look askance at the rifle. Then he paused and hurried to brush her cheek with his lips. "Do not fret," he said, then turned from the heat of the oven house to step back out into the milder warmth of the spring sunshine.

His father was engaged with a rather pompous, ruddy-looking buyer in full *Englisch* dress, including a piled white wig, and a coach and four waiting nearby with embossed doors and befeathered horses, the animals dancing with impatience.

Adam felt his father's eyes take in the gun as he passed and mounted Tim with the ease of long practice. Joseph's gaze was heavy upon him, but he knew that the prospect of a sale during the time of war would be more than a competing distraction from his doings, and he breathed another prayer of praise that took in the bewigged buyer. He nodded to Isaac, who returned a sour glance as he looked up from currying the mare.

Adam almost had to suppress a smile; it was rare that his *bruder* had to take over his work, and the small taste of freedom set the pace for the ride to Lena Yoder's. If he felt any remorse in not telling his would-be interested and chaste brother what he was about, it didn't show as he let Tim have his head. Isaac would probably suggest a sermon anyway, in hopes of avoiding any action that would lead to accountability. Adam ducked beneath a low-hanging limb and began to whistle as both tense excitement and a certain peace of mind filled him with a warmth equal to that of the spring sun.

Chapter 10

Lena straightened her back and rubbed at the faint ache that was a result of working in the kitchen *gorda*. The weather had warmed slightly, allowing her some early planting, and she had just cleared the leek bed, planning to have leek soup for dinner. The winter-sown broad beans were growing well, but there had been enough space to sow some early peas among them. However many peas were grown, though, there were never enough. It was her *fater's* favorite vegetable. She would not allow her thoughts to linger on him, though, and she turned to pace off a space where she might sow the early *reebs*, Hamburg parsley, and kohlrabi. The row where the spring *kraut* would go could do just as well now for a bit of fresh greens, and she could get the lima beans in as soon as she knew that the last frost had passed.

Three geese ambled over her footsteps in the dirt, all that was left of the flock after the soldiers had taken more than a fair share. She thought it a shame that the birds would probably be used for food and not for their abundant feathers, which graced the pillows of every Amish bed she had ever seen.

Ruth was in the house with the *kinner*—at least with Abigail and Faith and Baby Mary. John had run off somewhere as soon as the minimum of his chores was complete. Lena told herself that she could not concentrate on her work and worry about the boy at the same time, and she deliberately put him from her mind with a quick prayer.

She climbed the steps and dropped into a bent willow rocking chair, reaching to pick up a flat brim-shaped circle and to draw another length of straw from the oiled water where it soaked in a tall tin beside her. She needed to finish braiding the summer's new hats as quickly as possible in preparation for the season, and her nimble fingers flew at the task as she tried to thrust aside thoughts of Adam.

She looked up when she heard hoofbeats and almost sighed instead of feeling the normal clutch of fear that the sound of an approaching horseman tended to bring. In truth, she was weary and felt anyone might take whatever they wanted so long as they left the little family in peace. But when she recognized Tim and then Adam, her fingers froze in midtwist, and the straw slipped loosely from her hand. Perhaps he had changed his mind about their relationship.

He drew rein directly at the bottom of the stairs and she stared at him, almost level with his flashing eyes because of the height of the porch.

"Lena, there's no time to explain. I've had word that your *fater* is to face trial this noontime. I intend to go, and I wanted to offer you a chance to do the same."

The hat form fell from her lap as she rose to come forward to search his face. She saw the seriousness there and spun on her heavy-soled heel without a word.

She stalked into the house, not caring that she closed the door on Adam for the moment. He knew her well enough and could tell, she was sure, by hearing, that she had every intention of going with him. "Ruth?" she called.

"What is it?" the older woman asked, burping Faith with ease while Mary slept in the cradle.

Lena snatched off her work hat and pulled on the town straw, tying it neatly beneath her chin. She adjusted her apron and sighed aloud.

"It is my *fater*. He's to stand trial at noon. A—man brought news. I am going with him to town to see the outcome."

"A man, dearie? Do you think you should go alone with him?"

"Is it Adam?" Abigail asked matter-of-factly, looking up from scraping carrots.

Lena flushed against her will. "*Ya.*" She looked at Ruth. "Adam Wyse is . . . well, I thought once that we might build a life together. But he feels differently of late . . ." She trailed off lamely.

"What do you mean, Lena? We all love Adam," Abigail chirped. "Except maybe *Fater* . . . but I don't know why."

"Well, anyway, I will be safe," Lena declared, wishing she could silence her sister. She was not yet ready to talk about Adam with Ruth, or with anyone for that matter. And yet she knew her words to be true. She would always be safe with him.

She shook herself mentally for such thoughts while her father awaited his fate, then nodded to Ruth, patted Abby, and flew back out the door.

She came to an abrupt halt on the top step when she realized she'd have to ride with Adam in relentless proximity. He looked unconcerned at the prospect though.

"We must hurry, Lena. Do you wish to ride in front or behind?"

His innocent words conjured up images of herself in his grasp, his strong hands steadying her, the sinews of his arms encircling her . . . Or would it be less treacherous for her to place her own arms around his lean waist, to feel the warmth of his body through the linen of his shirt . . .

"Lena?" There was a faint tone of impatience in his voice. "We must not dally."

"Of course," she murmured, recovering some composure and uttering a silent prayer for forgiveness for her thoughts, only to allow herself to be engulfed in them once more. "I'll ride behind." *Where I'll be more in control of the contact . . .*

He shrugged and reached an arm out to her. "Fine, but astride, *sei se gut*. We must travel fast, and I've no time for you to slip off in a tangle of skirts."

She opened her mouth to protest, then closed it with a quick snap. She had ridden astride with him plenty of times in the past, and she could always have him deposit her at the edge of town where she could make a more proper arrival at the trial. It would most likely be held in public, in the town square.

She caught his arm and felt herself pulled upon the steady horse with ease.

"Hold tight. I intend to go as fast as possible," Adam warned as he turned the beast. Lena reluctantly let her hands slide along the thin linen of his shirt. He wasn't wearing a vest, so he must have been caught working when he heard the news of her father.

She tried to let the pacing of the horse beneath her soothe her tired mind. She felt torn inside between having very human emotions of passion yet feeling as stricken as an invalid in the face of her mother's death and her father's imprisonment. It seemed that life was to go on and that *Derr Herr* was carrying her, perhaps literally, through days that might have been slow and monotonous without the advent of Ruth and Mary and the tumult of Adam's rejection. Now, with her arms locked around him, she could not deny the effect he had on her any more than she could her own breath. She wondered if it would always be thus and tried to imagine some other man, a tall mysterious stranger, who might sweep into her life and wipe away the imprint of Adam from her consciousness. But try as she might, there was only the dark-haired man whom she held and with whom, she reminded herself, she should be very angry for his abrupt ending of their relationship.

"You are quiet," he said over his shoulder, offering her a glimpse of his tanned, perfect profile.

"As are you," she returned with conscious diffidence and a sniff.

"You think of your *mamm*."

It wasn't a question, just a simple statement of fact. His words dissolved the walls she had constructed surrounding her *mamm's* loss and left her heart and mind exposed and vital.

"*Ya* . . . I can scarce believe she is gone. I was—so scared. When she was dying, I mean. I had seen *Grossmuder* Yoder after she died, but this was so different. Her breathing—she labored so at the end." Lena sighed, realizing she had longed to express these small intimacies with someone, and now here she was, telling Adam, who had blantantly rejected her.

"I am sorry," he said after a moment of silence. "And that is sparse enough in its good, but my heart beats for you in what must have been a terrible situation. You did all that you could, I know. I would have . . . well, I would have been there with you if I could."

"Do you still have bad dreams?"

She was surprised at her own boldness in asking so intimate a question in the face of his rejection. But she felt the lean muscles beneath her hands grow tense and alert. She had often fretted when his eyes lost some of their glimmer and bruiselike shadows hollowed the contours of his face, knowing it was because of his dreams.

"Always," he finally returned.

The horse picked its way through an encroaching thicket where leaves and blackened walnut hulls were strewn across the road.

Lena drew a deep breath. "Before . . . when we . . . Well, you would never allow me to ask more than you were willing to offer. But I risk it now, since I have nothing to lose. Why is it, Adam? Why do you dream?"

She thought that he would cut her off in cold silence or with a clipped response, but instead his voice when it came to her was soft and husky with emotion.

"I do not know why it is that I dream, Lena. I—I have tried to wrestle with it within myself, before the Lord even, and I—"

The sudden and terrifying sound of a woman's scream echoed from the overhead tree branches above them.

Adam managed to hold Tim to a quick rear and simultaneously slid his rifle from the side of the saddle. Lena's heart beat with wild force in her throat. She knew that scream. It was the hungry battle cry of a mountain lion that had found easy prey.

Chapter 11

⌣

"That's not the way *Mamm* did it."

Ruth heard the treble threat of tears in Abigail's small voice as the child stared into the vat where old cooking grease and creek water needed to be rendered for the making of soap.

"Aye, she was bound to do it in the fall at butchering time, is that not so, dearie?"

The child nodded but didn't look up, and Ruth felt her heart more alive than she would have guessed it could be as she reached a gentle hand to the pale brow of the little girl, then went back to moving the paddle in the odorous mass.

"Soap making is as different as one woman to the next, Abby. Will you tell me how else your mum did it?"

In answer, Abigail turned and ran to a small barn where Ruth had seen earlier that tools and such were kept. The child soon came scampering back with a long, thin stick in her hand.

"It's a sassafras stick," she explained, holding it up to Ruth for inspection. "It's the only thing that you can stir the soap with proper, and you always have to stir in the same direction."

"Ah, I see now the error of my ways." Ruth smiled as she pulled the paddle from the vat and laid it aside to take the stick from Abigail.

She knew there were many superstitions as far as soap making was concerned, but this must be one peculiar to the Amish.

"You know, Abby, my mum died when I was a mite younger than you. I remember she always smelled like the sweet violets of England's vales. I can smell her still if I try hard enough."

"*Mamm* smells—smelled like herself. I cannot say a flower, but sweet. I can never smell her again, I think."

The needed tears spilled over onto the rounded cheeks, and Ruth waited. She knew from experience that there was no replacing a mother's touch when it was wanted.

She continued to move the stick in a careful pattern of direction, taking a step back from the open flame beneath the vat. She had no desire to singe her only remaining skirt. She thought about the fire that had claimed her home and knew that local farmers would sometimes let a fire burn an area of land the better to cultivate it. *Cultivate.* The words of the verse that Lena read echoed in her mind, and she tried to dismiss them. How could God possibly be "for her"? For any of this little family she had landed herself and her babe with? She shook her head and turned to the child whose tears had dwindled.

"Want to try and stir a bit, Abby?"

The girl gave an eager nod, and Ruth turned her mind to learning what else the Amish did in their soap preparations.

"If I let Tim run, the cat will only give chase through the treetops," Adam said, struggling to control the panicky horse. Adam's heart hammered in his chest, though his movements with the gun were slow and easy. He could feel Lena's hands digging into his sides, and he pushed aside the sudden graphic image of the cat leaping upon them. He didn't bother trying to get an accurate shot off; instead, bundling the reins around one wrist, he fired straight ahead, the sound a snapping echo. The responding telltale growl of the cat's shrill, shortened cry was followed by a heavy rustling overhead as the animal leapt away, deeper into the trees. Then Adam gave Tim his head, and the horse was off.

The whole occurrence took less than a minute, but Adam felt as though he'd been moving through dark molasses. It was normal for panthers or mountain lions, as they were called, to hunt closer to dusk. This was a bold animal indeed and probably should be dealt with by a hunting group.

"Are you all right?" he said to Lena, his throat dry.

"Ya." Her voice held a tremble, though, and he let Tim run on for another half mile before reining in at a local spring. He offered an arm to Lena, then fastened his rifle onto the saddle and jumped down beside her.

"Come, let's give the horse some water and have a quick drink ourselves. You need to calm down, and so do I." He let her fall in behind him as he led Tim to a place to drink from the nearby stream. Adam then cupped his hands to the bubbling wooden spout that someone had placed in the rock face and washed his face before taking a drink of the cool and refreshing water. He automatically scanned the ground for snakes, which often sunned themselves on the rock ledges, then turned to make room for Lena.

She brushed past him, and he caught her scent, like wild roses in the twilight, and he reminded himself that it was no longer his right to touch her. She bent and drank, then lifted the hem of her clean apron to her lips. She stepped away from him without meeting his eyes.

"I owe you an apology," he said after a moment. "I was . . . I was cold in my telling of my feelings the other night."

She took another step away as if casting about for something to do. "It is of no matter," she said in a cool tone.

Her distance provoked rather than dissuaded him, and her dismissive words were a prick to his ego that forced a wry smile from him. "I thought it a great matter."

She had turned her back to him, so that all he could see was an escaped tendril of her golden hair at the gentle bend of her neck and shoulder.

"I must go on, Adam, despite your words . . . your decisions. I have the *kinner* to think of." She drew a deep breath. "I will love again, if the Lord wills."

Her words struck him with brutal force, and again thoughts of Isaac came rushing into his mind. He wondered if something could dissuade her from any future idea of marrying his *bruder*. His mind was working out consequences even while his words came unbidden. "Are you so sure of that?"

She whirled to face him, her blue eyes snapping fire, her chin tilted upward, so that the fine line of her neck was exposed to his gaze.

"*Ya*, Adam Wyse. I am very, very sure."

He stared at her, the day in the barn following his whipping flashing with sudden clarity across his mind. "And yet a certain *mawd* told me once that a 'first kiss is forever.'"

He watched the delicate flush mount in her cheeks and longed to press his mouth to that gentle heat, but then her eyes filled with tears.

"You would turn a young girl's dreams against me . . . and you mock me yet, as we have never even had a first kiss."

He swallowed hard, remembering her mother's question. In truth, he had never given Lena that first kiss, and now she would have it from another. He knew he was wrong . . . knew it even before he stepped closer to her, but a sudden hunger pulsed through his veins, and he did not care to consider the outcome.

"I would never mock you, Lena," he said hoarsely.

"Then why would you remind me of all I hoped for?"

He reached an unsteady hand to thumb a tear from her cheek, and she didn't draw away. "Because I am wrong, most of the time in my life. Because I cannot be near you and think clearly. Because you are . . . were . . . all that I hoped for . . ." He bent his head, his words a hoarse whisper. "Let me, Lena, please . . . one kiss . . . just one . . . for remembrance, though I do not deserve it."

She sniffed. "No, you do not deserve it, Adam."

It was enough of a response for him, enough of an invitation, and he lowered his mouth to catch the dampness of her cheek. She let him, and he felt a stirring in his soul, like the wind before a storm. He let his eyes drift closed; he wanted to be gentle, wanted her to remember with tenderness and not regret . . .

———— ✦ ————

Lena knew she should not allow what was happening, knew it in the very core of her being. She would only hurt more later, only compare his kiss with that of any other man in the future. Yet she couldn't stop, did not want to stop. His mouth moved on hers. Tentatively she returned his kiss, breathing in the scent she knew to be Adam, and she heard him make a small sound of approval that sent shivers down her spine. She was, at once, both lost and found—the war, her *mamm's* death, everything seemed to drift to a fuzzy haloed background as she touched him with her lips, her fingers caught in the linen of his shirt.

When he pulled gently away, she felt bereft. She looked up to find his gaze shuttered, unreadable.

"What is it?" she asked, realizing she sounded like a little girl who'd had her sweet taken away.

"Lena," he said. "I cannot . . . You yield, and I am lost. Remember your anger toward me, for it will keep you safe. *Danki* for the kiss—our last in truth, for I cannot trespass upon your honor further."

"You lie," she said. She crossed her arms in front of her. "You do not care about honor, not mine, nor even your own. You used me now, and I will not allow it again, to be sure. I know you, Adam. I know that you desire me as much as . . ."

"As you desire me? *Ach*, Lena. You make me forget myself, forget everything that is noble and good."

He swooped like some careening hawk, and part of her melted with the familiarity, the feel of him, until she realized that she was returning his savage kiss with all of the mixed-up passion in her young soul. But then, it was as if he remembered that his lips had touched hers only moments before with tenderness, and his mouth gentled. She felt his frantic intake of breath drop to a low hum of satisfaction as he pressed his mouth against hers, and she was swept away into some simmering place of sensation and yearning and . . . peace.

She drew back at her traitorous thoughts, and he let her go so fast that she nearly stumbled. He steadied her arm, and her hand slashed out with instinct, slapping his cheek hard. She drew a sobbing breath at her action, knowing she'd never before struck a living soul.

He lifted his hand to touch the spot where she'd slapped him, looking puzzled, searching, as if he saw right through her. Surely her blow, for all its fury, did not hurt him to such an extent that he should appear dazed.

"Adam." She reached to touch his sleeve. "Adam . . . I'm sorry. Are you all right?"

He shifted his weight from one long leg to the other and stared down at her.

"All right," he murmured. "It will be all right." He swayed a bit from side to side, almost as though he sought to soothe himself.

Tears welled in her eyes. "Adam, I'm sorry for striking you. Please forgive me."

He smiled then, an odd, intense look, and she felt an eerie disquiet.

"*Ya*, forget it—forget something . . ." He trailed off and rubbed at his cheek and then at his temple as if his head ached.

"Adam, *sei se gut* . . ." She frowned in frustration, wanting to break the strange moment. "Adam, come. Let us go to town quickly . . . for my father's sake." She reached for his hand, her palm still stinging from her attack. His fingers closed on hers in almost a desperate grip. He thumbed the soft contours of her palm, rubbing again and again at the still sensitive spot. She took an instinctive step backward as a wash of sensation flowed from her hand to her mind. He held her hand—only her hand, but it was as though he were touching her everywhere.

"Please, Adam. I think that you aren't well. Let us go from here."

And then he was back. She knew it by the way he straightened up and by the mocking glint that fired his former vacant gaze. "And go from here so that I can feel your every touch as we ride together, making me want and you want and we both . . ."

She felt herself flush at his insinuation and spun without a word to march back to Tim. Adam caught her hand, and she tried to pull away, but he held her with a grip as strong as steel, as soft as velvet. She turned back to face him, sparked with defiance.

He smiled down at her. "I thank you, Lena Yoder, for your concern. But I do want to urge that you gather your passions before you meet again with any other man. You seem to . . . forget yourself, and hence, I find myself caught in love's talons." He let his long fingers play over the hand that had struck him, the one he now held with so much care. "Even talons as beautiful as these." He bent his head and brushed his lips across her hand.

Then he let her go and turned, walking away in silence, while she caught her breath and began to pray with fervor, his words licking like flames within the recesses of her mind.

She watched numbly as he moved to check the horse's saddle girth before swinging himself up. Then he reached his hand down to her.

"Come, your *fater's* fate awaits."

Lena felt color suffuse her cheeks once more that she should so be reminded of why they traveled in the first place. She placed her hand in his, pushing aside the feeling of warmth against her chilled fingers, and mounted the horse. She longed not to have to touch his body again, but there was no help for it, and she put her hand to his side.

Then he half turned, surprising her with his rough tone. "Do not think, Lena Yoder, that there is a day that goes by that I will not remember what we were."

Her throat burned, but she maintained her composure. "Well," she said, "do not think that there is a day that goes by that I will not remember to forget, Adam Wyse."

He turned Tim toward town with a mirthless laugh, and she wondered how she could ever be true to her own words.

Chapter 12

⌒

J oseph Wyse frowned. His day was not going well. First he'd lost the sale of the mare when the pompous buyer had refused to pay the reasonable sum he was asking, and now a fellow deacon brought disturbing news.

"A meetinghouse, you say?" Joseph sipped from the coffee that his wife had provided before she'd slipped from the kitchen to allow the men private discussion.

"*Ya.*" Abel Glick nodded, so that the tip of his beard nearly brushed the tabletop. "Many of the families have relationships that go back to the time of the sea voyages here. And they say they'd feel safer in a meetinghouse, what with the danger from the local army and the British themselves."

"We swore an oath to Britain," Joseph said, thinking aloud. "It would be double-minded of us to swear another to a government not even won. General Washington himself has written letters since the beginning of the war requesting that negative actions taken against the *freeda*-keeping sects be halted."

"A lot of good that has done in the past," Abel said. "I had no *glaws* left in my windows when we were down in Philadelphia once the Sons of Liberty passed through and I hadn't shown my support by having a candle lit and glowing."

"That is the past, Abel. We must forgive and move on." Joseph stroked his dark beard.

"And how do you suggest we move past the fine government of this state that no longer seems interested in William Penn's vision of religious freedom for all? You know the government has called upon all to 'associate' with the revolutionary cause via military companies. If we do not, then we are labeled Non-Associators—or worse yet, Tories! Imagine a boy of fifteen, still on the farm or newly married, called upon to learn the art of military, with no regard for his family or—"

"Peace, Abel. Peace. We must look and keep to our own. And there can be no meetinghouse built. We are not of the other peace-seeking peoples. We must keep to meeting in our homes, or part of why we came here, to this place and for this time, will be lost."

Abel had subsided back into his chair and took on an even glummer expression. "*Ach*, I fear we are lost at times already, Joseph. My own daughter just left us to marry a German Mennonite."

"Reliance on the other peacekeeping sects must be stopped. We must build an Amish community with Amish hearts in Amish homes. You should go and fetch her back."

Abel shook his head. "I kept too light a hand with her; it is too late. Do you know when the bishop is to come through?"

"*Nee*, but it must be soon. He visited with us last spring, about this time. I will ride about to investigate this idea of a meetinghouse. Needless to say, the matter must be resolved before the bishop should arrive and hear of such doings."

Abel looked worried yet. Joseph chafed inwardly at his fellow deacon's seeming lack of confidence, but he reassured him once more and hurried his guest on his way. As he waved Abel off, he noticed Isaac leading a horse to the foundry.

"Isaac! Come inside. I would speak with you."

His elder son was as tall as Adam but did not present the same taut strength. Instead he always seemed lost in thought, somewhere far from the moment at hand. Joseph sighed to himself as the boy approached.

"*Ya, Fater?*" Isaac asked, climbing onto the porch, his dark eyes passive.

Joseph held open the door to the farmhouse. "Inside, my *sohn*. It is an issue of some importance that will require the gifts of both your mind and body."

They sat at the dining table alone; Ellen was working in the garden. Joseph cleared his throat. "I would speak to you of the ways of women, Isaac."

Joseph saw the gleam of interest in the dark eyes opposite him with some relief. At least the boy was present . . .

"You mean the wiles of women, *Fater?* In the Bible, it reads—"

Joseph held up a hand and shook his head. "*Nee*, not a study of women, Isaac. The reality of them . . . the reality of Lena Yoder and your doings with her."

The boy looked shocked. "My doings, Father? I have not done—"

Joseph slapped a hand on the table. "Isaac . . . you have told your mother and me of Adam's decision to leave Lena behind. Do you not think this leaves a place for you to possibly wed the girl and aid her, as the Lord would see fit?"

The boy dropped his gaze. "*Ya*, if she would have me. But she is bent upon a selfish purpose, Father. A desire to run the farm alone, with the Lord's help, of course. I told her I would offer her counsel, but I do not know how I would make an offer of marriage. She is strong of will, though I believe that she could be brought to submit as is proper."

Submit, my right eye . . . The mawd is as wild-tempered as a colt and would lead Isaac a merry chase all of his days, should he be able to win her from Adam's hold . . .

89

Joseph let none of his thoughts show on his face, but simply nodded. "I see. It is very wise of you to give her time, my *sohn*. But she may need some persuasion of the *hartz*, some wooing as it were. Her feelings for your *bruder* will not disappear in a moment."

Isaac waved a languid hand. "She was still barely more than a child when she thought of a future with Adam; she did not know her own mind. The war, Adam's behavior, her *mamm's* death, and her *fater's* imprisonment have all worked, no doubt, to bring about a settled mien to both her person and spirit. Once she gets over this notion of managing things herself, she will see things differently."

Joseph longed to shake the casual attitude of the boy and opted for the obvious ploy. "You do realize, Isaac, that by engaging her to marry, you may well secure the sanctity of her soul by keeping her from any darker desires that might arise."

"You mean Adam again, *Fater?*"

Joseph spread his hands in a helpless gesture. "It is true that she may have changed, but I think your *bruder's* heart is still engaged with the past, and he might lead her down a path to some unrighteousness—even if she were unaware of that leading."

Isaac's dark eyes narrowed. "You are right, *Fater.* I should have thought of it thus before."

Joseph smiled. "It is not too late for such a revelation. But I wonder how you plan to go about pursuing young Lena . . . to win her to your cause."

"I will simply tell her outright, of course, what the Bible says."

"Do you know that I had to pursue your mother with great diligence?" Joseph leaned back in his chair. "'Tis true. She would not have my suit at the first, despite her father's approval. And I did try a rather forthright approach, only to be lost in my attempts at matching the Bible to the mind of a maid."

Isaac leaned forward. "You are saying that I should use cunning, *Fater?*"

Joseph shook his head. "*Cunning* seems a bit harsh in its meaning, my *sohn*. As I said before, a maid wants wooing before she will make her choice—gentle words, kind overtures. She has, after all, lost her *mamm*. There may be an emptiness in her heart and mind."

"Which I could fill!" Isaac exclaimed. "And in doing so, secure a sure soul for heaven's gates in her submission to my rule as husband."

Joseph leaned forward to clasp his son's shoulder. "You may be onto something *gut* in your thinking, my *sohn*. I will pray on it for ye, with proper intercession. Upon my word, I will pray."

"Thank ye, *Fater!*"

Joseph's eyes gleamed cold gray, and he rested with more ease against the back of his chair.

<hr />

Adam tried to count the pulse of the hoofbeats of the horse beneath him, tried seeing glimpses of shapes in the clouds above, then gave in to simply reciting the multiplication facts as he attempted desperately to concentrate on anything but the feel of Lena's touch about his waist. Why had he behaved as he did at the spring? He had dishonored his promise to Mary and sent Lena confusing signs of his true feelings. The sooner he enlisted and began this so-called new life the better, for he knew that he could not control himself any longer where Lena was concerned.

Chapter 13

Lancaster's bustle always stirred Lena's sensibilities until she found it difficult to concentrate on anything else—even the sting of her mouth from Adam's kiss. She had to remind herself not to hold him tighter as they entered the busy streets. She much preferred the country and was glad not to make the trek to town very often, even to fall festivals as some Amish did to sell handicrafts and wares.

"I would walk now, Adam. It is unseemly to ride astride, and with a man."

"And with me in particular?" He tossed her a smile as he drew rein to ease her off the horse. "Agreed. Please make a more ladylike entrance to your *fater's* trial alone."

There was a faint irony in his tone, and she realized that she did not want to be alone in the midst of the crowds, especially at the trial. She looked up at Adam to find him smiling down at her, waiting and obviously not going anywhere. *How well he knows me,* she thought with mixed ire and relief.

She stepped aside, nearly knocking into a buckskin-clad trapper with a coon cap, which he swept off with a flourish.

"My apologies, madam." His eyes twinkled with good humor, and

Lena allowed him a brief smile before looking away. Adam now stood beside her, and she sensed a change in his stance.

"What's the trouble here?" Adam asked, his voice distant and hoarse.

Lena turned to look up at him and saw that he was livid with anger.

"No need for jealousy, my friend," the trapper said with a smile. "Simply a greeting for a beautiful maid."

"Beautiful, yes, but not yours to greet."

"I'll greet whom I like," Lena snapped before she could think, then regretted her words as the grin spread on the trapper's face. Clearly, the man thought he was interrupting a jealous husband and a flirting wife. She pulled on Adam's stiff arm with a gentle tug. "Come, Adam. We must hurry."

"Yes, Adam, hurry along," the trapper singsonged.

Lena felt as though she could touch the anger emanating from Adam's arm. What was this about, that he seemed ready to fight with a simple stranger over nothing? It was not the Amish way, nor was it normal for Adam. And she did not like his proprietary air, even if she gained some comfort by it. Finally Adam seemed to come to himself and allowed her to lead them some distance from the other man.

"What were you doing?" she asked under her breath.

"Nothing. There's nothing wrong. Let's get Tim stabled safely and go to the trial. The sun is nearly overhead." He gently removed her hand from his arm to place it more formally in the bend of his elbow, and they walked on. They stopped only to pay what Lena considered a huge sum to have Tim stabled by a "reputable horseman"—as was advertised on a painted wooden sign.

Lena decided to dismiss the incident with the trapper and concentrated on not getting the hem of her skirt tangled against the press of other women as she and Adam moved on. She could not help but admire the color of some of the dresses, each so clearly defining a station in society. The crowd was like a moving patchwork quilt, and she realized how much the war had swelled the town's populace beyond the previously predominate Quaker settlers.

Indeed, Lena's eye was caught by the applied decorations of dress for both men and women—the ribbons, plumes, braids, ornate buttons, and laces stood in such contrast to the stark brown of her simple homespun gown. But then, she quickly reminded herself, dress wasn't what mattered. Outward adornment was not what was necessary in life, even if it was attractive to look upon.

Adam seemed to know the town well and led her with sure silence past a bakery that she had never seen before to turn the corner to the center of town. A mass of soldiers was gathered about, and a heavily decorated officer of the Pennsylvania Regiment sat at a simple table with a quill in hand and a stack of papers before him. A line of drab-looking prisoners stood nearby, their physical frailness apparent. No chains were necessary to hold them in their miserable stance.

"That is Major George," Adam whispered in her ear, nodding toward the seated officer.

Lena recognized her father as fourth in the line; his normally tall, lean form looked even thinner as he shielded his eyes against the sunshine. He was ill kempt and haggard, and she longed to burst through the crowd and run to him. Adam kept a steadying hand on her shoulder. She knew she might offer a plea on behalf of her father when it was his turn, but until then she must wait in silence. She studied the clothing of the prisoners more carefully and saw that her father was the only Plain-dressed man, clearly of a peacekeeping faith, even though dirt and filth had reduced his clothing to near rags. The others wore clothes of similar condition and appeared downtrodden and weak.

Suddenly Major George jumped from the table with a groan,

clutching his ear as if he'd been shot or stung. He issued immediate, hushed orders to the men assembled near him and they spread out, pushing through the crowd. Soon two boys, the taller carrying a slingshot, were dragged in front of the officer. Lena caught her breath as she saw the face of the shorter youth.

"John!" The cry escaped her lips, and she wrenched free of Adam's hand only to be hauled back with ruthless force against his strong form.

"Stop!" he hissed in her ear. "You will do more harm than good. If they realize that John is your *fater's sohn*, it may be perceived as a direct attack in attempt to secure an escape. That means hanging, Lena, sure and simple. Now wait."

Her eyes swam with angry tears at his reasoning, but she knew he was right. She took a deep breath and began to pray silently. She felt some of the tension unwind in her mind with strange peace and did not resist when Adam released her to step forward and push his way through the crowd. She watched him, head and shoulders above most, as he approached the edge where the townsfolk gathered.

The officer had ceased to hold his ear and held up his palm to the crowd, red with his own blood. Then he looked at the boys.

Lena saw the straight line of John's back and the lift of his head, but she knew that he must be terrified. She did not recognize the youth who held the slingshot and saw that he was dressed like a town boy. Then her gaze swung to her father, but thankfully, he did not seem to recognize John—or at least appeared not to.

The major came to stand in front of the boys. Lena's throat burned as she waited for the man's response. Gazing at the strange tableau, she realized that here was the way of things in her time. The rule of the land, holding father and son as prisoners, and the strange association of John and his companion, obviously not an Amish boy, standing as a sign of peace's companionship with war . . . Were the times to disintegrate into something like the Palatinate, that Old World place of Germany where so much of the reality of the *Martyrs Mirror* took place? Where the spilling of Amish blood was thought to be a blessing to *Gott* and the land? Her eyes skimmed over Adam as she thought of the officer's blood, and she knew that there was a struggle within Adam to break that hold of power, to challenge it. Perhaps she should have tried harder to understand when he spoke of joining the cause for freedom.

"A town pup and his country cousin, a pacifist mouse!" The officer's voice rang with an edged humor that curled Lena's toes in her sensible shoes.

"Amish!"

The major turned, and Lena nearly groaned aloud at the thin sound of John's voice.

"What?" The officer swiped at his bloody ear with a handkerchief and peered down at her *bruder*.

"I am Amish!"

"And proud of it, no doubt!"

The crowd rumbled with laughter.

"*Nee*, not proud. Simply what I am."

The officer moved like a snake's strike and grasped John by his collar, lifting him clear of the ground and shaking him hard.

"And what you are is a coward, boy! Companion to a sneaky sharpshooter here whom I might have use for. But you, you are worthless!" He dropped John so that the boy fell to the ground, and the crowd laughed again as the officer held a foot down on the hem of his vest, forcing him to remain in the dirt.

"Whose whelp is this?"

The major's keen eyes searched the crowd beyond the ring of soldiers. Adam stepped forward in a simultaneous stance with her father.

"Mine!" The two men's voices rang out in unison.

"Aha! Two fathers, have ye, Amish mouse? How many mothers were involved, then?"

The crowd roared at the ribald joke, and Lena clutched her hands together as Adam stepped with ease through the soldiers to meet with her father, who had stumbled from his place in line.

<hr />

Adam did not think twice when he claimed John as his own, but he hadn't expected the frail voice of Samuel Yoder to contradict him. Now, with his back to a merry crowd and facing the angry eyes of the Pennsylvania officer, he was unsure of what to do next. He turned to Samuel and resisted the urge to offer a hand to the older man, who appeared shaky but nonetheless came forward.

"The boy is my *sohn*," Samuel pronounced with a definitive edge that begged anyone to differ.

Adam caught the eye of the officer and smiled. "Fair enough. I relinquish my claim to parentage. But it seems that you have gotten three for the price of one here today. Two Amish . . . and myself, of course. A prisoner, a foolish boy"—his impassive gaze took in John where he still squirmed on the ground—"and a simple horse farmer."

The officer's eyes narrowed. "Horses, you say?" His voice was low now, as level as Adam's, and the crowd quieted, the better to listen.

"Aye, horses."

Adam waited, deliberation in his casual stance. It was a gamble, this lure of horses, and he wondered if he would see the tail end of poor Tim yet again.

The officer dabbed at his ear in thought, then stepped away to round the table and pick up his abandoned quill. John scrambled to his feet and looked ready for another outburst. Adam's hand came down on his left shoulder while Samuel Yoder's landed on his right, and the two men's eyes met over the boy's head. Adam ignored the fire that burned from the blue eyes, bleary as they were. He thought of Lena, waiting somewhere behind him, and gave a brief nod of deference to the older man. He withdrew his hand from John's shoulder with a warning squeeze and took a step backward.

The officer rifled through some papers with a frown on his face, then looked up. "Name, prisoner?"

"Samuel Yoder."

"Charge?"

A fellow officer stepped forward and pointed to a page; Major George nodded. "Ahh . . . resistance to the orders and privilege of the regimental army to confiscate lands and victuals as needed. What say ye?"

"I paid the triple tax assessed upon my land and willingly surrendered what was wanted. I have children at home and asked to keep one cow so that the family might have milk."

The officer laughed and met Adam's eyes. "Fair enough," he said. "A cow for a horse, I say. And freedom for these cowardly rebels . . . yourself in company, included."

Adam nodded graciously. "Myself included. And my horse is stabled yonder . . . so long as he hasn't already been . . . acquired by your reserves, sir."

"My second will see to it." He jerked his chin to the man standing at his right. "Go with him. Make sure he actually has a horse and see to its condition. Bring it round to my quarters if it proves a worthy steed. And you"—his eyes swept Adam's impassive face— "take your rabble with you. I know where to find you should this be some Amish ruse."

Adam bowed and linked an arm through Samuel Yoder's; the man was obviously resistant, but too weak to argue. John scowled as the officer began a conversation with his companion with the slingshot, and Adam herded him and his *fater* through the throng.

Adam smiled as he moved them toward Lena. He had won her father and brother freedom at a price God had surely arranged, despite Tim's recent changes in ownership. He glanced sideways at Samuel, expecting perhaps a slight lessening of the man's anger, but the older man shook his head.

"Pleased with yourself, no doubt, Adam Wyse. But I would as gladly have been sold for thirty pieces of silver as I would for your horse."

Adam ignored the cutting words and bent to whisper in the man's ear. "And I would gladly have my horse still, sir, instead of your spite. But I forgot to bring that much silver with me today. Come, show some spirit other than miserliness for your *dochder* and *sohn*."

Samuel Yoder grunted in response as they reached Lena, and she clasped her father in a warm embrace. She did the same for John, who squirmed in embarrassment, then let out a brief yowl when she stood back to box his ears.

Adam laughed out loud and felt that the world was a bit all right for once in a long while.

Chapter 14

I miss my *mamm*." Abigail's voice was a mournful sigh, and Ruth looked up from scrubbing the floor. She gathered her damp skirts and rose from her hands and knees to go to where the child stood, forlorn, next to the four-paned kitchen window.

After a brief moment of consideration, Ruth laid a wrinkled, reddened hand on the little girl's shoulder and was glad when she was not rebuffed. "I miss my man too. My best friend he was."

Abigail turned her bright head upward in consideration. "I forgot . . . the husband you have lost. Why does God let people die?"

Ruth floundered unhappily. What could she tell the child? What answer did she have that would be right and true? Something of the verse that Lena had read to her drifted across her mind . . . *"I am for you . . ."*

Abigail spoke with slow reasoning. "I mean, I know the answer *Fater* would give—that it is His will, but there must be something more. Do you not think so?"

Ruth swallowed. What was said to a child mattered, was remembered. She could recall her own quivering knees at her mother's tirades against men and drunkards and even God Himself. "God is for us," she finally managed, tightening her hand on the girl's thin shoulder.

Abigail's brows furrowed. "*For us* . . . You mean like with the war? For the Amish?"

Ruth grasped at her fast-passing thoughts and shook her head. "Nay. Not the war. Not this war—some way else. He's for us and He . . . He lets people . . . die because . . . because He loves us, I guess."

Abigail shook her head. "But that doesn't make sense . . . What does *Mamm* dying have to do with love?"

Ruth saw in her mind's eye Henry's gentle smile, and she stared out of the thick-paned glass of the window. She closed her eyes on the memory and answered with soft certainty. "Everything. Dying has everything to do with love, dearie. And that's the way of it. 'Tis all."

Ruth felt the child's disquiet with her answer, but then the girl relaxed and leaned against the bulk of her ample hip. Ruth drew a quick sobbing breath and encircled Abby with her strong arms. She drew the child close to the spot in her heart occupied by her husband and knew a certain measure of strange peace.

After the embrace, there was an easy spirit between them, and they finished the floor with laughter and wet skirts while Faith and Mary slept together in the nearby cradle. The afternoon flew by.

Ruth was wondering what had become of the Yoder family when she looked up from sweeping the porch and took in a bedraggled party unloading from the dusty back of an Amish wagon carrying potatoes. She recognized the tall, handsome Amish man who had first brought her to the farm. He gave a brief salute, then clambered back onto the seat of the wagon as it ambled off down the roadway.

Little John dashed past her into the house, but Lena approached more slowly, clinging to an older man. This must be Samuel Yoder. The father did not look as forbearing as his daughter, and Ruth reflected with a surge of regret that she would now likely be asked to move on. She took Faith from Abigail and walked down the porch steps to meet the party, carrying the blanketed infant in her arms. Her own babe still slept.

Lena released her father to grasp Ruth's arm with a gratifying squeeze.

"*Fater*, this is Ruth Stone. Truly, sent to us by the Lord—she and her baby, Mary. Ruth has been helping to feed Faith and to do all the chores that—well, to help us all."

Ruth felt herself studied by a pair of searching blue eyes. She realized, upon closer inspection, that beneath the rags and grime Samuel Yoder was not as old as she had first thought. More likely nearer to herself in age. She kept a steady look on her face and extended her arms so that he might see the babe's face.

"Your wee daughter, sir."

She was surprised when the man lifted well-shaped hands to take the infant from her with a gentle sigh. He cradled the babe against his dirty chest and tears filled his eyes. Ruth felt it too private of a moment and made to turn away when the man spoke.

"Wait . . . Do not go, Ruth Stone. Do not go anywhere, I beg of you. If Lena says that the Lord sent you and your babe, then surely it is so. I would say *danki* for the care you have given this child." He held the tiny form back out to her, and she accepted the bundle with confident hands.

"I would thank you as well, sir. For a roof, a place to sleep . . ."

He waved away her words with a lift of his hand. "Please, call me Samuel. Now, Lena . . . show me where you have laid your *mamm*."

Ruth stepped back to allow them to pass and hugged the baby close, breathing in the sweet smells of innocence and rosebuds that seemed to cling to the thatch of blond hair. She felt the urge to nurse and made her way with a grateful heart back into the house.

Lena felt like she was trespassing on an intimacy between her parents when her *fater* dropped to his knees at the simple stone that marked her *mamm's* grave. Some wilting wildflowers lay against the rock, evidence of her brief visit the day before, and she had to blink back tears as her father's hands tenderly brushed through the leaves to touch the stone.

He drew a deep, sobbing breath, and she wondered if she should leave him alone with his grief.

"It seems we are pressed to move on quickly in these days, when someone dies," he said.

"*Ach*, I know, *Fater*—so much to do, but I cannot and do not want to forget her. Though I must confess that some days her dear face appears blurry in my mind, and I cannot recall what she looked like. I do not understand this."

Her father smiled a bit and leaned back on his knees to look up at her.

"Do not think those thoughts are disloyal, Lena. In truth, when my own *fater* died I lost sight of his face for a while in my mind as well. I believe it's a blessing somehow, a way *Gott* has of taking some of that sting from death as I Iis Word promises. But I grew to remember my *fater* again, and you will grow to know your *mamm* again as well—a transformed beauty in the mind, a deeper knowledge of her than you ever had while she was here."

"*Ach, Fater, danki.* I do hope so." Lena stretched out her hand to him, and he caught it in a firm grasp.

"*Ya*, my child, you will see. The *gut* Lord can deliver grief into grace and bring great blessing from loss. Of this we must be sure, else how can we go on? Now help me up. I would go and see Faith once more."

Lena aided him to his feet, then walked with him hand in hand back to the house, his words of deep comfort resonating in her soul. Yet she wondered what he would say when he heard the truth about Adam.

Lucas Stolzfus was more successful at growing and selling potatoes than any other Amish man of the countryside, but he was an odd old fellow, known as "Nutter" to some behind his back. Adam could not help but think of the nickname now as he jostled along on the seat beside the older man, listening to his rapid-fire talk and suppressing a smile.

"Got fresh seed potatoes in from down Philadelphia parts, stole 'em out from under the Brits' noses. Expect they'll have turnips in their stews come winter. Sure is a pretty girl, that Lena Yoder. Used to think on pretty girls myself once, before the potatoes. Heard you want to enlist. Well, why not get it *gut* and over with then, instead of all this waiting around? When it's time to pick a crop, it's time to pick—don't ya think it so?"

Adam shrugged. "Maybe the crop's not ready yet."

"Well, now, bein' young makes you think young, so you don't know which end of your head is up. Neck-less, I like to say. Can't decide when a body's comin' or goin'. Me, now I'd join right off, but I'm too old. Though I don't like the thought of bein' an outcast either. Shunned, ya know. 'Course, you yourself ain't quite shunned . . . only a bit, mind ya. And yer *fater's* got a tight rein on you two boys. That *bruder* of yours, though. He thinks too much; head's going to explode like a tomato one day. Like to see that."

"Why would you fight?"

"Huh?"

"The war. You said you would fight . . . Why?"

Nutter scratched his cheek, then spit alongside the wagon wheel. "Got to know whot a body believes in. Got to know when to put the dog out at night, don't ya? Can't just go rambling along without any sense of why it is you got the privilege to ramble. If ya don't know why you can walk and talk and breathe free, well, then, you don't know much."

"I wish it were that easy."

"'Tis easy. Easier than settin' a spud to water and getting roots. You thinkers make it all about what it ain't. Whot's the Bible say? A time for war 'n' a time for peace. Well, explain that one . . . and King David, always a-goin' off to do battle 'cept that one time with Bathsheba . . . Don't hold much with bathing myself; makes a body ill, I think."

"You do not sound very Amish, Lucas."

"Ha! What's Amish? I know whot I am. Amish be part of it, yea. I knowed all about them martyrs in the mirror. Supposed to be for us to study on, look at. Would I want to be one, though? You bet not. Wouldn't make a *gut* martyr. Too ornery, too set in my ways. But I guess if *Gott* a-calls me to it, then I'd go. So you wait on His callin', jes' like my *mamm* used to call us young'uns in fer supper. WHOOP! WHOOP! WHOOPEE NOW! And we all come a-runnin'. Never missed a meal. Don't miss the meal, Adam Wyse."

The wagon slowed and Adam slid down, about to fish in his pocketbook for a coin.

"*Nee, nee*, now. You jest abide by my sayin's, and that's enough fer old Lucas, all right? Get along now . . ."

Adam watched the wagon drift slowly out of sight and turned to go into his home, the old man's strange words ringing in his ears.

Chapter 15

⌣

It had been nearly a week since her father had come home, a week in which Lena had quietly explained, as best she could, that things were over between herself and Adam. Saturday dawned fair and clear. The day before the family's worship always meant much to do in preparation.

Lena paused in the washing of a sheet against the heavy wooden slatted board as John skimmed down the steps and made to pass her where she knelt.

"John?"

He slowed with visible reluctance. "*Ya*, what?"

She did not like his tone or the sour expression he wore, but she kept her patience. She knew that *Fater* had talked for many long hours with John. Her *bruder* was struggling with his feelings about the other colonists and their persecution of the Amish. It was hardly persecution when compared to the times not so long ago in Europe, yet the boy wrestled with his feelings. Lena wanted to be mindful of this as she spoke in quiet return.

"John, you know that it will be a long time until we gather together with other Amish families for a day of communion. Yet, since we have *Fater's* safe return, I thought that we might do *fees wesha.*"

"*Ach*, Lena. I don't want to. It stinks."

Lena struggled not to smile. There was an odor at times when everyone removed their shoes and stockings, but that was not the point of the service. She wouldn't lecture the boy. "I know. But would you fetch the buckets from the shed, please? Make sure there's one for Ruth as well."

"Ruth? She will participate?" He looked even more disgusted.

"Yes." Lena spoke firmly. "She will be invited. You do not show *gut* spirit toward the woman whose cooking you eat and whose laundry you wear."

John turned away and headed for the shed, calling over his shoulder, "I told you before; she is not my *mamm*."

Lena sighed at the boy's resistance and returned to her scrubbing. A few minutes later, the sound of a dog barking announced someone's arrival. Lena sighed at the unexpected and unwelcome appearance of Isaac, then rose from her washing and struggled to roll her sleeves back down.

Isaac seemed to sense nothing of her feelings, though, as he approached her with a wide smile and a fair-sized package wrapped in brown paper in his arms.

"Lena . . . a *gut* morn to you."

She looked up into his dark eyes and nodded. "And to you."

"I brought you fresh venison. I've been hunting since dawn. I hate it, actually, but *Fater* insists. Here." He held out the package to her, and she hesitated before taking it. To be honest, she did not like to deal with fresh meat herself; she much favored the preparing of breads and vegetables. But she smiled just the same, hoping none of the blood would drip through the paper onto her dress.

"*Danki*, Isaac. I will take it into Ruth Stone and see if she might roast it for a meal today." She turned to go, and he caught her arm.

"Wait, Lena. I would . . . I mean . . . you look so beautiful today."

She glanced down at his hand on her arm, and he let her go. She sighed to herself, wondering what Isaac was about—it was unlike him to waste time on compliments or gifts.

"Thank you again, Isaac. Would you . . . like some refreshment before you leave?"

"I would indeed." He gave her a bright smile, as if she'd just given the proper answer to some unspoken question, and she turned once more to lead him to the house. She eyed her washing, wondering how long he would stay, and decided she would let her father visit with him while she did her many chores. Maybe they could speak of the Bible together. *Fater* had always favored Isaac's thoughts, in any case.

"I would like refreshment, Lena, but I would speak to you first."

She stopped near her wash bucket, turned to him, and shuddered at the coolness of the package in her arms. "What is it?" She squinted in the bright sun.

"This meat I've brought you . . . I would that it would be a symbol, a token, really, of the longing I have to provide for you, to give sustenance to your body and mind . . . and your soul, of course."

"Of course," she murmured faintly, wondering where he was headed.

He stepped nearer, and she couldn't resist comparing him to Adam. He didn't have his *bruder's* charged strength, though there was latent power in his broad shoulders and he had the same dark hair. Still, the vitality of spirit was lacking, for all of his professed spirituality, while Adam could simply stand near her and she would feel the electric current of storm and sea.

She choked on her thoughts and nodded to Isaac. "I appreciate your concern for my well-being. It is more than gracious, and I—I would return the goodwill."

"Would you, Lena?" he asked. "Would you return what I have to offer?"

She squeezed the venison tighter. "I mean that I would again extend the goodwill of refreshment to you."

"*Ach*, well, then . . . um, *nee*, thank you. I have recalled another thing I must attend to. I will bid you farewell."

She was surprised by his sudden turn of thought and the distinct look of a certain awareness about him, as if he had gained an insight into something . . . into her.

She shrugged off the annoying thought and smiled at him. "Farewell, Isaac. Thank you for the meat."

He gave her an intent look, then turned and sauntered off.

She turned, relieved, to climb the steps of the porch when she saw her father sitting in the shadows in a bentwood rocker. She wondered how long ago he had come silently to his place, well within earshot of her conversation with Isaac. He knew her well, and while he had always favored Isaac over Adam, he knew that she did not.

She felt a heavy burden in her heart to know that her words to Isaac would likely not bring him peace of spirit, even though she had not been forthright. She sat down in the opposite rocker, still holding the meat, and glanced at her father's reserved expression. Not knowing what to say, she sat in silence for a few minutes, then rose to go into the house.

"So you still hunger after one whom you know does not live by honor but by instinct? One who would leave you in an instant, leave his faith as well?"

Her father's voice cut with gentle force into her thoughts of escaping the discussion. She lifted her chin and wet her lips.

"*Fater, sei se gut,* are honor and instinct so far apart then?"

His eyes looked weary, and she wished she had not pressed the matter. "You do not understand, my daughter. Perhaps you do not even understand war for what it is."

She thought of the morning her mother died, and spoke with slow deliberation. "I understand enough of what it means to stand between life and death and to have both won and lost. Is that not war?"

He reached to brush her arm with tender fingers. "*Ya*, that is war in truth. But men do not fight by truths; they fight by instinct. And man's instinct is to wound, even to kill. Honor bids us to do something else, something beyond ourselves . . . something that glorifies *Derr Herr*. And I do not believe that Adam Wyse lives by such honor. There is something dark in him that calls. I do not know its source, but I know it is there—this dark instinct. Think. Search within yourself, and you know it to be true as well. And I do not mean to say that instinct does not bring appeal, Lena. I do not think it so easy for you to choose."

She bowed her head, images of Adam coming to her like shooting stars in a midnight sky. Perhaps her father was right; perhaps all that was between Adam and her was appeal—passion, and that was more than worldly. But could she ever bring herself to choose someone like Isaac? He was so pious and . . . *gut*. She smiled wryly to herself as her eyes filled with tears. Who was she to decide that *gut* was boring or something to be endured? She wanted to bring her *fater* peace and knew that her choice had the power to do so. And with *Fater* and Ruth at home, there would be no need for the other *kinner* to face Joseph Wyse and his strange disposition. She could do so alone—with God's help.

He spoke, staring into the distance. "My dear one, perhaps you do not consider in all your musings that you may yet help to save Adam Wyse's soul by teaching him denial and restraint, that he might come to trust in the Lord fully, not in himself alone, and thus gain his heavenly reward through our Savior."

Her *fater's* words caught in her vulnerable soul with all the ripping damage of hooks in linen. Suppose her choice could lead Adam to a deeper faith? After all, what was an earthly lifetime with Isaac compared to an eternity for Adam? Surely *Gott* would look upon such a sacrifice with grace and answer the prayer of her heart—that the wildness, the darkness in Adam would cease and he could walk fully in the light of God's love.

She lifted her head with solemn resoluteness, and her father turned to meet her eyes. "I—have never thought of Ad—of things that way." She lifted her chin with determination born of a sudden clarity. "I will try, *Fater*. I will try to choose someone like Isaac, perhaps even Isaac himself, and to choose honor."

He smiled at her. "Blessings on you, my *dochder*. You will see that the Lord will bring good out of this."

She nodded and tried to ignore the feeling in her heart that she was rowing far from land into a strange and tempestuous sea where the concept of self no longer mattered. *But this is submission in its purest form.* She tried to reason with the rising wall in her throat. *And submission will bring freedom from earthly desires,* she decided, ignoring the prick of conscience that said no teaching had ever told her this.

"You struggle, Lena."

He must have read the fleet of feelings that swam across her face.

"You struggle, but the Lord struggles with you—to do what is right. Together—the struggle can be won."

Lena nodded, wondering if she would regret telling him that she would try. Yet the look of peace on his countenance silenced her doubts, and she knew that she would keep her promise . . .

<hr />

Adam found his way to the Yoder farm with easy steps that afternoon, making little of the mile distance. He could not help himself; he had to check to make sure that all was well at the Yoder home. It was a habit of his, and he did not think that Mary Yoder would begrudge him this.

No one was readily about when he arrived, but instinct called him to one of his and Lena's favorite haunts down by the shadowed creek. He came upon her presence with drawn intent, like one who moves with gentle awe so as not to disturb a sleeping fawn in the weeds. She stood poised, staring into the waters of the creek.

"Lena." He kept his voice low, without the pressure of tenor or warmth. Yet she turned and looked at him with an expression of desperate flight, as though he were a wild predator and she the helpless deer.

He stopped still, afraid she'd move, until the only sound was the soothing gurgle of the creek cascading over moss-covered stones. "Lena, what is it?"

She shook her head, her fingers tangled in the unbound curl that so often fell with delicate grace against her cheek. "Nothing . . . It is nothing, Adam. But you shouldn't be here, not with me alone. I—I don't understand you. First you say that it is over between us, that you might enlist. Then you kiss me . . . and now you are here."

He took a step nearer, undeterred by her words. "'Tis all true, and I am sorry if I have hurt you."

She dropped her head with a sob. "Hurt me? You have done far more than hurt me, Adam. You have robbed my very soul." She turned to stare at him, tears glistening in her eyes. "But you should know the truth, Adam. I have given my word to my father, the promise of my *hartz*, to try and love Isaac, to give favor to him. To love honor."

<hr>

Adam could not help himself; he laughed. He watched her whirl away with a look of frustration, her hands fisted at her sides.

"Isaac? And honor? I suppose he could give a proper definition of the word if the case warranted, but as to exercising that noble quality . . . well, I doubt that he has ever had need to rouse himself—to put it kindly."

"He does not desire to make war."

Adam felt his laughter drift away and he moved toward her with purpose. "What did you say?"

"You heard me." She spoke over her shoulder.

He came up behind her and let his hands trail down to stroke her clenched fingers. "Look at me, Lena. Let us have this out once and for all. I cannot believe that you could ever be serious about my *bruder*." He struggled to keep the edge of urgency from his voice, as he contemplated what it would be like to let her go once more, this time forever.

She turned with slow grace, allowing her fingers to open into his, and he felt a surge of hope, until he looked into her eyes. They were dead steady calm, the still blue depths of cold ocean and windless sea. He felt a clutch of fear in his heart.

He lifted her now-unresisting hands to his lips, but saw no flare of response in her gaze. "Lena," he begged. "You must understand. I cannot—cannot explain why I must do these things."

She drew a deep breath, then lifted her hands from his grasp to touch his face. His heart hammered against his chest as she traced his brows, his eyes, and the contours of his mouth.

"What are you doing?" He swallowed, confused by her actions.

"I would remember your face for always," she whispered, almost to herself.

"'Tis not something that I would like you to forget." He tried to joke, but her eyes stood like steady beacons, threatening rocky harbors and unknown currents.

"You will forget me," she murmured, tracing the path of her fingers now with her soft lips until he felt he could scarce breathe or think.

"Never," he gasped as she kissed his cheekbone, stretching to find the tender hollow beneath his ear.

She slid her hands to his shoulders. "You will forget me, Adam Wyse. And you will be healed of what torments you—I have prayed it to be so, and God will honor my sacrifice."

"'Tis better to obey than to sacrifice,'" he quoted, and moved to gently press his mouth against the fair skin of her neck.

She drew back with such abruptness that he nearly staggered.

"I do both, Adam Wyse," she bit out, crossing her arms against her chest. "I both obey and sacrifice. And that was the last time you will touch me so."

He stretched forth a hand as if to comfort her.

"*Nee*," she snapped, whirling away. She looked at him once more, with all the fullness of her heart in her eyes, and then she lifted her skirt and ran, taking to the deer path as if pursued by wolves.

He stood by the stream, trying to think, to remember all that she had said, and then shook his head with a wry glance heavenward. "Women!"

Chapter 16

R uth rose early in the Sunday dawn to cradle Mary next to her breast and to allow herself to think for a few moments of the place she had come to . . . been led to, perhaps. She sighed as she shifted Mary's slight weight for a burping. She did not want to dwell overlong on the thought of God, despite her words with Abigail. She still felt hurt and angry at moments, though those times were getting fewer. Her eyes drifted to her skirts, which were soiled with the week's work. She had no other change of clothing and knew she'd have to go into town and buy something ready-made or else ask Lena for some fabric. She had a few coins that she had managed to save from the fire, but textiles and the like were at a high premium because of the war.

Today the family was to celebrate their worship, and although Samuel Yoder had asked her quite formally if she would like to join in, she wondered if it might not be better if she slipped away and did a bit of work outside. But then again, she'd been told by Lena that the Yoder family kept strict to the Bible's admonishment to rest and do no labor on the Sabbath. She certainly did not want to put a foot wrong there. She sighed a bit and laid the baby in her cradle next to Faith, pausing to rub a hand over both downy heads—one blond and the other red. A strange companionship in some ways, but the peace that lay between the babes was also a fair enough portrait of the peace that she herself was finding in this Amish home.

She rose to prowl about the kitchen, pausing to study the window box herb garden that seemed to burgeon with life, like a miniature Eden. She let her roughened fingers trace anise and balm, bay and borage, as well as the taller fennel and hyssop. It was a wonder to Ruth, who had never had much luck with a garden, that Lena could have such abundance growing right at her fingertips. It was probably the mother, their *mamm*, as the children called her, who had been the true gardener. She, Ruth, was really an intruder in some ways, a stoppage for death's hole in life.

She thought of Samuel Yoder's blue eyes, now growing keener with each passing day, and knew that there were times when his wise gaze seemed to see right through her. It wasn't a feeling she was entirely comfortable with, but it drew her just the same. She ran a finger down a tender leaf, then nearly jumped when the floor creaked behind her.

"I interrupt your thoughts, Ruth." Samuel made as if to back away, and Ruth shook her head. She took in his black vest and clean linen, noticing that he had gained some slight weight in the days since his release.

"Nay, sir. Come, I will toast ye some bread in the fire, and there's a new churning of butter from yesterday." She crossed the room near him to lift the toasting tongs from over the fireplace, when he caught her hand with gentle fingers and then replaced the tongs.

"'Tis the Lord's day, a day of rest for the body and spirit. You need not toast me bread, but I would have it fresh if you wouldn't mind."

Ruth's face flamed against her will. First his gentle touch, and then an equally gentle scold. She doubted she would ever understand the ways of the Amish.

He must have read her face because he followed her in silence as she made for the bread she and Lena had baked the day before. The loaves sat on the breadboard, draped in muslin like babes resting beneath a blanket.

She hesitated before drawing a knife from the chopping block, wondering if this too would be considered work on the Sabbath, when Samuel surprised her with a husky laugh.

"*Ya*, cut the bread, by all means, Ruth. It is only the unnecessary that we consider labor on the Sabbath."

She grabbed a knife with a *humph*. "Well, ye've sure got a body comin' and goin' to know what's what around here."

This time he laughed out loud, and she returned a smile. Just then she saw John standing at the edge of the room, his face stormy, and the smile slipped from her face. She understood the boy's expression; it reminded her again that she was trespassing on a family who had just lost their mother, no matter her own losses. She tried to concentrate on slicing the bread as she heard Samuel speak.

"*Sohn*, come in and break bread with us."

"*Nee, Fater*, I am not hungry. I would make sure all is prepared for today's *family* worship."

His emphasis on the word *family* caused Ruth to once more consider whether she should participate in the goings-on. She could always claim that Faith or Mary needed attention.

But Samuel spoke with quiet firmness to his son. "I am sure that you mean no offense to Ruth, my *buwe*, but *Gott's* worship is for all of His family, whether they be of this family's blood or not."

"*Ya, Fater*. I am sorry." John turned on his heel and walked away, not sounding the least apologetic.

Samuel Yoder made excuse for him. "He is young, Ruth."

Ruth pushed the honey pot toward him. "He misses his *mamm*, that's what. And I'm a sad substitute." Then she went on in haste. "Not that I'm trying to fill yer wife's place, sir. I just mean that ... that I ..."

Samuel patted her hand briefly with his large, work-worn one. "Peace, Ruth. I bid you peace. You are a blessing to this family. *Sei se gut*—please—remember that."

Ruth turned away at the sound of the warmth in his voice, her eyes filling with tears at the kindness. The verse Lena had read floated vaguely across her mind and brought relief to her tensing shoulders. *"I am for you . . ."*

Lena sat on the backless bench and listened to the soothing words of her *fater* as he spoke in High German. He presided alone over the small service, as there was no minister or deacon there to preach.

They sang from *The Ausband*, and seeing the bewildered look on Ruth's face, Lena reached out to touch the older woman's hand. She supposed that the tuneless, foreign words would sound strange to someone who had never experienced such worship. Yet it was the imitation of the voices of the martyrs for the faith, the laments and praises that compelled the singing. Lena prayed that some of this heartfelt emotion would communicate itself to Ruth, despite the language barrier.

As she sang, Lena struggled to keep her thoughts from Adam. She had tossed and turned all night, thinking about her resolve from the day before and wondering if she would be doing the right thing by considering to marry Isaac. Even so, part of her brain argued that she need not marry anyone at present, but she knew what a load it would lift from her family to have the strength of two households joined in community. And what her *fater* had said made sense. She caught her breath and almost stopped mid-singing when she realized that for all her professed anger at Adam, it could only be the deepest love that would inspire such sacrifice on her part. Her eyes welled with tears, but she reminded herself that the possibility of Adam gaining more insight and peace with *Gott* was more than worth any sacrifice on her part. Still, she wondered if denying him, restraining his advances would truly turn his soul toward *Derr Herr*. For all that she knew him, could feel him intuitively to the fibers of her fingertips, she did not know all of his faith.

If she were to be questioned about it, she supposed that she would have to admit that Adam found *Gott* to be capricious at best, and this thought made her want to weep. She did not know Adam in the way she should most, from a spiritual perspective. Yet Isaac's spirituality was like a steadfast light in the gloaming of life. She should respect the man for that, at least . . .

She nearly jumped when Abby touched her hand.

"Lena, it's time for *fees wesha*," her little *schwester* whispered. "And I want to do Ruth."

Lena smiled and nodded, then bent to slide the shortened buckets from beneath the benches. John had filled them with water the day before. She glanced at her father and John, who were removing their shoes and stockings, then bent to do the same. Abigail had stripped off her things in quick order and was now working to help Ruth lift her skirts discreetly. Lena could not help but smile at the strange expression on Ruth's face. The woman probably found them to be odd, but Jacob Amman, the founder of the faith, had long ago decreed that the service and self-sacrifice of *fees wesha* not be lost from the act of worship.

So the men washed each other's feet while the women did the same. Then each would rise and kiss each other on the cheek with a holy kiss. Lena found it a beautiful symbol of submitting to loving one another through Christ. And as she gently cradled Abigail's small, white foot in the bucket, she could not help but feel that *Gott* would give her the strength to serve, to humbly serve, Adam's life by marrying his *bruder* . . . no matter the cost to her heart.

Chapter 17

Joseph Wyse had no fear of retaliatory violence as he stood in the dark of night with a handful of stones. The only reason he had not been unduly pressed beyond triple taxes was the fact that he had paid off the tax collector and the sergeant in charge of commandeering stock and land. He kept these men satisfied with various bonuses and still did not fear for his coffers, for his family had come to the New World at quite an advantage and the horse farming had proved lucrative of recent years.

He aimed with a precise arm at the glass panes of the kitchen window. A second rock followed with its resounding crash, and he hunched his shoulders forward and made for the house steps as candlelight appeared from within.

Adam came out first, looking alert and angry, and Joseph met him when he would have gone off the porch into the dark after the supposed villain.

"'Tis too late, *sohn*. I heard the sound of hoofbeats fading on the night air. The miscreant cannot be caught."

"Then I'll go after him," Adam asserted, but Joseph caught his arm.

"Ye'll not upset your mother by some fool chase in the black of night. Now put your mind at rest. You can go for replacement glass tomorrow."

Adam backed off and was sweeping the glass from the floor when Ellen and Isaac came into the room.

"*Ach*, Joseph . . . are you sure things are all right?" Ellen asked worriedly as she bent to lift a smooth stone from beneath the table.

Joseph caught her close and smiled reassuringly. "All is as should be, as it always is. Now, *kumme*, let us all go back to bed. Adam can attend to this in the morning."

Adam followed his family slowly back to bed. He did not speak the words that pressed hard against his lips and played sleek havoc with his mind. He had not been asleep when the rocks had struck, but rather was moon-gazing on the fair but chill night. He had seen his father take aim at his own house and then cross the yard to appear as if he had been the first to arise. Adam turned the images over and over in his mind, like a child with a puzzle box, but he could make no sense of it. Why would his father strike against his own? And why hadn't Adam himself had enough courage to face the man and tell him what he knew? It was enough to keep him tense and sleepless on his bed for many hours to come.

When Monday morning dawned fair and clear, he had decided to dismiss the odd behavior of his parent out of hand and focus instead on driving the smaller wagon into town.

Adam always found it fascinating to visit the glass-making shop and furnace where sand and minerals were melted down to make glass for necessities like windows, but also for decorative toys and vases. Although he knew that such ornamentation was frowned upon by his people, he could not help but be drawn to the various samples of the revered art that were displayed in the shop. He had made friends with *Herr* and *Frau* Wistar, who owned the shop and who operated their business with a *gut* amount of cheer. He wished that this day they might bring some lift to his flagging spirits over Lena.

As he had hoped, *Frau* Wistar greeted him with a bright smile. "Adam Wyse, you come at a good time. Herman is in the furnace room and tries for a new color today. I know how you love to watch. You will go in, *ya?*"

He nodded and made his way to the back of the shop, leaving the measurements for the panes of glass in *Frau* Wistar's capable hands.

He entered the furnace room, the blast of heat taking him by shock as always.

Herman Wistar, a German immigrant and rotund, jovial man, looked across the long iron with its tip of fire that he held in an elbow-length glove and greeted Adam with a smile.

"Ah, Adam. You have come just in time, *ya?* The chemist got in a new supply of sulfur powders from Philadelphia this morn."

Adam grinned. "You'll try for the yellow again?"

The older man nodded happily, and Adam moved to where he could see the opened packet of powdered sulfur on a bench nearby. In times past Adam had watched his friend combine different compounds and minerals with molten glass to change its color from its natural aqua tint. Adam had seen success with blue-violet, green, and more predominantly, brown glass, but sulfur powders had yet to produce the elusive yellow glass so highly sought by wealthy households for doorknobs and servingware. Instead, at the irritation of the chemist who prized his mixtures, after four packets of powders only amber-colored glass had burned through. He hoped his friend would have better fortune this day.

Herman heated the glass in the stone furnace until it became molten. "Almost like liquid, *ya?*" he called, and Adam nodded, fascinated. "This time you try, my friend. Perhaps a younger hand will have more luck. Put on a glove."

Adam slid one of the leather gloves from the workbench onto his hand, then turned to the packet of powder. He had seen Herman combine things often enough to figure he knew how to give it a go. He tilted the packet of powder carefully into the palm of his gloved hand, then turned toward the small, molten orange piece of glass that Herman held.

Taking a step closer, so that he could feel the heat from the piece come to his face, he turned his hand and flung the powder into the liquid glass. It absorbed instantly, all orange still and glowing. Herman laughed as he twisted his arm and used a set of prongs to cut the glass into an even smaller piece, the shape of a teardrop, just large enough for a woman's pendant. He added a small hole for a tie as the glass cooled, but Adam knew they still couldn't be sure of the true color until the temperature had lowered completely.

Herman pulled off his gloves. "Now we wait, eh? And you tell Herman why you look so low, my young friend."

Adam glanced up, surprised. He didn't think that any of his true feelings showed, but Herman Wistar was wise and knew him well.

"What vexes all men's souls ails me," Adam admitted, sweeping his eyes downward.

Herman laughed and slapped his thigh. "A woman? You, Adam? Can you not have your pick of maidens both young and old?"

Adam sighed and shook his head. "'Tis only the one that has ever had the power to hurt . . . yet to catch a man's breath and steal it away 'til the wanting for air becomes delicious torture in itself."

Herman smiled. "Now that much I know and can understand. My fair Hannah, ah . . . she led me long about the chase." His eyes held the softened look of fond memories. "I love her yet, the answer to my heart's longing. And you too will find your heart's desire, Adam. Perhaps the answer lies in the glass."

He reached behind Adam and lifted a perfect translucent yellow teardrop from the cooling rack.

Adam stared at the glass in amazement, then broke into a grin. "It's yellow!"

"*Ya.*" Herman beamed back. "And it is yours . . . to give to what ails you, eh?"

Adam backed off, shaking his head. "Herman, I cannot take it. You've been waiting a lifetime for this, and the Amish do not wear such things, as beautiful as it is. Please keep it—or give it to your true heart, for that is what she is."

"*Ya*, you are right, my friend. The first yellow, I will give to her, eh? And you will join us for a meal to celebrate!"

Adam nodded as Herman hurried off with the clear yellow teardrop. He stood alone in the blowing heat from the furnace and thought of Lena. He knew that her heart would never be swayed by the fine things of earth. She was true to her Amish roots, while he . . .

He sighed aloud and fingered the cast iron edge of the tongs, thinking about the breakage his father had done the night before. It was enough to make Adam feel like he wasn't sure exactly what he was true to, what his heritage was.

Ach, he understood the Wyse lineage, the sufferings of his fore-fathers, and the work of his *fater* to bring about a new life in a new land. But who he was in Christ, as his father on earth exemplified Christ, remained as elusive an identity as the yellow *glaws*, as the mystery of his past—the childhood years that he could not seem to recall. His head began to ache, and he left his questions in the room, going into the shop to share in the Wistars' happiness.

On Monday morning Lena was digging in the winter rye, which she had sown herself last year to be a green manure crop for the carrots and parsley that would be planted soon. She considered the warmth of the sun and wondered if she might add a row of early potatoes to be grown under some of the green manure as well. She paused to swipe at her brow, feeling sweaty already though the day had hardly started. She did not really love the work in the kitchen *gorda* and much preferred to work among the grove of crab apple trees that were part of the farm's livelihood. But *Fater* saw the kitchen *gorda* to be women's work and did not want his daughter to work "afield." It was only during the business of fall harvest that she was permitted to handle the apples in the picking, selling, and drying.

She was just debating the merits of pruning the gooseberries versus setting out a few strawberry plants when Isaac came walking toward her from the forest. She thought for a moment that it might be Adam, and had to ignore the prick of disappointment when she recognized the different gait of the man. Still, she plastered a smile on her lips and called to him in greeting as he waved.

She laid down her spade and wiped her hands on her apron as he drew near, carrying his gun and bearing a bouquet of the first spring wildflowers, which he offered to her.

"Lena, I *kumme* early, I know. But I would have a word with your father, if I may."

She wet her lips and reached out an impulsive hand to touch his arm as she clutched the flowers. "Isaac, I know of what you would speak and how you mean to be proper, but to be truthful . . . Last week when you brought the venison, I spoke at length with my father." She went on in a rush, determined to have things done quickly, like the lancing of a festering wound, despite her spiritual resolve. "He—he made me see the—great value of you—and, not to be presumptuous, but the offer for

125

my hand. And I—I realized that it would please *Derr Herr* if I should accept any proposal you made to become your wife. I would consider it a great—honor and a privilege of my soul."

If Isaac looked amazed, then pleased, she barely noted it as he lifted her hand in his. She tried desperately to feel something, anything, beyond the simple warmth of another human's touch, but there was no sensation, no thrilling in her body in response to his nearness. But, she told herself sternly, that might be just as well. Perhaps all she had with Adam had been of the physical, of the world.

She jerked her mind back to the moment when she realized that Isaac was speaking.

"You will have no regrets, Lena. I will help mold your soul into the likeness of Christ's, and it will be my pleasure."

She looked up into his earnest dark eyes and nodded.

"May I kiss you?" he asked in a half-giddy voice.

She nodded again blankly. How strange a question. Yet Adam had asked, his voice hoarse and low . . . and then they simply had—

Isaac's mouth was on hers with a bruising pressure, a wet, driving lack of finesse, and she almost withdrew. Then she tried to guide him, to soften her lips, but he had finished. He stood back and stared at her, a glazed look in his eyes, while she resisted the urge to swipe her hand across her lips.

"I would speak with your father just the same. And you will wait expectantly, as a woman of *gut* character should, praying for his blessing."

She murmured her assent, turning to watch him go, as she felt the flowers fall from her limp fingertips to scatter on the ground.

Chapter 18

Adam left the Wistars' home with two panes of glass, a full belly, and an easier mind; he had ceased to question the actions of his father. And, most importantly, he knew how much he loved Lena. He knew it, and thinking on her words about obeying and sacrificing probably meant that she had some idea in her head about helping him in some way—with his dreams, his life. He thought this evenly and without conceit. There was some part of her that he understood with as much awe and inspiration as he felt when seeing a newborn foal, as if all the world, and worlds upon worlds, were twined and leveled upon the wonder of the small being. Lena was that to him, and that could not be lost. He would not allow it to be lost, even as he strived to keep his promise to Mary Yoder.

He crossed the busy, dusty street and hugged the brown-paper-wrapped glass close to his side. It would not do to have so much as a single crack in the valuable stuff to take back to his father. Adam was surprised at the density of the populous on the narrow walking street; it seemed that the war brought more and more people to what he'd heard called "the most important inland city of the day." He paused in this jostling crowd when he thought he heard his name being called.

"Adam! Adam Wyse!"

He turned in time to see Major Dale Ellis waving a long arm at him over the heads of the crowd. He turned, eager to meet his friend, when the protruding point of a lady's parasol poked him in the eye. He blinked automatically, but failed to keep a good hold on the package when the woman stopped to make apology. Her skirts bustled against him, and he steadied himself away from her only to be elbowed by a youth with a stick and hoop racing past. Adam dropped the glass and watched the package be trampled beneath a dozen or more passing feet. He sighed aloud.

The woman with the green-striped parasol seemed oblivious to the diversion she was causing, midstream as it were, and smiled up at Adam from beneath coy dark lashes.

"Forgive me," she mouthed over the din of the passersby.

He rubbed his tearing eye and nodded, sidling past her to where Dale Ellis met him a few steps away. The British major, still clad in his blue coat with clean linen, caught his arm eagerly.

The woman with the parasol stepped toward them both. "Gentlemen," she said, "please accompany me for some refreshment in exchange for the loss of your package."

Adam was already shaking his head when Dale spoke up in a cheerful bellow. "Our thanks, my lady, but we must attend to something pressing. Our regrets."

Adam had turned away with Dale when the woman let out a sudden screech. "Thieves! Thieves! Stop them. They've stolen my purse!"

Adam spun back around, his eyes alert, searching the crowd for any erratic movement, when he was hit forcibly from behind in the shoulder. Then he saw Dale take a strong blow to his cheek.

"'Ere now, what's this? Robbin' a lady? Now that ain't nice!"

Adam realized that a pack of four men, ragged and dirty looking, had formed a tough circle around Dale and himself.

"There has been a mistake," Adam asserted calmly.

"Right. That's why her purse is a-hangin' from your waist." The one who seemed to be the leader pointed a grubby finger at Adam.

Adam looked down in amazement to see a green velvet purse hanging by its looped strings on the top of his knife sheath. Immediately his eyes sought those of the woman, and she looked away. He had been tricked.

He unlooped the purse and handed it to the woman. She took it with a detached air of restlessness that made him uneasy. The ringleader looked to them with a half-toothed smile. "Now you gents need to pay yer fair share to keep this little thieving away from the eyes of the militia."

"I will not pay to—" Adam broke off when he saw Dale's flushed face. Of course he had to pay. If convicted of thievery or any other crime, Dale could be executed on the spot. Adam reached inside his vest for a bag of coins, noticing that the crowd had somehow thinned around them, almost as if people knew there was a crime being committed. They didn't want to be involved and had skittered away like water bugs on a pond.

Adam fingered the small leather sack that held his wages from two weeks of work, and something wild and fierce and flamelike swept through him. It consumed him, from his hair to his toes, and he had no desire to still the feeling. He had never felt such compelling rage, such power—and he thought of the unseen menace of the mountain lion that had attempted to prey on Lena and himself.

He thrust the sack of coins back into his vest and put his head down. With a low, guttural growl, he rammed into the leader, knocking him hard against the brick of the wall behind him. He felt the give of breath and flesh and hit the man hard again before turning to find Dale struggling with the others. Adam knew they would soon draw the eyes of the law enforcement, and with a blind, ruthless precision, he curled his fingers into fists. With fluid, animal-like movements, he watched, as if outside himself, as the others fell beneath his blows. He had his hand on his *messer* when Dale caught his arm and shook him.

"Enough. Enough, Adam. They are finished. We can go."

Adam clung to the very syllables of his friend's words, watching them flash behind his eyes as if illumined by some divine light. He saw the words and began to sob, low, guttural sounds that did not seem to be his own. The last thing he remembered was Dale slinging an arm round his shoulders and telling him things would be all right. But Adam was not sure, not of anything. It was as if the very earth had slipped from beneath his sensible shoes and he'd been transformed into the instinctual beast that all men could be. But worse, he had wanted it. He, an Amish man. He drew a shuddering breath. *I wanted it . . .*

———————

Lena tried to push the reality of her engagement to the back of her mind, as if it were some surreal thing that she could face later—much later. She reasoned that she had the time of courtship, until the bishop came through, traveling by mule, to perform the marriage ceremony. But the niggling truth that Bishop Mast could prompt his aged beast and even more aged self down through the Indian trails any day loomed as a very real probability. And then there was Adam to face . . . She thought he might have been told by now, though she had only given her consent that afternoon. What must he think of her? Then she told herself stoutly that it did not matter, so long as *Gott* knew the truth about her choice.

"What are you thinking of, dearie?"

Lena turned from the kitchen table to smile at Ruth. There was not a day that went by that Lena did not thank *Derr Herr* for the *Englisch* woman's miraculous appearance at the farm. And certainly, Faith was gaining strength and beauty by the day. Lena had even gone so far as to speak to her *fater* about something she had in mind to do for Ruth, but she had needed his permission.

"I am thinking of you," Lena said in a gay voice. "Won't you come with me into my *mamm* and—I mean, my *fater's* room for a moment while Faith sleeps?"

Ruth caught up the bustle of her ragged skirts. "Sure enough, love. Is there cleaning to be done then?"

Lena shook her head as she held wide the downstairs bedroom door. "*Nee.* Please come in."

Ruth followed into the room that neither of them had really visited since the day of Faith's birth. Lena had changed the bedding for her father in a brisk manner, lowering her gaze from taking in the sorrow of the room. But now she could smile a bit at the bright cream walls and the fading light of the day that fell in through the windows and across the wide-planked floor.

She went to the foot of the bed and knelt on the floor next to the simply carved large hope chest that rested there. "*Kumme.*" She motioned for Ruth to join her on the floor, which the older woman did with a grunt and a groan.

"Is this yer treasure chest then, dearie?" Ruth smiled.

"*Nee,* but it is a treasure of sorts." She raised the wooden lid, and the smell of fresh cedar filled the room. Lena could not help but think of her *mamm,* but she pressed on. She reached into the dim interior of the trunk and withdrew the three shifts that rested on top, pulling the fabric into her lap.

"My *mamm's* clothes and things," she said in a soft voice. "I spoke with *Fater.* We would like you to have them."

Ruth looked shocked and pulled back to rest on her haunches, her big eyes welling with tears.

"What? I cannot take any of yer mother's things. They're fer you girls and John's future wife to have as keepsakes, like."

Lena thrust the simple linen shifts at her friend and smiled. "A lot of good but for the moths would these clothes be as keepsakes. I know *Mamm* was smaller than you, but I thought we could use the fabric and make up at least one or two complete new outfits."

Lena tried to ignore the scent of her mother that wafted up from the clothes, but she could not, and a myriad of poignant memories seemed to swim behind her eyes. She thanked God again for the oddly mothering figure of Ruth Stone.

"You must take them with joy, Ruth, for that is what the Lord would have for you. And you have given me much joy since the Lord sent you here."

The older woman cleared her throat. "Well, as to that . . . mebbe He did send me. But the one who actually brought me was that tall Amish man I seen you ride away with on the day of your father's trial."

Lena looked at her in surprise. "What?"

"That tall fella, black hair, strange eyes. Real handsome-like. What did Abby say his name was? Adam something."

"Adam Wyse," Lena whispered.

"Well, now, that's all right then. Ain't Wyse the last name of the feller you'll be marryin', like yer father announced to everyone today? Ah, he's a keeper—I could tell right off—his seeking milk fer that little mite. Not an easy thing for any man to do, I would say. But he did it and brought me here. Well, dropped me off."

Lena stroked the homespun fabric of a dark dress and felt her resolve to marry Isaac dissolve a little, like ice melting from the edges of a pond. And she was in too deep a water to tread. She swallowed hard and forced a smile on her lips.

"Actually, Ruth, I'm to marry *Isaac* Wyse. Adam's brother."

"Oh." Ruth sniffed, clearly disappointed. "Well, I guess ye're old enough to know yer own mind. But marriage . . . that's a hard thing sometimes, even with the right person." She broke off, rubbing her hands together. "But now I miss even those hard times, I guess. It's foolishness, ain't it?"

"No," Lena said soberly. "There is nothing foolish about it. It is dear and wonderful and the way life should be together."

"Well, I wish that fer ye, luv. I do in truth."

"Thank you, Ruth." Lena moved forward to embrace the woman, turning her head into the strong shoulder so that her tears could fall unseen.

Chapter 19

Adam came to himself in the midst of dark shadows and a fetid smell. He sat in a secluded leather seat, and Dale was across the scarred table, watching him with intent eyes.

"So, you're back." It was a question from his friend, riddled with some current of knowing and anxiety at the same time.

Adam felt his hands around a cool tankard and knew a sour taste in his mouth. He nodded with a slow movement, feeling like his head might come off at the motion.

"When did you fight?" Dale asked in a low voice.

"What?" Adam wasn't sure he had heard right.

"Early in the war? For what side?"

"I do not—I have never fought before. I am ashamed," Adam confessed, feeling his face suffuse with color.

Dale shook his head. "Oh, you have fought. I've seen it before—what happened out on the street with you."

Adam leaned forward. "What happened? What happened to me? I am Amish; I do not fight. I lifted my hands to those men."

"And a good thing you did, too," Dale remarked dryly, taking a pull from his tankard. "I could not have handled their little scheme alone."

Adam sighed. "It was a trick. I should have paid them and walked away."

"I do not think you could have."

"What? Why?" Adam whispered.

"That look on your face, the bloodlust or fever—I have seen it in battle and in places far more civil. A man who has fought long and hard sometimes cannot recall . . . or seem to remember that he is not still warring, still killing. It is as though his mind sees another place, another time. That's how you looked, my friend."

Adam ran his thumb over the pewter handle of the tankard and longed for a drink of springwater. "And . . . this look . . . It went away?"

"After my nearly wrestling you into that seat and forcing a drink of strong cider down your throat, yes."

Adam stared at his friend. "I tell you again; I have fought no war."

Dale nodded thoughtfully. "No—perhaps not one that you can remember."

"You question my strength of mind?" It was not a challenge, but a wondering inquiry, almost that of a child.

Dale lifted his tankard. "I salute your strength of mind, Adam Wyse. Whatever you have been through, you have found a way to cope, to survive. And I respect that, my friend."

Adam lifted his tankard after a moment and knocked it into Dale's. The strong cider splashed over onto his hand, which he noticed for the first time was bruised and swollen. He lifted the drink to his lips but did not taste. He would not give tribute to a part of himself that was as savage as a mountain cat and as hidden as the minerals of the earth.

Joseph Wyse looked up from his Bible to encounter his wife's worried gaze. They were sitting together after the evening meal in bentwood rockers near a low fire in the hearth, while Isaac had gone upstairs with his books.

"*Ya*, Ellen, what is it?"

"Isaac's announcement about himself and Lena . . . Do you think it wise?"

Joseph closed the Bible and began to rock in the chair slightly. "Why ever not? She is of *gut* stock. And you will be able to look forward to *grosskinner* to dawdle on your knees."

"You know I think of Adam. It will drive him away surely."

"And what of that? Perhaps it is time he made his own way in the world. The boy is long past marrying age himself."

He noticed that Ellen did not drop her gaze as she was wont to do, and he frowned.

"Joseph, I try never to vex you, but Adam is unmarried for reasons you well understand. And to have him lose what he holds most dear may break him in entirety."

"I think you will find that—" He stopped speaking as the front door opened wide and Adam stepped inside.

Ellen gasped at the boy's disheveled and bruised appearance and rose to hurry to him.

"Adam," she whispered, so that Joseph could barely catch her words. "Have you been in a fight?"

Joseph had wondered many times . . . if Adam were pushed to the edge of violence, would he recall those minutes so long ago?

"It's nothing, *Mamm*," Adam soothed her. "Please don't worry. I am well. I would simply go to bed, if it would please you both."

"You have brought the *glaws* back, *sohn*?" Joseph called from his chair.

"*Nee*, sir. I dropped it in the crowds of the street. I will go again tomorrow."

"*Ach*," Ellen cried in despair. "Forget the glass. Let me give you some liniment for those bruises."

"Again I tell you that I am well. I bid you both a good night."

Joseph stirred and raised his voice. "Before you would lie down, *sohn*. Some news of celebration for the family . . ." He heard a soft sigh escape Ellen's lips and turned his head to see Adam standing wary and alert. "Lena Yoder has done your brother the honor of accepting his proposal to become his wife. We will celebrate the happy marriage when the bishop rides through."

If Joseph hoped for some visible reaction, he was disappointed. His *sohn's* strange golden eyes never wavered. Adam merely nodded and made for the stairs, leaving Joseph to finger his Bible under his wife's worried gaze.

Adam felt the steps beneath his feet, turned to the right toward his room, doing all as if it were the most natural thing in the world—the most natural thing when his world had imploded into a vague nothingness in the pit of his belly. *Lena is to marry Isaac.*

He passed his *bruder's* open door and stopped, staring at Isaac where he reclined on the bed with an arm under his head and a book in his hand while a mangy pup curled about his feet.

"'Tis the courting hour, is it not?" He heard his own voice from a distance, surprised at its normality.

Isaac looked up with a lazy smile. "You have heard then. *Gut*. I want there to be no ill will between us, Adam. I believe what Lena felt for you was a dream of childhood, well past. While I—"

"Do you love her?"

"What?" Isaac lost his page.

"Do you love her?" Adam repeated the question, turning a figurative knife in his abdomen, wanting to feel even the pain to know that he was still alive.

Isaac gave a derisive sniff. "Love is for young swains who would sneak about in the night and charm a woman's virtue from her. 'Tis better for the man to be *fond* of a woman and to let her dabble with all of those emotions so common to humans but so far from the real love of *Derr Herr*. I would not want—"

"Love her," Adam commanded in a harsh growl.

Isaac sat up in the bed. "What? Do you threaten me?"

"Love her. And may *Gott* have mercy on your soul if I ever discover that you do not."

"Adam, I—"

"You heard me," he muttered, then swung the door closed with a quiet snap. He continued down the hall and fell into his bed, still fully dressed, unsure if he would find the will to wake upon the morn.

Chapter 20

"I would not alarm *Fater*," Lena whispered to Ruth on Tuesday in the early morning light of the kitchen. John stood nearby, tapping an idle foot and balancing a long rifle with ease between his hands.

"Well, ye alarm me, that's what, luv!"

"Shhhh," Lena said, snatching up her basket and tying the strings beneath her straw hat. "Ruth, please, you know we need sewing supplies if we are to make your dresses. John and I can be to town and back in a few hours. John found out yesterday that Timothy Stolzfus can give us a ride on his wagon while he goes to fetch some hides from the tannery. We will buy our few things and walk back before the sun is high overhead. And John will take the gun."

Ruth shook her head. "If ye've a mind to do it, I cannot stop a body. But I know how short coin is around here. Since we will be sewin' fer me, you'll be taking my coin." She raised a warning finger as Lena opened her mouth to protest. "And not a word . . . I saved a bit from the fire, and ye'll take it or I'll drop two kettles on the floor and have your father out here in the curl of a cat's tail."

Ruth had bustled to the small shelf where her belongings were kept. Lena watched her gather a few coins together, and then she came and pressed them into her hand. Then she approached John, who frowned but did not look away. "I may not be anything near as good as yer mother was to you, John, but I was young once myself and enjoyed a good licorice pull. Take this coin and buy a treat for yerself."

For a long moment Lena feared her *bruder* would refuse, but then he shifted the gun and took the coin with a brief dip of his head and a mumbled thanks. Ruth smiled.

"All right, go on with ye both then. I'll keep yer father's mind from worryin' if I can."

Lena slipped out with a grateful smile, followed by John, just in time to catch the passing wagon, which was piled high with the hides of many animals, the results of a winter's trapping. Lena disliked the woodsy smell, but gamely let her legs dangle next to her brother's out of the back of the wagon. The day was hot but beautiful, and she enjoyed looking at the trail in the woods disappearing then turning on itself as the wagon progressed. It seemed they were in Lancaster in no time, and she thanked their distant neighbor with a curtsy and a bow of her head.

She had to hustle John away from the various shops where he was wont to wander, but she had a short list and made her way through the crowds with a brisk step. They arrived at one of the many dry goods shops in Lancaster, and she agreed that John might be permitted to wait outside so long as he did not slip off somewhere.

"I mean it, John. You be right here. I will only take a few minutes."

John rolled his eyes at her but gave an obedient nod.

Once inside the shop, Lena was overwhelmed by the number of items and the cavalcade of scents. She had not been in such a place since she was a child and *Fater* had taken them on a trip to town. Now she gazed surreptitiously around at the shelves full of china, pottery, textiles, wooden ware, brass, and all sorts of sundries.

She passed a display featuring fine soaps, scents, and powders, labeled from around the colonies. She was surprised to see products being sold for men's grooming as well, in addition to men's hats in strange shapes and materials.

In spite of her good intentions, her eye was drawn by a glass counter revealing jewelry, mirrors, bottles, ribbon, decorations, and other necessary means for making a woman fashionable. Then she saw ready-made clothes for men and women, which seemed very strange to her considering that all she wore had been made by hand at home. But there were stockings, shifts, shirts, gowns, short gowns, petticoats, and so much more.

She thought about John when she saw books and materials on watercolors, penmanship, and art. She looked at candles in decorative holders and picked up something labeled a "sachet," which really seemed to her a fancy word for naturally dried herbs and spices stuffed into small burlap bags. She was considering how she might make such delicate things herself at home when she realized that two women, fashionably if oddly hatted, were studying her simple garb and head covering.

"A farm girl," one woman hissed, wearing what looked like a powdered meringue cookie on her head.

"We had a hired girl like her . . . Amish . . . stole my best string of pearls," her beribboned companion said a bit overloud.

Lena flushed. She clung a bit harder to her basket and turned her back on the two women, instead moving to the textile counter where a middle-aged man with a great mustache gazed at her with a cheery smile and warm eyes.

"Hello, miss. Havin' a sale on tobacco cloth. Makes right nice curtains and valances, if you like."

Lena shook her head. "No, thank you," she murmured. "We do not make window dressings and the like."

The shopkeeper smiled. "That so? Say, you're Aim-ish, right?"

Lena nodded, wondering if she would be met with the same derision as the two female customers had offered her, but the man went on in a pleasant manner.

"Well, then, what can I help you with today?"

She studied the textiles available behind the man. Of course, some of the cotton and linen wefts and warps she could have made herself at home, but she had precious little time for weaving, and Ruth needed clothing now. She decided on a fine tow fabric in black that seemed to match one of her mother's dresses and a bit of *dobbelstein*, a checkered blue and white, for an apron; there was no need for Ruth to dress like an Amish woman.

"Got some linsey-woolsey on special sale," the shopkeeper remarked as he cut her fabric choices with large shears and a deft air.

Lena considered. Linsey-woolsey had a linen warp and a woolen weft, a combination of fibers that produced a warm, durable cloth more often used for winter clothing. She thought a warm apron would not be amiss for Ruth, no matter how long she stayed with them, and bought two yards.

Back on the street with her wrapped packages, she realized that there was no sign of John and she sighed. After the goings-on in the shop with the unkind women, she simply wanted to get home and away from the crowds.

She allowed herself to drift past the next few shops, standing on tiptoe to see if she could catch a glimpse of her *bruder*. Then she remembered his behavior at their father's trial and she felt a growing sense of alarm. Suppose John had found his town friend with the slingshot again? She turned back toward the store, unsure which way to search. A green parasol passed her line of vision and she felt herself hauled with ruthless suddenness away from the crowd and into the darkness of an alley. A large, dirty hand cut off her scream with brutal force . . .

"I still believe I might have gone after them," Samuel Yoder remarked to Ruth as they stood in the burgeoning kitchen garden. He had told Ruth that he needed a few days more to get his strength back before setting to mulch the apple trees, and in the meantime, would help out in the kitchen garden.

Abigail was busily sowing onions, humming softly to herself as she kept the row even by using a long, thin board.

Ruth stepped lightly between rows of growing things. "No fretting now, Mr. Samuel. They're probably on their way back right now."

"I suppose you're right. And please, you know me a little now, Ruth. I wish that you would call me Samuel."

There was some unidentified current of warmth in his voice that caused Ruth to look up from the brassicas that she was pulling to chop and compost, but then she decided that she had imagined such a thing, as his back was already turned.

She watched him from the corner of her eye, noticing that he had an excellent hand among the plants. He was laying out the hay and buckets to force the sea kale and rhubarb in a manner she might have liked to try herself. She thought about the seed potatoes she'd seen on the back porch.

"I wonder if we might get the wee potatoes going in the same way you're doing there," she ventured and was rewarded by his gentle smile.

"An excellent idea. Abby, run and fill your apron with seed potatoes and we will try something a bit different with them."

The child scampered off to obey, and Ruth suddenly felt nervous standing alone with the man. She cleared her throat. "I . . . uh . . . I must go and check on the babes inside."

"Wait, please, Ruth." He held up a hand and rose from his work among the buckets. "Lena told me of your losses . . . your husband and home. I just wanted to tell you how much I admire your strength of spirit and willingness to go on, and appreciate your love toward Faith."

Ruth pursed her lips. "I thank ye, but what else is there but to 'go on'? I'm thinking you must have lost a great deal yerself in a wife who helped you create all of this." She made a sweeping gesture with her arm, then looked down at the ground, wondering if she'd said too much. Menfolks did not seem to talk about their lives as readily as women did.

Samuel smiled at her with a sad steadiness. "*Ya*, I miss Mary. But the Lord's will allowed Faith . . . and you as well."

"I would not have you be deceived, sir . . . Samuel. I get a mite mad at the Lord now and then for Him doing His will."

To her surprise, he laughed, displaying even white teeth. "*Ach*, Ruth, you speak the truth that plagues all human souls. Do you think that simply because I accept the Lord's will I do not grow angry or frustrated at His choices at times? I would not be flesh and blood if I did not."

"I—I didn't know," she said in a soft voice. "I thought maybe the Amish were able to . . ."

"Have some will that was more than divine? *Nee*, Ruth, I am very much like you."

His voice had lowered, and she felt him studying her. She had a sudden longing for a new comb or mobcap for her unruly hair.

But again he seemed to read her thoughts. "*Nee*, Ruth . . . It is not the outward adorning of a person that matters, but the heart inside. And you have a gentle heart that is—"

"I got the potatoes, *Fater!*" Abby called, tripping gaily over the dirt clods.

Ruth turned with Samuel to smile at the child. But as she made her way to the porch, she longed to know what it was he might else have said. Risking a glance back round, she saw him watching her. She flushed and hurried into the house, feeling as flighty as a young chick.

Chapter 21

N ow ain't this a ripe berry for the pickin'?"

Lena's eyes swam with tears at the pain of the man's grasp across her mouth. She began to pray for her attacker in quick, mentally breathless gasps, even as the man let a hand trail down her shoulder, tearing at her kerchief.

From far off she heard a woman's scornful rejoinder. "Bruce . . . it's one thing to rob a man, but takin' a girl from the street is wrong, and I won't stand here while you do it."

"Then go on with you—git!" Bruce snarled, turning his ratlike eyes back to Lena's. She heard the retreating high-heeled boot steps of the other woman and thought desperately how she might escape. Surely to stay calm mattered most.

"Stop. Let her go. Or I will shoot."

Lena recognized John's voice and began to struggle in earnest. She broke her mouth free. "*Nee*, John. Do not. 'Tis wrong."

The man called Bruce laughed in a menacing tone. "Got a boy to yer rescue, eh? You'd better shoot straight, whether 'tis wrong or right, or I will snap her pretty little neck."

"I think not," intoned an older, dry voice. There was a whizzing sound in Lena's ears, and she saw a stone sink into Bruce's neck with a dull, sickly sound. He let her go and fell to the ground, writhing in pain.

Lena looked over to see a man in a blue frock coat with blond hair standing behind John. He had a slingshot in his hand and a grin on his face. "Madam, if you'll come this way. I'm Major Dale Ellis. British army, I'm afraid, but glad to be at your service."

Lena hurried toward John as Major Ellis spoke to her *bruder*. "Blow the powder from the pan in the gun, son. You did well."

John obeyed, a faint smile on his lips as he lifted the gun, but Lena frowned.

"John . . . you would not have shot, would you?" she asked in desperation as Major Ellis herded them back out onto the street and into the crowd.

"'Course I would have," the boy said. "I wouldn't let some sc— some man lay hands on my sister."

"Brother and sister then," the major said with a smile. "And Amish, I think."

"*Ya*," Lena murmured. "Forgive our manners. Thank you for your help. I'm Lena Yoder, and this is my brother, John."

"My pleasure. Now, if you would allow me, I believe some light refreshment might be just the thing to settle everyone's nerves."

"Oh, we could not intrude," Lena said, wanting to get home.

"It would be my pleasure, ma'am. My wife back in England would insist on tea, I am sure. Oh, but here's someone from your own faith, and a good friend of mine. Come, I'll introduce you." He shepherded them across the dusty street to the glassworks store, and Lena caught a sharp breath that the major did not seem to notice as he went on cheerfully.

"Adam Wyse. Meet Lena and John Yoder . . ."

"What happened to you?" Adam asked, urgency tingeing his voice as he stepped forward and caught Lena in his arms.

"Oh," Dale said brightly. "Perhaps you know each other."

Adam lifted the piece of Lena's torn white kerchief between his fingers and something swam in his brain, like fog on tilting glass. He could not understand, but he knew that he was about to slip again into that darkness and despair, all because of a torn kerchief. He snapped himself upright as Lena pulled away from him.

"Adam," she said low. "I am fine. It was just a man in an alley."

"One of our mates from the other day, I believe," Dale interjected.

"Are you hurt?" Adam stretched to run his hands down her arms, and she shook her head.

"I am fine."

"She's fine; the boy's fine. I know. Since we're all together, let's have a bit of a picnic outside of town."

Adam turned to stare at the major, sensing Lena do the same.

John spoke up. "*Ach*, let's, Lena. We have not had a picnic in forever."

Adam watched her prepare to refuse, but then something softened in her face as if she saw her brother for what he was, half man, but still half boy.

She smiled then, and gestured with her basket. "But we have nothing to eat."

Major Ellis clapped Adam on the shoulder and bowed low before her. "Please, allow me. I am sure that the kitchens of the White Swan will be more than able to prepare a quick but luscious repast. I will return shortly. John, would you like to come along?"

Adam watched as the boy nodded eagerly, handed Lena his gun, and scampered off after the major's long strides. Adam took the gun from her and laid it inside the back of his covered wagon. He moved slowly, not really wanting to look at her when she had such a vulnerable air about her. He was amazed at his desire to do harm to the man who had attacked her.

"You are sure that you are well?" He turned, his body tense.

"Adam . . . I prayed for the man. He didn't harm me. 'Twas only a bad scare, that's all."

He nodded, looking at the small tips of her shoes peeking out from beneath her skirts. "Only a bad scare," he murmured. "'Twas how I felt when I first heard news of you . . . and Isaac."

"I tried to tell you that day at the creek."

He watched her cross her arms defensively and longed to smooth the troubled frown from her brow. "*Ya*, what was it you said about obeying and sacrificing? Do you fancy that you are making some offering of self, Lena? Do you believe that is honorable before the Lord?"

"We are all to offer ourselves to the Lord," she snapped, then lowered her voice, color flooding her cheeks. "I do what I do of God's will. I do not expect you to understand, nor is it any of your business to understand. It is between *Derr Herr*, Isaac, and me."

Adam snorted. "Sounds like a good union, in theory."

"'Tis the way that all marriages should be, Adam."

He felt the rub of her words and would have rejoined when John ran between them.

"Here he comes," the boy laughed. "He's got a whole basket full of goodies!"

Dale followed, bearing a huge wicker hamper. "Cheerio, Adam Wyse. Let us pack up and go."

Adam took the hamper with a reluctant smile and watched as Dale offered Lena his arm and helped her trim form up onto the wagon seat. Perhaps a picnic wasn't a bad idea after all . . .

Lena sat shyly on one of the linen tablecloths that Dale had procured from the hotel while the two men unloaded the hamper. She glanced around, enjoying the feeling of simply being still in the spring air, and admired God's handiwork in the fresh green grass, golden forsythia, and burgeoning bushes. Adam had found a spot that was isolated enough from the main road, yet still allowed them visibility of the wagon and horses.

She listened to the rumbling voices of the two men and realized that they must have been friends for some time. Here then was another secret of Adam's, one that her father might call dark—that he, a peacekeeper in theory, should befriend a British prisoner of war. She supposed, watching his fine features without appearing to do so, that men were simply who they were to him; no matter the color of uniform they wore or their station in life.

"I say!" John bounced down beside her, having come from shooting Dale's slingshot at trees. "Look at the spread!"

Dale laughed, but Lena shook her head reprovingly. "Be polite," she ordered in an undertone.

But the major smiled. "I've got three lads back in England, Mistress Lena. The eldest is about John's age here. I miss the exuberance of my boys, and I would have to agree with John. The hotel put up quite an array."

Lena agreed, laughing, and wondered how much coin the major had to pay for the display of fresh pasties, two kinds of pie, breads, cheese, and crocks of various spreads. There were also bottles of soft cider and root beer, glistening with condensation from the icehouse to the sunshine.

The four made a merry repast, then sat about, full and talking.

"So do you know each other because you are Amish and meet together?" Dale asked, looking at Adam, where he sat a distance from Lena.

John laughed. "You might say that about these two, though Lena's dead set on marrying Adam's brother."

"I see," Dale said, clearly confused, but polite.

Lena threw her *bruder* a daggered glance. "Yes, I am to marry Isaac Wyse."

"But she likes Adam Wyse," John went on, his mouth full of cookie.

"Quite a dilemma." Dale smiled, but he shot a serious glance at Adam, then turned to John. "Have you heard the latest ghost tale, lad?"

John shook his head. "*Nee*, do tell. Please, Lena. May he?"

Lena, like many of the Amish, was superstitious enough to disagree with a ghost tale on a rainy night, but there seemed to be no harm in the broad light of a sunny day. "If it pleases you, Major. But perhaps I will take the chance for a bit of a walk."

"Call me Dale . . . and by all means, let me entertain the boy. 'Twill do my heart good."

"Thank you, Major—Dale. I am sure we will hear a good many variations of the story you tell come this winter. The Amish love storytelling around the hearth, and John excels at the art."

"You are most welcome, fair maid." Dale grinned as John begged for him to begin.

Lena rose, and the men scrambled to do the same. "*Ach*, please, sit back down. I will just take a brief walk among the pines."

"I will follow," Adam said lazily. "No need to be threatened again by a panther or ruffian . . . or the latest ghost."

"Panther?" Dale asked, looking alarmed.

Lena heard John begin to tell the major tales of the woods and panthers as she drifted off into the trees. She knew Adam walked behind her, but tried to concentrate on the heady scent of the stand of tall pines instead.

"I would have it from your lips alone," Adam said finally, without any apparent attempt to make her feel guilty.

"I have told you already," Lena whispered, knowing what he meant. She bent to pick up a pinecone and squeezed its jagged edges hard against the palm of her hand.

He took it from her absently, tossing it away and catching her hand to rub at the marks the impression had left. "Then tell me again."

She pulled away from him and stared up at the towering pines that surrounded them like straight-backed soldiers, never wavering on their course to reach the sky. If only she could be as old as the trees so that she might have knowledge and wisdom enough to know what she was doing, what she had to say.

"I will marry Isaac," she heard herself murmur. Then she took off running through the lines of pine, as if she were a child again and could be free to play and scamper like a wild deer. She wanted to forget about the man whose steps she knew followed hers, muffled by the rich and cushioning layers of pine needles.

Then the tree line broke and they were in a small circlet of green grass. Lena stopped and stared at the ground in wonder.

"*Ach*, Adam, look. A faerie circle." She gestured to the ring of violets, vibrant purple with yellow throats, surrounding her. Of course, she was too old to believe in faeries, but the beauty of the place was mesmerizing.

Adam stepped into the ring of flowers very near her, and she almost moved away, but he caught her hand. "Tell me the old story about the faerie circle, Lena," he cajoled with a smile.

She looked down. "You already know it."

"*Ach*, but I would have it again from someone who can still find wonder in such things."

"I do not . . . ," she started to protest, then sighed. He knew her too well for her to lie. She lifted her gaze and met his strange golden eyes, shrouded now by some emotion she couldn't quite fathom, but it absorbed her, drew her, like a moth to flame. She wet her lips. "Superstition says that if you stand in a faerie circle with a man . . ."

"Just any man?" he prompted.

"The man of your heart," she said. "That time will stand still for you both, that you will have all of eternity to be . . . together while the rest of the world goes by."

Adam smiled. "Would that we could live in faerie circles forever. You will make a *gut* mother, to have such fancies to spin into tales for your daughters."

It was too much to imagine daughters with eyes that did not glow like the light of a candle, and she stepped out of the ring of violets, breaking the clasp of his hand, intent on hurrying back through the pines.

But Adam caught her back. "Lena—tell me another story."

"What?"

"A new story . . . about a *mawd* who follows her heart and not her head. Who carries the scent of roses and dew about her like the charm of a spring eve. Who is strong but soft, tender but—"

"Adam, stop." She shook her head, trying to shake away the spinning of his words. She'd even taken a few steps back closer to him, led by his gentle hand. "I have no new stories to tell, no myths to believe anymore. I know what is real."

He bent his head, drawing her even nearer. "Do you, Lena? Do you know reality beyond the flame of fear, the touch of death? *Ach*, let your heart sing and find hope once more."

He moved as if to kiss her, and she drew back sharply, the tension of the webbed moment snapping when he spoke of hope. How could she hope, knowing that he might enlist? It was he himself who had broken what they might have been.

"*Nee*, Adam. I have no song to sing nor story to tell, none but what you have taught me yourself. And I will not dance to that tune again."

She turned from him, not caring if he followed, and made her way back to the picnic spot.

"Ah, we've just finished," Dale called when he saw her.

"You will have to hear the story one night at home," John said, his face alight with a smile.

"That will be *gut*," Lena murmured, trying to regain her composure.

Adam brushed past her with a grin as he went to help gather up the picnic. "Keep your pretty fancies, Lena, no matter the denial of your lips. Some fantasies may yet turn out to be real."

Chapter 22

The week waned to Friday, and Lena rose from the floor of the keeping room where she had been cutting out the pattern for one of Ruth's dresses. She enjoyed sewing with Ruth, finding her to be a nimble and jolly seamstress who was capable of talking as well as keeping her needle flying.

"Did you sew much with your mother, luv?" Ruth asked as Lena stretched her back.

Lena smiled. "*Ach*, all the time. One of my earliest memories is carrying a swatch of fabric around and practicing my stitches. I remember being close to the floor as I walked, so I must have been very young. I was so proud of the little pinpricks on my fingertips. *Fater* would kiss each one at night and tell me that I would be an excellent *hausfrau*."

She paused then, wondering if Isaac would kiss her fingertips. And then, like the sudden flush that companions a fever, she imagined Adam kissing her fingertips. They would be outside, the green of the burgeoning land a backdrop for the senses, and he would press long, slow, heated kisses on her fingers that would send triggers of sensation from her hands to her heart.

"*Your fingertips only will I kiss, my sweet, this day.*" She imagined his deep voice and how he'd bend his dark head to make good his word and send her heart pounding. *"Not your full lips, nor your white neck, nor the blush of your cheeks or the sweep of your brows . . . just your fingertips. Denial is good for the soul."* Then he would grin at her and she'd slap playfully at him and they'd run together, hand in hand, through the trees. They'd come breathless upon a patch of dark blackberries, full and ripe with summer's sun, and Adam would catch her fingers to his lips and select a fine, moist berry and . . .

"Be ye all right, child?" Ruth's voice broke into her thoughts just as the sound of a wagon approaching reached her ears. For a brief moment, she wondered if it might be Adam, then blushed at her thoughts of a moment ago.

She peeped out the window and recognized Isaac and told herself that she was not disappointed to see her betrothed. She forced a smile to her lips and turned to Ruth.

"I am well, Ruth, but 'tis Isaac. I would run and change my gown, if you do not mind seeing him in?"

"Go on, dearie," Ruth said with a comfortable nod.

Lena stepped with a light foot to her room and pulled out her best dress, a rich burgundy weave. She'd finished pressing a fresh kerchief and apron only that morn, and she knew that she would be looking her best. Isaac deserved that, she told herself stoutly. She dressed in a hurry, knowing his lack of desire to be kept waiting, even if he was dropping by unannounced. Then, noticing her pallor in the small bureau mirror, she pinched her cheeks to bring forth color and straightened her prayer covering. She was back down the steps in minutes, finding Isaac standing stiffly, with his back turned, while Ruth nursed Faith.

"*Ach*, Isaac . . . I am so glad to see you. Come, let us walk outside for a bit."

He glanced at her over one shoulder. "Actually, I have come in hopes of bringing you home with me for a meal. *Fater* suggested that he would enjoy your company, and *Mamm* is making *schnitz* and *knepp* that we might all celebrate our engagement. I will, of course, bring you back before dark."

"Go on, dearie," Ruth called. "It will be just the thing."

"Well," Lena said with some reluctance. "All right." She did not want to deny Isaac, but the thought of breaking bread with Adam made her both nervous and excited. She decided she needed to spend more time in prayer on the matter.

Ruth agreed to let her father know, and Lena followed Isaac to the wagon, where he helped her up with a decorous arm. She held on, wondering if she should sidle closer to him as he drove, but decided from the set look of his face that he must be concentrating fully on driving. She felt anxious to create a peaceful atmosphere between them and cleared her throat.

"Um, Isaac . . . now that we are engaged . . . perhaps you might . . . let the horses graze a bit, and we could walk together."

He glanced sideways at her. "Whatever for? *Mamm* can use your help in the kitchen, I am sure, so we should get home as fast as we can. And I hope to finish a certain translation of the Book of James that I've been puzzling over. There is no need for a walk."

And that is that, she thought, put nicely in her place. She patted absently at the rough-headed dog that nosed its way up from the wagon back between them and tried not to notice the soothing tones Isaac used as he spoke to the animal—much more soothing than he had ever used in speaking to her. She wondered how she would ever spend a lifetime with the man who was beside her, but in no way *with* her . . . then told herself that all things were possible through Christ.

Adam watched Isaac drive in with Lena and felt a jolt of jealousy stab through his chest. He tried to concentrate on the mare that he was training, but he couldn't help but glance at his brother and then at the woman he loved as she clambered lightly from the wagon. He had a sudden and deep longing for peace in the whole situation. Peace for once with Isaac, an understanding and acknowledgment of the differences between them. Peace with his father, which seemed so very much out of reach, and more than anything, peace in his heart when he thought of Lena.

He had not yet made any move toward enlisting, toward seeking out that new life that would supposedly allow him, by his own word, to court her again. But the engagement between Lena and his brother had been a shock too heavy to comprehend, and every time he prayed about joining the army, he encountered again and again that still, small voice from *Gott* that told him to wait. But wait for what?

He brushed his hand down the mare's side and considered that love had to have something more to do with freedom than cost, had to be something that liberated and did not hold with crushing power. He did not understand why it was not as simple as crossing the paddock to Lena and taking her in his arms . . .

And then the Lord spoke to him again, softly, tenderly, and Adam thought, for the first time in a long while, beyond himself. Perhaps love really mattered in terms of how he responded to it, how he received it, and not by his trying to force what he wanted onto situations, onto others. It was an idea that he knew he should cling to . . . and then his mother hailed him from the edge of the grass, with Lena standing tentative and still in the background.

"Adam! Lena's kindly offered to help with the dinner preparations. But we cannot reach those upper shelves of the cabinet. Would you mind?"

157

Would I mind, he wondered curiously, *being so near to Lena in such close proximity as the kitchen?* Maybe he could try out his new thought and relax, be in Lena's presence without wanting, without pushing . . .

He turned the horse to run loose in the field and accompanied the two women back to the house. "Where is Isaac?" he couldn't help but ask.

"Working," Lena replied stiffly. "On a translation of the Book of James."

"Ahh," Adam said softly. "James . . . the brother who did not believe in his older sibling, did not find Him special . . . until after the cross."

Mamm nodded. "That is so. And so should we learn to look for what is God-given and special in each other before time on this earth runs out and we must give account for our actions in heaven."

They had reached the house, and Adam held the screen door open. Lena passed under his arm, and he closed his eyes on the desire to kiss her, cajole her, whisper to her . . . *Nee, I will simply accept the situation,* he told himself as he headed for the kitchen. *How hard could it be?*

Lena noticed the seeming perfection of the Wyse kitchen and down-stairs rooms. She supposed that since the advent of Faith she had let little messes run away from her. She resolved to do some spring cleaning when she returned home, waking the place from its winter's sleep in preparation for the life of the seasons to come.

Adam hauled the bench over from the table and balanced easily atop it, stretching his long arms up for the platters used at special times. He handed them down, one by one, to Lena. She then passed them to Ellen, who busily scrubbed the dishes in a pail of soapy water and then rinsed them.

Standing so near to Adam put Lena about eye level with his lean hip, and she couldn't help but notice the fine line of his body's strength each time he stretched. She told herself that she was wanton, and when the last platter had been sent down and put back, she spoke out with abruptness.

"Uh, *Frau* Wyse . . ."

"Ellen, my dear, *sei se gut.*"

"Ellen . . . may I see Isaac for a moment?"

She felt Adam and his mother's surprise and blushed a little, sensing heat creep into her cheeks.

"In his room, dear?" Ellen asked with hesitancy. "Or should I call him down?"

"Call him down," Adam snapped.

"In his room," Lena said.

Ellen shrugged with a frown on her face that Lena chose to ignore. "Top of the stairs, dear. Last door to your left."

"*Danki.*" Lena brushed past Adam, who still stood on the bench, and took to the stairs like a water bird in flight. She was determined to do right by Isaac and get her thoughts under control.

So she clambered up the steps, holding her skirts high, then smoothed them with some measure of decorum as she marched down the hall and knocked on Isaac's door.

"*Ya, kumme!*"

He sounded faintly irritated, probably at being disturbed while he worked, but she slipped inside anyway, closing the door behind her with firmness.

Isaac turned from the desk that sat beneath his window and stared at her. "Lena, what is it?"

She swallowed and pressed her back against the sturdiness of the door, steadying her breathing. She allowed her eyes to soften as she looked at him. A one-eared cat on his bed regarded her with a lazy eye.

"Would you wish a moment's rest from your studies, my betrothed?"

He shook his head. "I do not understand. I am deeply engaged in a particular passage, and I—"

He broke off as she advanced with coy steps across the room, coming to stand before him. The breeze from the window played against the back of her kerchief and neck. She studied him objectively. He was not unattractive, but he simply was not Adam. She suppressed the thought, then bent forward to twine her fingers in his dark hair.

"I would have a kiss, Isaac. If you would desire it also?"

She felt him stiffen with shock, but she didn't care. She had to do something to banish thoughts of Adam from her mind. With a faint sound of despair, she bent and pressed her lips tight against his mouth, concentrating. After a few seconds he pulled away, sliding his desk chair back so that it screeched against the hardwood floor.

"Lena Yoder, what has come over you?"

"We're going to be married. I would spend some time with you, 'tis all." She advanced on him until he almost tilted backward.

"I think that you need to pray and ask *Derr Herr* to . . ."

She bent and kissed him again, trailing her fingertips down the back of his neck, closing her eyes. He made a strangled sound in his throat that might have been passion or outrage, but she could not let it matter. He scrambled away from her and stood up.

"Uh . . . *Mamm* is . . . calling . . . downstairs . . ."

"Oh no, I don't believe she is."

"Heard her . . . got to go . . . get help. I mean, go help . . ." He scooped up the cat, flew to the door, and was out within seconds, closing it behind him with a slam.

Lena began to laugh so hard she had to sink down on the edge of the bed. Then her laughter turned to weeping, and she held her head in her hands and sobbed.

Adam had left the kitchen once he was done helping his mother and gone back to stand along the fence, watching the mare. He could not fathom what it might be that Lena had wanted with such urgency from Isaac, but again, maybe it was not his business. Maybe he should simply relax and let peace reign in his body and mind.

"Adam!" Isaac puffed, coming up alongside him as if he were being pursued by a specter.

"What's wrong?" Adam asked, trying to tamp down irritation at the interruption.

His brother hung over the fence and caught his breath. "I—I must ask you—rather a personal question, I think."

"Well, do not think; ask." Adam frowned. He was not used to Isaac being unnerved by anything, and he worried that Lena might have had her feelings hurt by his elder sibling.

"All right." Isaac leaned closer. "It's about . . . a girl."

"You mean your beautiful betrothed?"

"Very astute." Isaac patted his arm. "*Ya*, Lena. Well, did she ever demand . . . or insist that you . . ."

"What?"

"Well, kiss her," Isaac hissed. "I mean, I have kissed her before, of course, but . . ."

Adam's hands tightened involuntarily on the wood of the fence at this revelation, but Isaac rambled on.

"I am talking about demands for kissing, and then . . . well, she . . ."

Adam rounded on his brother with gritted teeth. "Isaac, if you do not get out what you are trying to say . . ."

"Right. She kissed me. Bold and full on the mouth. Two times, and I was not even willing."

Adam relaxed a bit and tried to suppress a smile. "Scared you, did she?"

"*Ya*, in truth, she did."

Adam nodded. "Well, she is a handful—there'll be no taming her, I'm sure. Likely she'll want kissing all the time, even when you're trying to study. You will probably have to give up your books and your pets . . ." He let the idea drift with just the right amount of regret.

Isaac's shoulders sagged. "Give up my books . . . my animals . . . for the sake of kissing? I cannot do such a thing. Why, 'tis not even right before the Lord."

"*Ach*, I don't know. I think the Lord means for a husband to tend to his wife," Adam mused.

Isaac goggled at him. "Tend her, *ya* . . . but not . . ."

"All the time?"

"*Ya*."

"I imagine you will grow to forget your books."

"Forget my . . . Adam, I am going to have to pray very hard about this wedding."

"You do that. Likely you'll find comfort in prayer now. You won't have much time later."

Isaac groaned and turned to stagger from the fence while Adam struggled hard to contain his mirth. But then the reality of the proposed wedding, with all of its necessary intimacies, washed over him, and he was filled with a sorrow as vast as the sky above.

Chapter 23

Joseph glanced down the table at Lena seated next to Isaac, directly across from Adam, and smiled with pleasure. He felt confident, given Adam's moody manners during the meal thus far, that it would not be long before the boy would quit the farm and flee somewhere far away. He had come to the conclusion that Adam's departure was the best solution to his own fears. Toward this end, the faster Isaac married Adam's true love, the better.

"So how is our happy couple?" Joseph asked, reaching for his drinking glass with a smile. "I do hope that the bishop arrives soon. Of course, you've had little time to court, but that shouldn't matter—you know each other well enough, I'm sure."

He watched Isaac staring at his plate and wondered what addled the boy. His wife had served a traditional Amish favorite dish, *schnitz* and *knepp*, which was usually a fare of celebration, but Joseph noticed that only he himself seemed to be eating with any appetite.

"A *gut* meal, Ellen," he said, and his wife nodded her thanks. Lena murmured her agreement. *At this rate*, Joseph thought, *I might as well be eating alone.* Yet Adam, although not happy, did not seem overly put out, and this too worried Joseph.

He decided he would enliven the group with a recitation or two.

He prided himself on his excellent memory and oration skills. It might not hurt to bring the table's occupants back to a more pertinent domestic frame of mind.

"I've heard a new speaking in Lancaster as of late. 'Tis on the topic of the care of a home and marriage, so it is most fitting. Would you have me recite?"

Lena nodded almost frantically. "*Ach*, yes . . . please do . . . My *fater* often tells a *gut* story at dinner."

"Very well, my dear. 'Tis called 'Huswifery.' Thoughts about the sharing of life's work that must be done before the Lord." He cleared his throat, then began:

> "Make me, O Lord, thy Spinning Wheele compleat;
>   Thy Holy Worde my Distaff make for mee.
> Make mine Affections thy Swift Flyers neate,
>   And make my Soule thy holy Spoole to bee.
>   My Conversation make to be thy Reele,
>   And reele the yarn thereon spun of thy Wheele.

> "Make me thy Loome then, knit therein this Twine:
>   And make thy Holy Spirit, Lord, winde quills:
> Then weave the Web thyselfe. The yarn is fine.
>   Thine Ordinances make my Fulling Mills.
>   Then dy the same in Heavenly Colours Choice,
>   All pinkt with Varnish't Flowers of Paradise.

> "Then cloath therewith mine Understanding, Will,
>   Affections, Judgment, Conscience, Memory;
>   My Words and Actions, that their shine may fill
>   My wayes with glory and thee glorify.

Then mine apparell shall display before yee
That I am Cloathd in Holy robes for glory."

He stopped and there was a disjointed amount of applause, and he frowned. "Adam, what think ye of the merits of the poem?"

Adam looked straight across the table at Lena. "I suppose that it is inviting God to be the designer of one's life, one's garments of repose or action. I suppose it to mean much more than I can fathom—like the rich heart of a woman can be."

Joseph chewed his lip. The boy was practically wooing the girl across the dinner table, and right beneath Isaac's drowsing nose. He was about to speak when a loud crash of thunder suddenly boomed from outside. Lena startled, and an idea crossed his mind. He ate with renewed vigor, then put his fork down as the storm continued to increase in intensity.

Joseph rose from the table. "Isaac cannot possibly see Lena home safely in such a storm as this. She must stay." He gestured to his wife. "Ellen, if you might go with Lena and Isaac and prepare the bed with the bundling board . . ."

Joseph felt the weight of the guests' various expressions as he uttered the words and suppressed a smile.

Lena looked as though she might bolt into the stormy night, and Isaac for once appeared very awake, if not alarmed. Ellen's pretty mouth was slightly open in surprise, and Adam stared in fixation at the butter crock on the table as though it had sprouted thorns.

Joseph clapped his hands. "*Ach*, bed courtship is a *gut* thing, I say. A chance for couples to talk but not touch in private. Every young person who plans to marry should spend some time thus together."

No one responded until Adam's spoon clattered with a jarring noise against his plate. Joseph smiled at the sound.

Lena had forgotten the controversial custom of bundling that persisted among some of the Amish and many of the other colonists. Sometimes the man of the engaged couple was sewn into a linen sack, and a bolster was placed between the couple to prevent physical contact. In truth, she knew that her own father might not approve of bundling despite the engagement. It was really a controversial issue; the efficacy of a bundling board to prevent touch really rested on the couple's honor. She hoped that Isaac was as honorable as he purported to be. But there was no telling what he would do after her behavior that afternoon in his bedroom.

<hr />

There was no denying that the thought of Isaac lying abed with Lena was the most torturous experience that Adam could ever remember. He stripped off his vest and shirt and went to open the window casement to stare out at the storm, careless of the rain that dampened the waistband of his breeches. He could not change custom, the very thing that helped shape the world he lived in—but, *ach*, such a custom. He stared at the dark, moving clouds and wondered if she would take her hair down. He could see its rich fall brushing over the edge of the bundling board, free for Isaac's touch. He wondered wildly what they would speak of and realized that this was the reality of his future if Lena really went through with the marriage. And it appeared that she would, for she made no demure to the bundling.

There had certainly been no bundling for him and Lena, Adam considered with bitter thought . . . They had barely progressed past a second kiss. He rocked his head against the window frame, pressing until it hurt. Mary Yoder's promise held him with fingers beyond the grave, with the eyes of heaven. Yet he could not lose Lena . . . would not . . . He turned to stare at his room with vacant eyes, and then he remembered something. He threw a grim smile over his shoulder at the display of the storm, then reached for his shirt.

———— ◆ ————

Lena tried to ignore the rather desperate glance that Ellen Wyse gave Isaac and her as she left the bedroom, allowing a single candle to burn. The bundling board was nothing more than an eight-inch-high slab of wood down the middle of the bed, bolstered by rolled quilts. Fully dressed, something she'd insisted on, refusing Ellen's tentative offer of a night shift, Lena accidentally bumped the board with her elbow as she reached to worry with the usual curl of escaped hair from her prayer covering.

"Are you knocking?" Isaac's voice came sleepily from the other side of the board, and Lena hugged her arms against herself as the thunder crashed outside the window.

"*Nee*," she answered in quick denial, not wanting him to know that she was terrified, both of the storm and of the thought of it being him and not Adam who would have the right to share a bed with her in the near future, with no bundling board in place.

"I look forward to the time when you are my wife, Lena. I realize that you were simply . . . overwrought . . . by the idea when you . . . this afternoon . . . up here . . ." He broke off, sounding shaken.

She found her voice with difficulty. Should she tell him that she was looking forward to it as well? But that would be a lie, no matter her intent to go through with the marriage.

"I am sure that you will be a *gut* husband, Isaac," she managed finally.

"Do you know the bundling poem?" he asked after a moment.

Lena swallowed, knowing that some bundling poetry could be quite heady, and she wondered where he was leading with such talk.

"Noooo," she told him.

He began to recite in a singsong tone:

> *"Nature's request is grant me rest,*
> *Our bodies seek repose;*
> *Night is the time, and 'tis no crime*
> *To bundle in your clothes.*

> *"Since in a bed a man and maid*
> *May bundle and be chaste,*
> *It does no good to burn out wood,*
> *It is a needless waste.*

> *"The sacred Book says wives they took,*
> *It doesn't say how they courted,*
> *Whether that they in bed did lay,*
> *Or by the fire sported.*

> *"Since bundling is not the thing*
> *That judgments will procure,*
> *Go on, young men, and bundle then,*
> *But keep your bodies pure."*

Isaac laughed. "What do you think?"

"'Tis fun," she admitted, wondering if she could relax with his jokes about purity and judgment.

"I think so too." He yawned again, then was silent.

Lena sought desperately for something to talk about when her ears were met with the distinctive sound of an echoing nasal snore.

She blinked her eyes in surprise, leaning upward cautiously to peer over the board. Sure enough, Isaac was sound asleep, his mouth slightly open, his snores shaking sounds that competed with the thunder.

She waited a long while, until she was sure that everyone must surely be asleep, then slid from the bed and caught up the guttering candle as the storm increased in fury. She slipped from the room without looking back.

———— ◆ ————

Lena pressed against the dark, jar-filled shelves of the *tzellar* of the large house and cringed as another crash of thunder seemed to shake the shadowy timbers of the foundation. Then the sound of footsteps coming nearer drew her ear, and she shook for fear of being discovered in such a silly position. But she'd always feared a bad storm, and going to the cool of the cellar had seemed a blessing of hiding to her in days past.

She thought of dousing the lantern she'd found, but she knew its glow had probably already been seen, so she straightened her spine and waited. Adam walked into the circle of light, and she exhaled with relief.

"*Ach*, it's you," she said.

"And it is you, my dear soon-to-be sister-in-law." His voice was moody. "I thought I might find you here. I remember how you hate storms. I assume my brother, your beloved, snores peacefully asleep."

She ignored his pricking comments and swallowed at his close proximity, trying not to let her eyes trace the breadth of his shoulders in his loose linen shirt.

"How was bed courting with my *bruder?*"

"You make it sound so awful," she cried before she thought.

He glared at her. "Then I assume it either went very well or very quickly downhill."

"I will not answer," she announced.

She did not meet his eyes. She was engaged to Isaac and forced herself to conjure up a blurry recollection of his face when the thunder came again with fierce power. She scrunched despite herself, and Adam took a step forward, his hand outstretched, then stopped.

"What you need, my sweet, is a distraction." His voice had warmed in the moments between storm crashes, and she now felt as caught as a mouse in the applesauce as he reached outward. But he stretched over her head to pull down a small jar from the shelf behind her.

"Blueberry jam. I helped *Mamm* put it up last summer. I remember it was so hot." His tone was lulling as he pulled off the brandy-soaked leather lid and popped the waxen seal.

Lena did not like his tone or the sensation of warmth that spread across her shoulders and down her back. She should flee . . . but the storm still rumbled. She clutched the lantern with sweaty palms; its warm glow played on the beauty of the iridescent-like glass of the jam jar and caught on the length of Adam's tanned fingers.

"Adam . . . ," she managed in a warning croak.

He looked at her, his eyes simmering gold in the lantern light, full of a range of emotions that did little to calm her spirit.

"What? I seek but a taste of jam. Is that so bad?"

"*Ya . . . Nee.* You know what I mean."

He smiled and swiped a finger across the top of the fruity substance, then drew a long taste.

She tried to put a rein on her thoughts when the thunder came again in a terrible roll and nearly caught back a sob at the desperation of the situation.

"*Ach,* my manners," he chided. "What about you, sweet sister-in-law? Would you care for some jam?"

She knew exactly what he thought; that she would not be having a taste. And, indeed, she knew she probably shouldn't. But he had no call to tempt her thus when she was willing to sacrifice so much to aid his soul. She put the lantern down with a clink, and he raised a dark eyebrow in the half light. She crossed her arms and lifted her chin. "Thank you," she whispered. "I would love some."

She almost laughed out loud at the half frown that formed about his handsome lips, but then he stepped forward, swiping two fingers in the jam this time. She watched him extend his hand to her and tried to focus her sensibilities. She was merely having a shared taste of jam. She closed her eyes with determination and tried to pretend that it was a spoon he held out to her.

⚬——⚬

Adam bit the inside of his mouth until he tasted blood. He knew the game had ceased to be his when the last stain of violet blue was gone and she opened her eyes to stare up at him, cool and waiting.

The thunder crashed overhead once more, and the lantern suddenly guttered out at their feet. Adam welcomed the darkness to hide his disconcerted state, but he knew it would only worsen Lena's fears.

"Lena," he whispered. He bent his back and dropped his mouth, landing a half kiss on her temple when he'd meant it for her mouth.

He heard her quick indrawn breath when the storm rumbled again, and then his mouth closed unerringly upon her own. He tasted the summer-sweet weight of the berries on her lips.

He almost dropped the jam jar when he felt her withdraw from him.

"The storm is passing. Can you hear it, Adam?"

He couldn't speak and nodded in the dark instead.

He felt her bend down and heard the clinks as she fixed the lantern, and light spread in a soft pool at his feet once more.

"Adam, thank you . . . for helping me through the storm."

"'Twas nothing," he said stiffly, feeling as though he had been used to bring momentary comfort, like a doll to a resourceful child.

She tapped the jar he'd forgotten he held, and then she picked up the lantern.

"'Twas delicious jam, Adam. The fruit of your labor captured in a single passing moment."

He glared at her, feeling stormy and heated and out of sorts. "The storm does indeed pass," he said with irony. "Glad to have been of service."

She smiled at him. "*Danki* again, Adam."

And then she was gone, swinging the lantern, its light bouncing off the cellar walls, leaving him standing in the cool dark and longing for the storm to return.

Chapter 24

Adam eased into his bed, resisting the urge to make sure Lena had found her way safely back to his *bruder's* room. He sighed when he considered his behavior—so much for not forcing things in love. He turned over and thumped his pillow, knowing he should dismiss the whole incident in the *tzellar* and his blasted idea about the jam from his mind, but at the same time he longed for the luxury of dwelling on the images. He drifted off into pleasant lassitude until he started to dream . . . his nightmares of always.

Ruth looked up in surprise from her dawn feeding of Faith to see Lena slip inside the front door and close it firmly. The girl turned, out of breath and a bit wild-eyed.

"What's wrong, luv?" Ruth asked, rising to settle the babe back in her cradle.

"Nothing." Lena's teeth chattered.

"Ye look like you've been chased by wolves for a good mile. Do you want some herb tea?"

"*Ya* . . . please."

The two were soon seated in comfort round the kitchen table.

Ruth waited, sipping her tea, to see if Lena might speak of what had her so riled.

"It was quite a storm last night," Lena offered.

"Aye, yer father said you would most likely stay the night at the Wyse farm. Said you hated storms."

"I do hate them, but it—it was all right."

Ruth saw an accountable blush stain the girl's cheeks.

"You must not have stayed long for breakfast then," she said, sliding a plate of fresh bread and the honey pot in front of the girl onto the table.

Lena met her eyes and then dropped her gaze. "*Ach*, Ruth. It was terrible . . . in some ways."

"They did not treat you right?" Ruth asked, bristling.

"*Nee* . . . I . . . had to bundle with Isaac."

"Oh, well, that's all right then. Enough to make any girl feel strange. He didn't try anything to harm ye, did he?"

Lena shook her head. "He snored . . . and snored. And then there was the storm . . . I usually hate storms . . . Finally, when it was almost light, I left. I know it was rude. But I made my farewell to his *mamm*, who was starting breakfast. I told her that I was homesick and had to go."

"Well, she might have wakened the snorer to bring you home. You could have been hurt coming all that way alone."

"No, I know the forest trails. I had to escape."

Ruth sighed. "It might not be my place, Lena, but I have to ask you if you believe in that verse you read me the one day."

"That God is for us? *Ya*, I believe."

"Then answer me something else. Do you truly want to marry Isaac?"

Ruth watched the struggle on the beautiful young face.

"I don't understand what those two questions have to do with each other."

Ruth stirred her tea. "Well, seems to me that if you believe God is on your side, then you don't have to try to be your own god, or make your own decisions based on what you think is right, but maybe not on what He wants . . ."

"I—I am not doing that."

"And I'm not saying that you are, but I know one thing." Ruth looked at her directly. "Sometimes the most dangerous advice in life comes to us from those who love us the most, the people who care for us and want to protect us. Maybe they love us so much that they want to keep us from . . . what was it? Being 'cultivated and sown'? They want to spare us that, so they give us advice that might not quite be lined up with God's plough."

Lena blinked. "You mean my *fater*, don't you?"

Ruth shook her head. "I told you before, I'm no Bible studier as it may be, but I know this: your father loves you very, very much."

"Ruth." The girl leaned across the table and caught her arm. "I thank ye for your talk, but I have to—I must believe that what I am doing in marrying Isaac is right."

"What happened between you and Adam Wyse?"

Lena sank back in her chair. "It was when my *mamm* died. He told me he was going to join the militia and start a new life. He said it was over between us."

"Hmm. That is a heavy weight for shoulders as young as yours. But again, God is fer you."

"Well, *Fater* has never trusted Adam, although my *mamm* liked him."

"Sometimes folks differ on such things, but it don't always make one person right nor the other wrong."

Lena smiled sadly. "I suppose not . . ."

"Whoop! Hiya!"

The two women looked up as Samuel called suddenly from the front door.

"The bishop's come! Let us welcome him!"

Ruth squeezed Lena's hand. "So your bishop's here. And that means your ceremony can take place?"

Lena nodded with troubled eyes. "It must."

Ruth sighed and rose to make more tea.

Chapter 25

The early morning sun made a slatted patchwork on the floor of the Wyse kitchen as Adam came to sit down at the table. He reached for a chunk of bread and caught his *bruder's* eye. "So where's your future bride?"

Isaac lowered the book he was reading and yawned. "She told *mamm* she was homesick and ran back this morn."

Adam dropped his spoon. "You mean you let her go alone, through the woods, at this hour?"

"Boys!" their *mamm* pleaded. "Keep quiet; your *fater* is having a bit of a lie in this morn."

"*Ya*, Adam, truly," Isaac said. "When I wed Lena, are you going to keep up this incessant babble over her? You act like a moon-eyed calf." His tone wasn't challenging, simply matter of fact, but it was the straw that snapped the mule's back for Adam.

He rose and leaned across the table, calmly took the book from his brother's hands, and stretched his arms forward to grab his collar.

"Adam," his mother exclaimed in alarm, coming over from the sideboard to the table. "Adam, *sei se gut*. Take your hands from your brother. 'Tis sin."

"Is it?" Adam asked in a quiet voice, ratcheting up his grip so that Isaac was now inches off his seat.

"Yes," his father's voice intoned nearby. "It is. Put him down and go from the table. I will speak with you out by the barn."

Adam dropped his hold so fast that Isaac almost fell backward off the bench. Then he stalked from the house without his hat, not meeting his father's eyes.

Lena was surprised to see Bishop Mast looking pale and aged. The man was normally bursting with good health and vitality, but now he required her father's help to lift him down from his faithful mule, Bud.

"*Ach*, I took a bad fall last week. Tried to tend it a bit, but I am afraid it's got a *gut* hold now. I've had the fever and chills too."

Lena and Ruth rushed to fluff up the pallet before the low fire in the hearth as *Fater* and John brought the bishop in and eased him down onto the pile of blankets.

"*Ach*, now this is comfort. I thank you, Samuel. Ladies. Where is fair Mary?"

Her father cleared his throat. "Our Mary died in childbirth, but the Lord blessed us with a new daughter. Faith, Mary named her."

The bishop closed his eyes for a moment. "Samuel . . . I am sorry for your loss."

"*Danki*," her father murmured.

"Shall we tend your leg then?" Lena asked, and the older man nodded.

"*Ya*, do whatever you might."

Lena glanced at Ruth. "I am not so skilled in healing," she murmured, her mother's death all too familiar in her mind.

Ruth patted her arm. "Let me have a look then."

Ruth knelt and unwrapped the makeshift bandage that covered the lower leg. Lena caught the sickening smell of diseased flesh and steeled herself not to turn away. "What do you need, Ruth?" she asked.

"I must clean this first, but it will hurt a bit, I am afraid, sir."

The bishop waved a weary hand. "Your hands are gentle, mistress. Do what you need."

Lena brought rags and water, and Ruth cleaned out the deep wound, causing the bishop to grasp Samuel's hand tightly.

"Now," Ruth announced. "John. Run to the creek bed with a bucket and dig down deep beneath the stones and water. Bring back the darkest mud you can find. And, Lena, I need cobwebs."

Lena flushed. "I—I do not think the house that messy, Ruth."

The other woman laughed. "Nay, from the outside porch corners, maybe. They will work to bind the wound together and bring about healthy clots."

Lena hastened to gather cobwebs from the porch, brushing the disgruntled spiders out of her way until she had a whole handful of the sticky stuff. She went back inside, and John soon arrived, huffing with the wet bucket.

Ruth unceremoniously scooped a handful of the dark, earthy-smelling mud from the bucket and slapped it into the wound. She continued until all of the reddened skin was covered, then added Lena's layer of cobwebs. Then she drew a piece of muslin tightly about the whole area, and the bishop breathed a sigh of relief.

"Now," Ruth admonished, "you must rest and keep this leg up a bit. No traveling on your mule 'til I see some pink and healthy skin a-growin'. Do you hear?"

Lena flushed at Ruth's tone. Didn't she know she was speaking not to a child but to the leader of all the regional Amish? But to her surprise, Bishop Mast responded with a polite and deferential nod.

"*Ya*, mistress. I will do as you say."

Ruth got to her feet. "Call me Ruth, good sir. Everyone else does hereabouts. Now how about a hard cider to help ease the pain a wee bit?"

Lena cringed again and looked to her father. Everyone knew that hard cider was not something the bishop would partake of.

"I would love some hard cider, Samuel," Bishop Mast said with a sigh. "If you have any on hand . . . for medicinal purposes." His blue eyes twinkled.

"*Ya*, surely." Her father hurried off to the cellar, while Lena considered that things were not always as they were expected in life.

———— ✦ ————

Joseph walked outside to the barn area and found Adam splitting wood with ruthless abandon. He decided that things must be handled delicately at this juncture. He didn't want to push Adam too much.

"You cannot lay hands on your brother, no matter your feeling," he began with caution.

"Yet you have found it an easy enough pleasure to lay hands on me over the years," Adam ground out, hefting the axe.

"One thing has nothing to do with the other. When you have *kinner*—"

Adam caught his eye over the axe handle and shot him a wicked grin. "When I have *kinner* I can feel free to beat them as I please? Sorry . . . don't plan on having any." He let the axe fly again, and Joseph resisted the urge to take a step backward.

"I understand why you are angry, *sohn*."

"Do you? I think not. You don't understand the first thing about love. Somehow you managed to wrangle *Mamm* from her family without their being aware of what a tight-handed wretch they were letting her go to."

A splinter of wood hit Joseph's cheek, and the flame of anger began to grow in him at the boy's words. "So that would make you the *sohn* of a wretch, would it not?"

Adam threw the axe so that it landed in the woodpile, then swung to face his father, gold eyes glistening. "I know you, *Fater*. I saw you break the windows in the house. I don't know why, but I have a *gut* idea that it was to keep our family's nose properly bent in front of the other Amish. It must mean that you've paid off someone here or there, while other, truer men sit in prison."

It took everything within him for Joseph not to strike his son. Instead he caught Adam by the collar and pulled him close.

"You will shut your mouth or leave this land. Do you understand? You will remember who it is that governs this family and offers you the protection of a roof and labor. You will stop abusing your *bruder* and losing your head over a skirt. You will grow up!"

"*Fater!* Stop!"

It was Isaac, walking with purposeful strides toward them. Slowly Joseph let his hands drop.

Isaac came close and studied Adam, as if looking for some sign of abuse. "*Fater*, you will not lay hands on Adam. He serves you well—in truth, better than I, for he wrestles with his temper and I can't even seem to find mine—until now. I tell you that if you ever again hurt Adam physically, I will pack my things and leave without looking back."

Joseph looked at his sons, reading the disgust written on both of their faces. He knew he should make some response, show some sign of power to squelch this uprising, but he couldn't seem to think. He turned on his heel and stalked toward the house.

Adam stared at his *bruder*, wondering what had happened, surprised at the dark intensity of Isaac's gaze. "Isaac . . . what are you about? You mustn't damage your relationship with our *fater* over me. This was nothing."

"I have been less than a man, Adam. I've watched him beat you for years, and I tell you that this is not the way to treat a *sohn*. If I had more character, I would have stopped him long ago, but I did not. I was afraid for my own place. The Bible tells us not to fear. Anytime a man makes a decision based on fear, it produces bad consequences. In this case, I have slept blissfully through the years while you have endured the brutality of the lash and much else. I ask for your forgiveness, though I do not hope that you will give it. I do not deserve it."

Adam was silent for a long moment. "There is nothing to forgive, Isaac, else I, too, would have to offer my apologies. I have been jealous of you for years—jealous of your place in *Fater's* heart, jealous over Lena. Perhaps we both have lessons to learn in becoming better men."

Isaac nodded and extended his hand. "Then have my hand, Adam, that I will become better than what I have been to you."

Adam brushed his hand aside and pulled him into a hard embrace. "Nay, *bruder*, take the offer of my heart that we will both move on to honor—and friendship."

Chapter 26

Joseph stood in front of the small, cracked mirror in the master bedroom and forced himself to look into his face. He was getting old; it was easy to see the silver threads in his dark hair, matching his cold eyes. He gripped the edge of the bureau that he'd carved himself years ago and sought for solace in squeezing the steadiness of the wood. But still, inside he shook.

Isaac's betrayal was something that he could not understand. Had the lad been at the hard cider? Or been overlong at his books? In his heart Joseph knew that there was no excuse beyond what it was—Isaac had defended his *bruder*.

He held the wood harder beneath his fingertips, as if it would anchor him somehow to the present, but soon he was swallowed in the familiar rush of memories, the assaulting images flashing like a tempest in the back of his mind. His *fater's* hamlike fist raised . . . his *mamm* cowering against the balustrade . . . the popping sound of wood splintering . . .

"Joseph, are you well?"

He swung with a fierce glare, gasping for breath, as the reality of Ellen's presence materialized behind him.

"What?" he gasped.

"I asked if you fare well. I saw Isaac go outside this morn. Do the boys trouble you?"

He heard the quiver of fear in her voice and hated himself for it. He leaned back against the bureau and drew a deep, steadying breath.

"I am well, Ellen. You may go."

"I thought some herb tea might perhaps—"

"You may go."

He watched her nod, her pretty face sad, but there was no help for it. He was what he was—a monstrous slave of his past. And Ellen must never know. She must never know . . .

—◆—

Adam ran as long as he could along the Indian trails, pushing himself beyond breath, heartbeat, and thought until he dropped in a mossy copse and lay with his face to the earth. On one hand, he felt renewed by the exchange he'd had with Isaac, but then he closed his eyes against the image of his confrontation with his father because it made him feel lost again somehow. It was a bitter irony that in close proximity to the man who helped give him life he lost all sense of being. When his father had shaken him, had been so near his face, those elusive and fractured images of darkness flashed again somewhere in the back of his brain. Perhaps he was mad . . .

He rolled over and stared up at the blue sky. Yes, perhaps he was truly mad. Had he not only yesterday come to a decision that he would receive love, not force it? Yet he had laid hands on his brother over the breakfast table. He upset his mother, insulted his father . . . Perhaps he should enlist now, or go away somewhere. But where? Where without Lena? For surely he would wander the earth like a marked Cain, and all would see him for what he was . . . a creature of loss and lament. He half sobbed at the thought, but knew he could not withstand the torment of living under the same roof with Lena as his sister-in-law. He would dishonor her with his mind, of that he was certain. What did the Bible say? Flee from temptation? Perhaps he should flee . . . enlist . . . as he should have done days ago. But something held him again, bid him wait and hold a bit longer, and he gave in to that calm, still Voice and turned back over to sleep against the moss.

He woke to the strange sensation that he was being watched and sat up with abrupt concern. To fall asleep in the woods was not a wise idea, and thoughts of the stalking panther made the hair stand up on the back of his neck.

Then he saw John Yoder sitting cross-legged, regarding him with a sober and considering expression from the blue eyes that were so like his sister's. Adam relaxed and leaned back on his elbows, allowing himself to stretch out.

They sat in companionable silence until a hawk screamed overhead and broke the moment. "He's found his breakfast," Adam remarked, gesturing with his chin to the sky. "Did you have yours?"

John shook his head. "I have been up for a while."

"'Tis a danger to run in these woods alone and unarmed."

"Or to sleep in them?"

"True enough. So tell me what troubles the heart of a ten-year-old man," Adam said lightly.

"Eleven," John answered calmly. "Today I'm eleven."

Adam looked at him, at the fine features that would come to fruition in years, at the speckling of freckles that would disappear or stay to charm his first love. *His first love.*

"I must congratulate you then, John Yoder. Eleven years is nothing to scoff at, with the perils of this new world." Adam was serious and lay back fully on the grass, staring up at fluffy clouds between the treetops.

"The Brits would take me at eleven, at ten even," John said softly.

Adam sat back up and turned on his hip to face the lad. "What are you talking about?"

"Going to fight."

"And kill your *schwester* with worry? I do not think so."

"What do you care? She'll be married to Isaac."

Adam sighed. "*Ya*, there's the rub. 'Tis enough to make me consider the fight as well." He shouldn't have admitted his feelings to the boy; it might sound like he was giving permission for an early enlistment. "I did not mean that."

"Yes, you did," John said flatly. "I heard you the evening you talked to Lena about it . . . heard you leave her. Everyone wants to run away, I should imagine. Why not you?"

Adam blew out a breath of air and half chuckled. What was he to do with a prophetic muse in the body of a child whose very eyes seemed to penetrate his soul? "The trick is learning not to run, lad. To stand . . . and to fight from where you are."

"Are you preaching the Bible to me?" John asked solemnly.

"No," Adam said, alarmed. He did not want to appear as Isaac to this boy; that would drive him off entirely.

"Yes, you are. Stand and fight . . . fight the *gut* fight. Isn't that what the Bible means about accepting things in life?"

Adam felt something twist in his heart. "*Ya*, fight the good fight. I think you be too smart for your own age, eleven-year-old."

The boy grinned at that, and they rose in mutual accord.

"*Kumme* home with me," Adam invited. "My *mamm* will feed you."

"*Nee*, I had better get back. But, Adam—"

"*Ya*, what is it now?"

"Adam, the bishop came this morn."

The boy's words flashed through Adam's mind with the rapidity of lightning, then simmered like hot oil and sank in. The bishop meant marriage . . . and soon; he usually only stayed a few days.

Wait . . . A few days more . . . The calm voice of his Creator murmured deep inside, and Adam reluctantly began the walk home to obey.

———— ◆ ————

Lena stole some time from her chores to go and kneel at her mother's grave site. How she longed for the gentle presence of the woman who had raised her, for the sweet voice that always knew with calm deliberation exactly what to do.

Lena sighed and began to speak aloud softly, not caring if her *mamm* could hear her words or not. She wanted to talk.

"I miss you," she began, then uttered the words again and again like a litany until she was spent of the permeating feeling of loss for the moment and could move on. "*Ach, Mamm,* you cared for Adam, found him to be a righteous man in God's sight. You spoke out confidently for him when *Fater* had his feelings of doubt. But Isaac . . . what did you think of Isaac? I do not suppose that I will ever know. We never spoke of him, simply in passing. But I am to marry him, *Mamm.* Marry him. How I wish I might be younger again, like Abby, like Faith, that I might move forward *knowing* instead of doubting. How I wish I might have saved you that morning . . . I am so sorry. I didn't know what to do. But I guess it's not my burden to save you— not then, not now. That is hard to know, *Mamm.* It is so hard to know a lot of things . . ."

"I feel like that too."

Lena jumped in surprise at the low voice.

"John! You frightened me."

He dropped to his knees beside her and laughed. "I am sorry,

Lena. I heard some of what you said. It makes me feel *gut* . . . feel less alone when you talk to *Mamm* like that."

Lena reached to squeeze his hand, and he squeezed back for a second. "That's *gut*, John."

"I heard you talk about Isaac. Lena, I don't understand why you want to marry him when Adam—"

"I do not wish to talk of Adam." Lena swiped at her eyes and rose.

"I saw him this morning."

Lena paused. "You did? Where?"

"I thought you didn't want to talk about him." He squinted up at her, a grin on his pale face.

She turned her skirts in a huff.

"*Nee*, Lena, wait. I think . . . I think he is ready to do it now. To enlist."

The words caught at her like cruel fingertips, and she stood still. "Why do you say that, John? Is that what he said?"

"No," John said. "Not exactly. But I could tell he was restless like, and I think he might, that's all. And why shouldn't he, if you marry Isaac?"

Her brother's words made her face flame, and she closed her eyes against the thought that by her actions she might inadvertently send Adam to his death. She could not speak.

Then John rose and patted her awkwardly on the arm. "Never mind, Lena. I shouldn't have said that. I thought, though, that maybe you . . . Well, never mind."

He started to walk away and she called after him, staring down at her mother's grave marker. "John . . . John, wait. Happy birthday. I forgot, but I guess *Mamm* reminded me somehow. We'll have a cake."

She turned, and they walked in sober silence toward the house.

Chapter 27

Samuel had gone out to the apple trees and Lena was sewing when Ruth noticed that the bishop had wakened from a nap, and she went to test the strength of the bandages on his leg.

"How are ye now, sir?" she asked.

"I am much better in body and spirit, thanks to you. May I ask who you are?"

Ruth bowed her head before the wise eyes of the older man and longed to say that who she was did not matter anymore. To the people of this house she was "Ruth," and to Faith she was sustenance and love.

"I'm Ruth," she said simply.

Bishop Mast nodded. "And, Ruth, how came you to be here?"

His voice was layered with time, it seemed to Ruth, as if he had heard all and seen all that there was to be seen in men, yet still found enough reason to persist in life.

"I am a wet nurse for the babe . . . a stopgap for the loss of their mother. Miss Lena believes God is for me, but given my past, I do not know."

An aged and blue-veined hand came down on top of hers. "You have lost all, have you not? I have met many women like you in the mountains and countryside. War is unforgiving; it stretches wide arms to encompass the land and sweeps all away, like crumbs from a tabletop."

"My crumbs were my husband, my home." Ruth's eyes filled with tears, which she swiped at hastily with the back of her free hand.

"I am truly sorry for your loss, and yet I do not think that is what troubles you most, Ruth."

He waited, and she was amazed at his depth of perception.

"'Tis true," she whispered finally. "I fear I sin here."

"How? How can you when the Lord is for you?" The man's eyes were kind and steady.

"I—I think I grow to love the family too much." She bit her lip.

"The family?" he asked gently. "Or the head of the family?"

She met his eyes, the truth bare in her own, when the front door opened and Samuel came in. Ruth nodded her thanks to the bishop and made haste to rise, swiping once more at her face before turning to greet Samuel.

"You are finished with the trees already?" she asked, carefully steadying her voice.

"I felt a break might be good. I also wanted to check on the bishop." He glanced toward the pallet bed.

"The bishop is much more himself, thanks to your Ruth here," the older man called out cheerfully.

Ruth flushed at the use of the word *your*. She busied herself pouring cider and heard the bishop beg Samuel to come over and sit awhile.

"So, Samuel, have you heard about General Washington and his interest in apple trees?"

"I know he is rumored to be interested in the New York apple nursery . . . trying to import new varieties instead of the usual crab apple."

"Oddly, it's the one thing the British and the colonists seem to agree upon. I have heard that both armies have posted an amicable guard around the New York orchard to protect it from any warfare."

Ruth could not help but laugh. "'Tis strange that it was the taste of an apple that caused so much trouble in the Bible, and now the fruit works to bring men together."

Both men chuckled, and the bishop waved a hand at her.

"Come and sit, Ruth," he insisted when she had brought them refreshment. "Come and talk a bit, for I would enjoy the company."

Ruth perched cautiously on the edge of a rocker next to Samuel and hoped the old man would not reveal any of their conversation. She needn't have worried. The men discussed everything from the weather to the crops to news from other Amish farms. She was invited to give her opinion more than once and relaxed back into her chair.

Then Bishop Mast cleared his throat and caught Samuel's eye. "So are there marriages for me to perform hereabouts as part of my duties?"

Samuel nodded, clearly pleased. "*Ya*. Isaac Wyse has asked for Lena's hand. I have given my permission."

"Hmm. I see. But was it not Adam Wyse the girl fancied?"

Ruth wanted to speak, but held her tongue. Lena must make her own choices in life.

"*Ya*," Samuel answered soberly. "But that has passed."

"I see . . . Well, then, name me the other marriage to be performed." The bishop took a sip of cider as Samuel looked at him confusedly, then glanced at Ruth.

"I've not heard of another couple. Did you hear something from another farm?"

The bishop pursed his lips, and Ruth felt a jitter of nerves when he did not reply readily. Finally he put his cup down and looked at both of them. "It seems you miss what is right beneath your nose . . . uh . . . heart, Samuel Yoder."

Ruth sneaked a glance at Samuel and saw that he had flushed red over the top of his beard.

"Sir?"

191

"Must I spell it out, man?" Bishop Mast demanded. "There is a woman of good report, a kind, homemaking, generous woman, comely still, who works from dawn to dusk, tends to the *kinner*, builds a good home . . ."

Samuel's voice came solemn and trebled with an excitement that Ruth could feel down her spine. "I know this woman," he admitted. "But—"

"I'm not Amish," Ruth finished for him, then clapped a hand over her mouth at her outburst.

Both men laughed in good nature, and she joined in.

Then the bishop spoke seriously. "Ruth, you live as mother and mistress of this fine home. Should you choose to accept what I believe will be a proposal from Samuel Yoder, would you learn the tenets of the Amish faith and seek to join the church?"

"Oh, I would," Ruth exclaimed, feeling a strange sense of belonging. Then she glanced at Samuel and spoke with hesitancy. "But, sir, I would not have Samuel Yoder driven into a marriage for which he has no desire. I am glad to continue on . . . as we are."

Samuel turned to her and caught her hand in his. "Upon my soul, dear Ruth . . . I have wanted a union between us and have thought much of it of late. If . . . if you would have me?"

He bent and kissed her lightly, and the bishop laughed. "I think we have cause for celebration. And perhaps a mite of hard cider?"

Ruth lifted her head to see that the older man was teasing, but his attitude made her feel welcome, and she found that she had renewed vigor for living as Samuel kissed her again.

Lena watched John's face when the surprise engagement of Ruth to her father was announced. Lena was pleased herself, having grown to cherish Ruth, but John fled outside as soon as he'd gained permission to do so. She wanted to follow him, but she wasn't sure what good it would do. Ruth was not trying to replace his mother, but John was still child enough, despite his birthday, to resent the situation. She decided not to speak, but to pray for him, when Abby tugged on her hand.

"Lena . . . will you come outside with me?"

There were a thousand and one things that she could be doing, like preparing her clothing and Ruth's for the upcoming weddings—though even as the word *weddings* crossed her consciousness, she longed to shudder. The bishop would not be well enough to preach on the morrow, but had decided to stay until the following Sunday to preach to as many Amish who would come, and to perform the marriage ceremonies. And besides the fact that her wedding was a week away, she had to accompany her father and the bishop to the Wyses' home that afternoon.

A thousand and one things, but the pleading, freckled face of her baby *schwester* was too sweet to deny. After all, how long would it be that she would have time to dally and play? So she gave in with a smile.

They walked hand in hand past the now-blooming kitchen *gorda*, and Abby danced about like a butterfly on a string as she swung Lena's arms. The sun fell on their straw hats, and Lena had to laugh when Abby's chin strings kept coming untied. As she bent to tie them for the third time, she caught her little sister's face between her palms and kissed her.

"I pray that you will always be as happy as you are right now," Lena whispered.

Abby giggled. "Are you happy, Lena?"

Lena straightened her back and wondered if it was given to her to be happy. Certainly she had joy at her father and Ruth's union, and John's birthday, and Abby's freckles, but ever since Adam had told her of his decision to leave, she had not been as happy as she might be. And now she was deciding, choosing, to make a sacrifice that she could only hope would bring abundant life here on earth and eternal joy later.

She had to blink in the sunshine because her reasoning somehow seemed faulty to her own mind. She told herself sternly that perhaps she had best not play but act like the grown woman she was. Yet still she lingered with Abby, troubled but helped by the child's carefree movements and her joy in simply being alive.

Chapter 28

The following Monday afternoon, Adam decided to test the bounds of his cautious new feeling of friendship toward his brother. He realized that it had been his father's encouragement of a feeling of jealousy between the two of them that had kept him from ever looking to Isaac for support or companionship. But today, after a hesitant request to exercise two horses, Isaac had responded with surprising alacrity, spilling his books in the process. It was enough to humble Adam's heart.

They set out on two fine bays, crossing the meadow at a pace fit for conversation, and Adam cast about for something to say. He need not have worried; Isaac was an engaging companion when he wanted, and Adam wondered how life might have been different if he had known this about his brother sooner.

"I say, Adam, I wish we had taken rides like this together when we were younger."

Adam looked over as Isaac echoed his thoughts. "Me too. Tell me, Isaac, what is it like to know you are called for a purpose in life, that *Gott* cares for what you become . . . like a bishop?"

Isaac shrugged. "I have never known things to be otherwise. I have always been drawn to books—I love the way they smell and the weight of them in my hands. I suppose I sound a bit mad."

"Only a bit." Adam grinned.

Isaac laughed out loud. "As for being a bishop . . . I do not really know how *Gott* will work all of that out for me. I simply trust that if He desires it, then it will be so."

Adam shook his head. "You yield your life so easily." It was not an accusation, but a statement of wonder.

"*Nee*, that is not the truth, Adam. I could let you think that it was so, but that would be being my usual pious self, and I would like things to be more real between us if we are truly to be friends."

"So what is the truth?" Adam asked, surprised at this startling bit of self-revelation from his brother. He wondered if he would be willing to bare his own faults so readily.

"The truth is that I am angry much of the time. I judge people— for their actions, their looks. I do not yield easily, but care too much about what others think to show otherwise."

Adam was silent for a moment, absorbing the weight of the words. Then he cleared his throat.

"I am about as jealous as a trout over you and Lena. It burns within me. I—I do not think that I can stay once you are married." *There. That was a fine dose of truth.*

Isaac nodded, then his horse shied. He kept an excellent seat, and Adam scanned the ground as his own mount began to prance nervously. "It's a deer carcass. Only half gone." He gestured to the ground nearby.

"Then why the anxiousness of the horse?" Isaac asked, regaining control.

"Look at the mud by the deer. Those are fresh panther tracks. Big ones. A cat gave me a scare awhile back, in daylight too. We need to take a hunting party out to find this animal before somebody gets hurt."

Isaac shrugged. "I suppose. Likely it'll range off, though."

"*Nee*," Adam said. "Too much game here . . . too many people, which make for easy prey."

They led the horses around the carcass, and after a moment Isaac spoke.

"So where will you go if you leave? What has the Lord called you to?"

"I have no idea. The war, I suppose. Survival in the face of the odds . . . all those things."

"She loves you, you know."

"What?"

"Lena. It's you that she loves."

Adam felt at a loss. "Then why would you marry her?"

"Because I am willing to settle for the opportunity for *Gott* to grow a love between us over time."

The answer cut to Adam's core. Could it be that the Lord would grow such a love between them? If it were so, then he must leave forever, for he did not think he could bear to see love shine in the turquoise blue depths that he longed to be his own personal sea.

After a bit, Isaac drew rein. "I must go back, Adam, and fetch Lena and her family in the wagon. They are to come over to discuss wedding plans."

Adam nodded, starting to turn his horse when Isaac extended his hand.

"*Danki*, Adam—for the truth of the ride."

"*Ya*," Adam agreed quietly. "For the truth."

They rode home in silence, the only sound their horses' hooves on the grass beneath, marking the passage of time.

Ruth climbed the steps of the farmhouse to the second floor. As a rule, she ignored the simply carved balustrade, coming up only to do dusting or to change linens. She had felt that the second floor was John's domain, and she did not want to intrude or push in on the boy. But, she told herself, if she were to be mistress of the fine home, then she should feel a part of it, on all levels. And she knew that John had gone outside somewhere, so her walking about upstairs would not bother him.

She felt the floorboards creak beneath her weight as she crept down the hallway, feeling a bit spooked, like a little girl on a hunt for a mystery. When she passed John's room she noticed that the window was open to the sunny but breezy day, and that papers were strewn about his desk and floor from the air blowing. She bit her lip, then ventured inside, wanting to straighten things up.

She tiptoed and caught up the paper nearest her and then the next. She tried not to look, but the bold black ink drawings drew her eye. She stood amazed at the pictures the boy had drawn—a rabbit poised in perfect, natural posture, its very nose seeming to have movement against a backdrop of tall grasses; the farmhouse in stark relief, down to the detail of the last stone in the foundation; the forest, deep and darkly mysterious with the trunks of trees done to twisted familiarity. Then she lifted another sheet from the floor, and her eyes filled with tears.

It was a very definitive battle scene . . . two opposing sides caught up in a heated fight, weapons poised and ready.

"What are you doing in here?"

Ruth turned, the page in her hand, startled for a moment by the angry thread in John's voice, but then she looked at his flushed face. She saw the vulnerability there as well as the anger.

"I'm sorry, John. I wasn't trying to hurt you and didn't mean to be searching your things. The wind blew the papers off the desk." She slowly extended the drawing of the war toward him. "The war troubles you greatly, don't it?"

He snatched the drawing from her. "What of it?"

"I don't know much about pictures and the like, but that one is special. They all are, but the one of men fighting . . . I understand. The war between life and death . . . My Henry could be one of them men."

John snatched up the other drawings from the floor and brushed past her, turning his back to her and standing taut at his desk. Ruth was glad he had not yet thrown her out completely.

"It's not only about the war," he explained. "It's about this country— the country and the way my people are treated."

"I didn't see it that way." Ruth nodded. "I am not so good at art and such. But I wonder—are you in that drawing?"

John drew a deep breath, then turned to face her. "I'm in the middle . . . can't pick a side between the British and my family."

"The British?" Ruth asked, surprised, as she now noticed the small, lone figure of a gunless boy standing in the background of the battlefield.

"Yes," he snapped, suddenly fierce. "The Brits do not persecute us, us Amish anyway." He lowered his head. "I know your husband died fighting. I do not mean to offend you."

Ruth could have sobbed for joy at this kindness from the lad. And she began to understand his way of thinking. "So you think the Patriots war in vain?"

He shrugged. "Of course not. But why do they not leave us alone in the process? To not fight with them is not to fight *against* them."

"Isn't it? I mean, from their view? The Brits have an army a mile wide, and they'll take a lad as young as ten. At least the test laws leave the colonists' boys alone until they're fifteen. But we . . . the Patriots . . . need every man who can fire a rifle if we're going to win."

"But why do we have to win?" John asked. "William Penn's experiment in providing a place for us to worship freely was working. Sort of."

"Your sister read me something from the Bible, John. It said that 'God is for us.' I asked her then, kind of like you, what that could possibly mean in a war? How could He be for both sides? Or any side for that matter, but what I figure is that He is for you and me and everyone as a person, a believer in Him. He works things out in our lives—not like we're part of a side, or standing alone and lost, but He works with us each one. Maybe you should let Him work with you."

John shrugged. "What would He do with me?"

"Look what He does with you," Ruth exclaimed, indicating the drawings. "You can do things with your mind and hands that I have never seen the likes of before. You are wise and deep beyond your years. And I—I like you, John. Not because I ever want to take the place of your ma, but because I want us to someday have something special together . . . some kind of together-like way, if you see what I mean," she finished lamely, unsure if her impassioned speech would even touch the boy.

The world stood still as the wind lifted another paper from the desk. John caught it with a deft hand, then gestured with his chin to a shelf behind her. Ruth turned to look at glass jars filled with vibrant colors.

"See there. That's all paint that my *mamm* got me. We were supposed to do a floor painting when she—when she felt well after Faith was born."

Ruth did not stop herself. She went to him and embraced him in a brief but heartfelt hug, and he didn't pull away. "I am truly sorry, John. I wish I might have known your mother." She stepped away from him and noticed a blush on his cheeks. "Tell me about this floor painting. Did you already draw it out?"

"*Ya.*" He turned for a paper, then showed her a design of simple but beautiful detail—flowers, scrolls, and stark but striking lines.

"We will do this, John. We'll do it on Thursday, this week, while the bishop is here, and we'll make a real party of it! We'll invite the Wyse family too."

John shook his head. "The bishop is likely to say it's not plain enough to suit."

Ruth laughed. "Not if he's half the man I think him to be. Come, let's show him this—together."

She felt like she moved on feet of air when the boy took up a stride beside her, and she knew she would now always be welcomed on the second floor of the home.

━━━━◆━━━━

Adam had decided that he would wait a few more days . . . for what, he wasn't sure. But he knew enough about his faith to understand that it was better to obey that heart echo of a Voice than to ignore it. Then he would enlist; the Patriots needed all the help they could get, and he had begun to feel that somehow he would be keeping to the creed of his faith. Somehow fighting for their freedom, protecting his family and Lena, made sense. It meant little that he would sacrifice his own life in the process, now that he did not have the love of his heart. He pushed aside the sudden inspiration that perhaps *Gott* was the One who was meant to fight, to protect . . . not man. He sighed aloud.

He looked up as Isaac returned in the wagon with Lena, the bishop, and Samuel Yoder. They were coming to discuss the wedding plans, as Isaac had said, and Adam knew he didn't have the stomach for it. So he took himself off to hoe the sprouting corn and to remind himself to keep his place . . . which was not beside Lena.

He was much surprised, then, when Samuel Yoder came out to

him in the field. Adam paused in his labor and pulled his hat off in deference to the older man.

"*Ya, herr?*" he asked, wondering if he were to get some personalized invitation or warning regarding the upcoming nuptials. But the blue eyes that beheld him were steady, somber.

"Forgive me," Samuel said, and Adam almost dropped the hoe, thinking that the sun had addled his hearing.

"I'm sorry . . . What did you say?"

"Ruth told me that it was you who brought her to us," Samuel said. "She has agreed to become my wife. I also cannot help but think of the nourishment I received in prison, and how that came to be."

Adam dropped his gaze, and the older man went on. "I have prayed for you of late, knowing that this union between your brother and Lena would be difficult for you. And the Lord has convicted me that I have been wrong about you. You would have claimed John as your son at the trial. I—I wasn't thinking at the time, but I've had time now. Forgive me."

Adam shrugged, trying to drink in the deep and utter resonance of peace that the man's words brought to him. He did the only thing he knew to do—held out his hand, only to be taken in the other man's arms for a bone-crunching embrace that did much to bring balm to his soul.

Samuel turned to go, then turned back again. "If things could be different . . ." His voice broke, and Adam knew he paused to steady himself. "If things were different, I would have been proud to call you *sohn.*"

Adam nodded and returned to hoeing the earth, his eyes wet with tears.

Chapter 29

~⟪⟫~

"S o I told him I was wrong, and now I make the same confession to you, Lena. And I ask your forgiveness." Her father's words rang in her ears as she stood poised with a tray of cookies she had baked for the paint frolic the next morn.

She felt her world spin away and come back again in some proper alignment as she gazed at her father with wonder. "You mean that you would give your blessing to . . . to a marriage between Adam and me?"

Her father shook his head sadly. "*Nee*, Lena. You and I have both given our oaths before God and man. And Isaac is a good man."

"*Ya*," she whispered. "I suppose he is at that. *Sei se gut*, excuse me, *Fater*."

She put the tray down on a shelf with a calmness that she did not feel, then turned and walked from the kitchen. Words came to her lips that she longed to speak—angry, frustrated words that would only be dishonoring to her father if she spoke them. As soon as she gained the front door and closed it behind her, she lifted her skirts and ran blindly in the direction of the apple orchard.

She felt her breath come in gasping halts as she struggled with a rage she had never known before, let alone against her own parent. She fell to her knees, heedless of the messy ground, and tried to pray. But the words would not come, and she sobbed aloud. She cried for her mother, for Adam, and for the girl she had been—the girl who had loved with a passion beyond words, but who had been thwarted by her father's best intentions.

She caught a sudden tight rein on her thoughts and knew she could not proceed with such dishonor, even in her mind, against the man who had helped to give her life. She reached out and caught the supple strength of the tree trunk in her hands and felt a peace begin to move over her, covering her negative thoughts and deep anguish like cool linen on a summer's night. She remembered that the Bible promised that if no prayers would come, the Spirit Himself would make intercession . . . would groan for her. She held to this anchor of the soul even as she clung to the tree, and slowly she became aware again of her breathing, soft now and shallow.

She bowed her head and asked *Derr Herr* for forgiveness for her anger, then allowed the power of the Lord to lift her gaze to the sky above. She rose on shaky legs but with a calmed heart. *God is for me . . .*

She would do what was right and honor her promise to Isaac, would do what her father had believed was best. Surely the Lord would bring good out of it somehow.

Joseph lounged in his chair by the fire, feeling unusually chilled.

Ellen came and stood over him with concern.

"Shall I make you some hot tea?"

"*Nee, danki.* I will have a bit of a rest here before seeing to my chores."

She sat down opposite him, and he noted her tense posture.

"What is it, Ellen?"

"The paint frolic tomorrow, Joseph. Do you think that you will be able to attend? It will promote *gut* relations between the families, and even Adam has agreed to go."

"Adam? Ha . . . a brute for punishment the boy is, then."

"Yes," Ellen whispered.

"What was that?"

"Nothing, Joseph."

"It's come to my attention that some in our community are trying to build a meetinghouse in the woods north of town. I must go tomorrow and investigate, and if need be put a stop to it. I can't attend such frivolity as a paint frolic before I take care of this."

"*Ya*, Joseph. I'll go make that tea now." She rose and went to the kitchen.

Joseph closed his eyes, allowing himself to nap for a bit.

And then he was dreaming, something he rarely did, rarely allowed himself. Usually he would force himself awake when he felt a dream coming, but this afternoon he was unable to resist.

Ellen was in her wedding clothes, her long blond hair unbound as she waited for him after the celebration. Her family's house still echoed with gaiety downstairs. Joseph walked toward her, wanting her beauty, her touch, her gentle hold, but suddenly a knife was in his hand. He felt the urge to lift it, wield it, in horror, defense . . . maybe in love. And Ellen was speaking, calling to him through the veil of her blond hair . . .

"Joseph? Joseph. Your tea."

He woke with a strangled gasp, then relaxed back in the chair, his wild eyes taking in the room, the fire, his wife. He nodded.

"*Danki*, Ellen."

He accepted the hot cup and tried to still his hand from shaking.

Chapter 30

⌒

The night before the paint frolic, Adam decided that he would enlist the following day. He felt he owed a good-bye to Dale Ellis. He would miss the man's friendship, but once he enlisted, they would be at war with each other. It didn't bear thinking about, so he thanked the traveling tinker for the ride and got off the rattling wagon at the White Swan Inn. Center of Lancaster's hospitable waysides for travelers, the White Swan had, by rumor, hosted George Washington himself. It seemed perfectly in keeping that Dale would seek rooms in such a place for its ironic humor.

Adam decided to enter at the back, unsure exactly where he was going or if he'd be welcome. He saw a clutch of women in the shadows, and a scent of lavender and lemon of an intensity he found uncomfortable wafted toward him. He made to pass them with a quick tip of his hat.

But a bold redhead, her shoulders gleaming white and bare from the half light of the inn's side window, sidled next to him, blocking his path.

"A fair evening, if you will excuse me," he said, realizing that he'd got himself tangled in a nest of women of ill repute.

The redhead pouted and stretched to twine her arms round his neck. He removed her with firmness, thinking idly of Betty from his youth and wondering what had become of her when she had left the family's service.

"'Tis a Bible man, girls," the redhead tossed over her shoulder as he held her off. "Ain't you ever read the Song of Solomon, eh?"

Her cohorts laughed, and Adam sighed and reached to withdraw coin from his pocketbook. "Please, ladies, allow me to pass and take this in good faith. I would find Dale Ellis's rooms, if I could."

The redhead snatched the coin from him and flounced a shoulder. "Major Ellis, the Brit? Why, he's whot you are, a Bible man. No fun at all."

Adam felt somehow relieved at this piece of information and waited.

The redhead frowned. "Go up the back stairs, last room on the second landing."

He tipped his hat again and smiled. "My thanks. Use the coin for food, ach, and less finery."

They giggled like a group of lost little girls and drew aside, leaving him to find the back staircase in the dark. Fortunately, candles flickered in wall sconces on the second floor, and he made his way to the door the woman had described. He gave the wood a quick tap, waiting, until a brisk voice bade him enter.

Adam went into the room, stepping across the wide-planked floor with its luxurious carpet, and saw his friend bent over the bed stuffing things into a satchel.

"Adam Wyse? 'Tis good to see you. God has sent you to me for mercy's sake, and also to save me a bit of postage."

"Where are you going?"

"Home," Dale said. "Home to England and out of this forsaken land—my apologies. My father has somehow arranged a buy-out of my service and imprisonment, and it is one thing for which I cannot fault the old gentleman, for I long to see my wife and children. But you, you I will miss." He indicated a velvet upholstered chair. "Please, sit down."

Adam sat, wondering if he should tell his friend of his own plans. He gazed about the luxurious room, and his eyes lit on a side table. He rose again, drawn with surprise to the incredible workmanship in carved wood that he saw. Children's toys, a perfectly round ball of cedar, a clock case, all standing beautiful and poignant among tools and curled shavings of wood.

"This is your work?" he asked in wonder.

"Aye." Dale chuckled, pausing in his packing to come and join Adam at the table. "'Tis been time on my hands that bids me back to my boyhood dream to be a wood-carver. Father had other plans for a son, though. Only the military would do."

Adam fingered the curve of the small clock case. "Your father was wrong."

"Indeed, I believe he was. But no matter. Here." Dale handed him a chain of carved links. "I had planned to send it to you."

Adam held the smooth wood, admiring the strong curves and tangle. He could not see how the carving had been done to chain the links together without seeming end or beginning.

"It's remarkable."

"It is for you, Adam Wyse, carved from a single block of wood."

"It is perfect, but surely your children—"

Dale turned to face him fully. "'Tis no toy, never meant to be. It is the chain that holds you, that enwraps your heart and mind, perhaps your very soul."

Adam stared at him, frantically shuffling through their times together to see what he might have said or done to expose his true self to the other man.

Dale smiled. "It is the Lord who has revealed this to me. And now bids me tell you that it is He Himself who is revolutionary . . . not this heavy war, nor the stand you take. Nor the one I imagine that you are about to take. Going to fight, probably got your possessions bundled up like some boy on the run. Do not, Adam. Know instead that it is only God who can change the heart, who can even change the past."

Adam stood, holding the chain, thumbing the initials *AW* that had been burnt into the wood. His heart stirred.

"Keep the chain as a reminder that personal freedom does not have to come at a cost you cannot bear. Our Lord has paid the cost, and freedom waits for you if you will but ask."

Adam sighed, turning the links between his fingers. "I have asked, for years now. And always I am met by this darkness that holds me."

"Perhaps you do not ask aright," Dale said.

Adam stared at him, feeling his heart begin to pound. "What do you mean?"

"Ask . . . with your father in mind."

"My father, but why . . . ?"

Dale shrugged, then clapped him on the shoulder. "Again, the Lord convicts, and I but speak. Think on it, my friend." He dropped his hand and began to scoop up the carved toys.

Adam helped him to pack, then faced his friend once more.

"I will think on all you've said."

"Good. Well, until we meet again, Adam Wyse."

"Ya . . . fare thee well." Adam returned the hug of goodwill and had a sudden wish that he might have shared the past few minutes with Lena.

He bowed his head as he left the room, the chain clutched tightly in his hand. He stood still for a moment in the dark of the staircase. "*With your father in mind . . .*" It didn't seem to make sense. Perhaps all of Dale's suggestions were but the talk of an enthusiastic man, giddy with relief at going home. Yet something convicted Adam's heart, made him go over his friend's words again and again. *"With your father in mind . . ."*

━━◆━━

Lena couldn't sleep. She thirsted for a drink of the cooled cinnamon-spiced cider that was in a small wooden keg in the kitchen. She bit her lip as she eased from the bed, intent on not waking up Abby. Then she pulled on a housedress over her nightgown, should the bishop awake and find her traipsing about the house in the predawn.

She tiptoed in bare feet across the wood floor and turned the notch on the cider keg, filling a pewter cup.

"A bit of that would be most welcome, my child."

Lena jumped at the sound of Bishop Mast's cheerful voice, and some of the cider splashed out of her cup and over her hand. She glanced toward the low-embered fire to see the old man sitting up on his elbows, a smile on his face.

"Of course." She hastened to wipe her hands and fill another cup, then hurried to take it to him. He had moved into one of the rocking chairs and gestured to the other chair.

"Would you join me, Lena?"

She did not want to, having felt that she had wrestled and won a victory in the orchard with the Lord's help. She knew that Bishop Mast had a way of turning life matters upside down. Yet it would be rude to refuse. She fetched her cup and sat down on the edge of the rocker, curling her bare toes into a crack in the floor.

"I remember when you were eleven, like young John is now," the old man said, stroking his beard and staring into the jewel-like coals of the fireplace.

She smiled. "It seems long ago, yet not in a way. So much has changed."

"Your *mamm* was a fine woman, Lena."

"I fancy that she still is." She bit her lip, wondering if she sounded irreverent, but the bishop laughed in agreement.

"'Tis true as the pines stand, child. But then—you are child no longer, hmm? Soon to marry . . . make a new life, in a new home. The Deacon Wyse can be a stern man, I believe. Have you thought of how you will cope with this new household?"

Lena breathed a silent sigh of relief. At least he wasn't discussing Isaac or Adam.

"I expect I'll adapt. And the distance between the farms is not so difficult to traverse."

"*Ach*, but there is distance of land, and then the distance of the heart."

She felt the ground of the conversation begin to slide from beneath her feet and wondered if she might take her cider back to bed.

"*Ya*," Bishop Mast went on, almost to himself. "Sometimes we can be close on one level and worlds apart on another. I once met a man and wife up in the mountains who had divided their cabin straight down the middle with a bit of chalk. He lived on one side and she on the other. Made for an inconvenience getting in and out of the door, but there you have it."

Lena had to smile. "Really?"

"*Ya*, 'tis true. So I wonder what lines of division will lie in your own marriage, my dear?"

She clutched her cup tighter. "You jest with me. Surely there are no divisions early on in a marriage?"

"*Ach*, but that's the romantic idea of marriage. Everyone who lives together in marriage must find some matters to work out at first—the chores, the *kinner* . . ."

Lena closed her eyes briefly against the image of carrying Isaac's

211

child. How could she do it? Always looking into little dark eyes and expecting them to be gold? Always wondering where Adam was, if he were safe, alive even . . .

"I trouble you, Lena?"

She met his eyes squarely. "*Ya*. You are wise with the grace of *Gott*, Bishop Mast, and as you have said, 'tis been long since you have known me. You should know that I agreed to marry Isaac to please my father, but that I love Adam, his *bruder*."

"Adam Wyse—who would enlist when the time is right? Hmm?"

"*Ya*. I cannot take such a risk with my heart, a risk to lose him to the war. I have lost my *mamm*. The other would be too much."

"Real love is always too much, Lena, and always a risk."

"I will not be swayed."

"You say that you marry to please your *fater*, but do you, I wonder, please your heavenly Father in the process?"

"Of course," she said, fiercely pressing her toes into the wood of the floor.

"Well, then . . . you choose aright. And that is that. I think I shall retire now, my dear. Thank you for the drink and the talk."

He extended his empty cup to her, and she took it reluctantly, somehow wishing he might continue, might push her further. She felt churned up and awake inside. But the man had already closed his eyes, and by the time she had cleaned the dishes she could hear his faint snore.

Chapter 31

⌒

Ruth burped Mary in the early light of dawn, then moved to watch Lena's confident and quick movements about the kitchen. "What are you making?"

"Pretzel soup. You crush the pretzels and add them to a boiling kettle of butter, flour, milk, and water. Then you add salt and pepper. It's very hearty."

Ruth sniffed. "Sounds thick to me."

"*Ya*, it is."

Ruth put the babe in the cradle. "Well, you're movin' so fast this morn, dearie, that I can hardly catch up. What would you like me to do?"

Lena gestured with her chin to the outdoor bake oven through the window. "If you would, Ruth, go and check on the cookies. I made some horse shapes for the *kinner* and in honor of the Wyse farm. They should be nearly done."

Ruth left to comply, feeling the moistness of the dew on the grass round her ankles. She so wanted the "paint frolic," as everyone seemed to call it, to be a success for John, but it left little time to think about the wedding. She wondered what she should wear and, lost in thought, burned her fingers on the cookie sheet as she entered the bake oven house.

She let out a yelp and put the fingers to her lips when a strong hand caught her wrist.

"Allow me, my dear," Samuel said in a hoarse voice. Ruth blinked at him when he put her fingertips to his lips and slowly kissed the burns.

"Any better?" he asked after a few delicious moments.

Ruth could only nod.

"You should be more careful with these hands, Ruth. They are beautiful to me."

"These? Red and rough," she said.

"Strong and skillful . . . and ready to serve and love. Now, what were you thinking on so hard that you burned yourself?"

Ruth sighed. Men did not usually understand the value of clothing— her Henry certainly had not. She could have worn a potato sack and he would have thought it grand.

"Oh . . . the wedding. What to wear, actually." She gave him a sheepish grin. "Silly, I suppose."

"Not silly," Samuel said as he caught her close. "In fact, I know a secret about this very issue that might ease your mind."

"Well, tell me then!" She stared up at him.

"For a price, woman. A single kiss, if you will be so kind."

Ruth thought about the young girl she once was, how she'd practiced kissing on an old pewter plate, her reflection blurred and nonsensical. Kisses with Henry had been quick things, as they'd both been too tired to think at times when they were indentured. But Samuel's kind blue eyes beckoned to her, and she stretched on her tiptoes, feeling young and giddy as she placed softened lips against his own.

She drew back and looked at him expectantly, surprised to find his face aflush and his eyes half closed. Her own face felt hotter than the heat from the bake oven, and she decided she would win her secret from him.

"Well?" she asked.

"Delightful."

"Nay . . . the secret?"

"*Ach, ya* . . . Ellen Wyse told me when we went over the other day that she was making you Amish wear to have for the wedding as a surprise. I suppose it will take much time and sewing."

Ruth's eyes filled with tears. "That is so kind of her. You Amish understand how to be neighbors and friends better than anyone in the world, I imagine."

"*You* Amish," he reminded her, and she had to laugh.

"Aye, I guess I will try my hand at this neighborliness. Got a talent for making biscuits, I do, and for keeping bees. I might get you to help me set up a hive, and then I could give Ellen some honey."

"That would be *wunderbarr*, my love. And now, for sweetness' sake, how about one more kiss?"

Ruth smiled and complied with enthusiasm.

Adam looked up in surprise when Isaac came to stand in the doorway of his bedroom.

"You're up early this day," Isaac said.

Adam looked down at the clothing he'd been folding on the bed, trying to sort out what was best to take for a time of sleeping in tents in a regiment.

"*Ya.* I have things to be about."

"So you plan on leaving in truth then?"

"After the paint frolic, I guess."

"So you can see her one last time?" There was no sarcasm in the tone, only a genuineness that stole at Adam's heart.

"*Ya*, if you do not mind."

"I would never begrudge that from you."

"*Danki.*"

Isaac nodded, then straightened. "Hold on a minute, Adam. I'll be right back. I have something to give you." He returned shortly with a single page of a book in his hand, one side of it clearly torn. "Here." He reached across the bed.

"You tore one of your books—why?" Adam took the page and looked into his brother's eyes.

"It's a page from the Bible. Fold it up. Don't read it now, but I marked a verse there on one side. Perhaps it will give you peace in time of trouble one day."

Adam slowly folded the page, then slipped it into the pocket of his vest. "*Danki*, Isaac. I—I will keep it always."

His older *bruder* nodded. "I will miss you, Adam. It has always seemed the wrong way round with us, like you were the elder, someone I looked up to and admired. I still do."

Adam came round the bed and caught him in a fierce embrace, then pulled away, his eyes damp. "And I have been wrong so often, Isaac. Making fun of you and your studies . . . I pray that the Lord will bless you and keep you."

"He will."

Adam nodded. "I will see you at the paint frolic then."

"At the paint frolic."

Adam stared at the empty doorway for a long time once Isaac had gone and wished he might bring back time to make things different.

⚫

Lena mindlessly gathered the ingredients for potato soup. Onions, carrots, peas, herbs, all found their way into the pot without her really thinking about the matter. She had determined to concentrate on cooking that morn and not on her coming guests, but she found that her mind wandered of its own accord.

Abby was soon up and wanting to help, so Lena set her to filling the sugar bowl with brown sugar from the barrel in the corner of the room. Next John rose, and the bishop came in from a brief hobble out onto the porch. He was using a heavy stick and seemed to be making *gut* progress. Lena did not want to think of their nighttime conversation, so she smiled gaily at him and asked what he and everyone else wanted for breakfast.

"Bacon!" John said.

"Hotcakes!" Abby cried from the corner.

The bishop laughed. "Perhaps, for the sake of your *schwester*, who is the cook of the day it seems, we might all settle for bread and butter and some dried apples."

Lena gave him a grateful look, while John and Abby groaned. "An excellent idea. Please help yourselves."

She went on about her work while the cheerful voices bubbled in time to her thoughts. She wondered what was keeping Ruth, then looked up in surprise to see her father enter first, carrying a tray of cookies, followed by a red-faced Ruth who had a more than tender look about her.

Lena smiled in surprise, recognizing that expression from her own experiences with Adam, then had to force herself back to the present as Abby piped up in excitement.

"*Ach*, Lena, the pot on the fire boils over!"

Lena rushed to the soup, fearing on some dark level of her mind that it was not a good start to the day.

Chapter 32

J oseph rode confidently through the woods and onto the Indian trails, contemplating how good life would be once Adam had gone. He had noticed his son packing when he had passed the boy's bedroom that morn. To be free of the pursuing feelings of guilt and fear of exposure at last . . .

He reached the clearing where Abel Glick had suggested there might be building going on and pulled rein on the horse. Sure enough, several Amish men were working at the stone foundation of a half-formed structure. Joseph watched for a moment from behind the cover of the trees, then moved forward.

"Gentlemen, how fares the day?" He kept his voice level, engaging. He did not recognize the men and wondered if they were outside of where he roamed. Then a man with a hammer lifted his head, and Joseph knew it was *Herr* King, the father of the children whose puppy he had attended to. Joseph was surprised; he'd thought the King family a stable lot.

"Caleb King, a *gut* day to you."

The other man nodded, clearly embarrassed at being caught in what he was doing. But Joseph also recognized a spark of defiance in his eyes.

"We want no trouble, Deacon Wyse," Caleb said. "'Tis only for a time that we would build a structure to worship together in peace and safety."

Joseph nodded, stroking his beard. "I see. But the way of the Amish, the home church, what of that?"

Caleb looked around for support, and another man chimed in. "This is easier. No need to move benches and such. And it presents a safer place in a way, a sounder structure than some of the homes hereabouts."

"You do realize that this is why the Amish took to home churches? Because of the persecution they faced when they tried to meet in groups?" Joseph answered, strolling closer. "It is truth that some churches were barred and set alight, so that all within perished. How then can this structure you build in secret be a blessing of a place to worship? Do you think the Lord cannot see what you do?"

"*Ya*, He sees and maybe approves, Deacon." The man twisted the last word of his speech, and Joseph had to suppress a feeling of anger at being questioned in his authority.

"Well, as to that, why not let us consult Bishop Mast? He is even now at the Yoder home. And though he's been injured in the foot, I am sure that he would like to have a look at what you are so sure is approved of in heaven's eyes."

There was a prolonged moment of silence, and then Caleb King dropped his hammer in surrender. "I do not need to see the bishop to know what he would say, and he is a fair and righteous man. What we do here for the sake of convenience is wrong and goes against our history. And I would not like to think of either side of the war setting this place alight with my wife and *kinner* inside. I say we have laid the last stone. Let us pray and walk away from this."

The other man scowled. "You give up because this man disapproves? I would like to see the bishop and hear what he has to say."

"Fine," Joseph said. "I will fetch him here."

"And I will go back to my home. Deacon Wyse, a *gut* day. And blessings on you." Caleb King walked to his horse and mounted, riding away through a line of trees.

Joseph too turned his back and went for his horse. "I will return with the bishop in *gut* time. Please, feel free to keep on with your work, holy that it is."

He laughed at the grunt from the other man and set his horse off at a brisk pace toward the Yoder farm.

Adam saw that the furniture in the keeping room had been moved out and that about a nine-by-twelve-foot space on the floor had been painted a cheerful pumpkin color already. He watched John completing the stencil sketch on the space and was amazed at the boy's talent. Jars of paint in red, blue, yellow, and black surrounded the area, and Lena sat on the floor beside her brother with a round bristled brush in her hand.

Adam decided he might as well make the most of the last time he would see Lena. He grabbed a brush from a nearby table and eased himself down next to her. She looked at him with a soft smile on her lips. He longed to tell her that he was leaving, but he was content simply in that moment to sit by her . . . to see her familiar and beautiful eyes and the tempting tendril of hair that always worked itself loose from her prayer covering.

The painting began in earnest, with even his mother wielding a brush. Jars of paint were teasingly fought over, and the design began to take wonderful shape. Then Adam noticed that Lena's hair had somehow become dipped in the red paint. He reached an automatic hand to the curl, then froze as if the earth had opened up before him and he teetered on some precipice between truth and sanity. He fell . . . vast, wrenching depths that snagged at his mind and tore like splinters from a rock face. He made a strangled sound of despair in his throat as the scene flooded back to him with utter clarity. He was standing in snow, staring at a lock of blond hair across a man's chest, tainted with blood . . .

Somehow he got to his feet and dropped the brush.

He staggered from the farmhouse and down the wooded road; he felt devastated and moved as though his body belonged to someone else and he was but a mere captive to the space he occupied with each step. In some distant, alive corner of his mind, he sensed that Lena longed to follow him, but everything seemed to be swallowed into the dream that took slow formation of reality in the shock of his mind. *His father was a murderer . . . and he himself, a young boy, had helped to dig the victim's grave . . .*

Adam finally collapsed to his knees and stared up at the blue of the sky between the treetops. He wondered with fleeting awareness how the earth could continue to move, how the sky could be normal when he felt as though all that he knew of his world was crashing apart in bloodied fragments of consciousness. A hoarse, primal cry came from the back of his throat as he stared at the sky. "*Gott!* Dear *Gott* in heaven! Help me! Help me!" And then, from the depths of his heart, something Dale had said reverberated through his body, and he cried out once more. "Dear Lord, help my *fater!*"

Chapter 33

Lena ignored the mingled stares of her family and her betrothed as she hurried to the door, which Adam had left gaping behind him.

Then she heard the heart echo within that compelled, *nee*, commanded her as clearly and loudly as a bell on a crisp autumn day. *Go! Go after him!* And she knew the blessing and freedom to follow her heart.

"I beg of you all," she called as she gained the open door, "forgive me, but I must follow him." Her eyes swept Isaac and her *fater* for one blazing moment of truth. "I must always follow him."

She spoke with ringing clarity, then closed the door as she raced across the porch and down the steps.

"Well, now, here's a fine pickle." Ruth stood and clapped her hands together, feeling like she should do something in the abject quiet of the room. "Who wants more cookies?"

"Uh . . . *ya* . . . cookies." Ellen Wyse took up the trail. "Children?"

But John and Abby sat transfixed, their mouths slightly open.

Bishop Mast cleared his throat. "Well, now may be an opportune time, Isaac Wyse, for us to talk about your future goals. I understand that you desire to serve the Lord as a bishop one day."

The gaze of the room swung to Isaac, who was sitting on the floor, frozen, with a blue-tipped paintbrush dripping onto the knee of his breeches. "*Ya* . . . a bishop."

"Hmm . . ." Bishop Mast stroked his beard. "Since your impending nuptials seem to have taken a turn for the . . . er . . . difference, might I invite you to accompany me instead, and study as is proper training for a man aspiring to your position?"

Isaac's face took on a reverent glow from Ruth's perspective. He dropped the brush and rose to his feet in excitement. "You mean it?"

"I never say what I do not mean, *buwe*. Of course I mean it. We travel by mule far and deep into the mountains. I have sort of a base home in a small cabin, where an elderly woman and her granddaughter tend to me as the widow did with the old prophet in the Bible. You will have to be willing to face hardships, though. Closed folks and troubles."

"When can we leave?"

"Isaac," Ellen Wyse gasped, clearly confused by the rapid-fire turn of events.

"It is all right, *Mamm*. This is what I have been praying for, hoping for . . . You know that."

"But what about Lena?" she said.

Isaac laughed, the sound seeming to break the spell that held the room. "She loves Adam, *Mamm*. Always has. Always will. And I find that I would rather have a *gut* friend of a *bruder* than the half heart of a wife."

Samuel spoke up clearly. "*Ya*, 'tis right. Only I was too prideful to admit it, except to Adam and Lena. *Gott* has His hand on this day, to be sure, and I will not interfere."

Ruth smiled at him, then moved to pat Ellen's shoulder. "Come, have some hot cider."

And then the room was an excited babble of talk and questions as Ruth served the soup, praying silently that Lena and Adam would return home soon.

— ✦ —

He heard her soft voice from somewhere far away, like an echo in a dark cave, and he tried to cling to the sound.

"Adam . . . *ach*, what has happened?"

He felt her touch his shoulder, an ocean away, as he rocked himself back and forth on his knees. His words came haltingly, broken and forlorn.

"We were hunting . . . my father and I."

"Today. For the panther? I did not know."

He shook his head and felt the roaring in his ears level to a muffled drone, like he'd heard in a seashell once.

"I was nine. Just nine. We hunted, but found nothing . . . until him."

He saw her blue eyes level with his own, swimming with tears, concern. He wanted to be lost in the blueness, swallowed whole, but the scene kept playing out with relentless profusion in his mind.

"Him?" she asked.

"*Ya*," he sobbed, then began to talk as if outside himself, telling a story like a distant narrator, saying his own name as though it did not belong to him . . .

— ✦ —

"Run back to the farm, *sohn*. Now."

Nine-year-old Adam knew better than to hesitate when his father gave him an order, but there was something wrong with the moment that stilled his feet in their snow-covered moccasins. He and *Fater* had been hunting without success for nearly an hour when Adam heard the rustling in the underbrush. He'd readied his small bow and looked to his father for direction.

Then a trapper, dressed in bloodstained buckskins and a coon cap, had stepped from the woods, and the sunlight caught on a long golden lock of hair tied to a thin piece of leather hanging outside the rough man's cloak. There was no mistaking the hair. Adam's *mamm* had hair that rivaled sunshine in full summer—not that she ever revealed it unbound to any but the family. But a drifting trapper had torn her hair covering from her head and cut a lock from her waist-length curls when she'd been alone in the farmhouse nearly a week ago. She hadn't been hurt, only badly frightened. The family had counted it merciful that *Fater* had returned from the fields when he did, leaving the intruder to flee without a trace.

"Adam."

Fater's voice held a low undertone of warning, and Adam hastened to turn, though he wanted badly to stay and see what might be said between the two men. Of course, he knew that only words would be exchanged, and the attack most likely forgiven. It was the steadfast way of his people not to retaliate against evil or take up arms to hurt another. The Amish followed the way of Christ—but Adam didn't know if the trapper cared about such things.

He decided to hurry as he trudged back through the snow to fetch his older brother, Isaac, whom *Fater* had told to stay at home with *Mamm*. But he'd gone no more than thirty feet through the vast forest when the strangled groan of a man reached his ears. His heart began to pound as he turned back, running as fast as he could, terrified for his father's sake. He staggered into the small clearing, gasping, then stopped dead still.

The trapper lay on the ground, crying out, in a widening pool of crimson against the white of the snow. *Fater* was stabbing the man with his great hunting knife again and again. The trapper's groans turned to choking gurgles, and then there was no sound but the wind through the pines. *Fater* leaned back on his heels, the bloodied knife still in his hand. He looked up and saw his son.

"Adam. I told you to go back."

Adam's mind was rushing like a swollen creek at springtime. His father had killed another man.

"I—I heard a noise. I thought you might need help . . ." The boy broke off with a sob of distress, unsure what to say, but longing to sink to his knees.

His father rose, his cloak covered in blood, and came toward him. Adam wanted to run in fear, but fear itself held him fast.

"*Sohn*. What you saw here, you must forget. You must count it as never happening."

Adam swallowed as his father neared; he could smell the strange warmth of the trapper's blood.

"But our ways, *Fater* . . . you have taught me; we cannot kill." His voice quivered, and he swiped at a half-frozen tear along his cheek.

His father's voice came again, quiet, sure . . . unrepentant.

"That man took from your mother. Just a lock of hair, *ya*, but he might have taken more. He did not deserve to live to continue in such behavior."

"What—what will you tell the bishop?"

As soon as the words had escaped his lips, Adam knew it was the wrong thing to have asked. His father drew back a large, bloody palm and with calm deliberation slapped Adam's face so hard that the boy felt his spine rattle. For a brief moment he saw black-hewn stars before his eyes and felt the warmth of lifeblood stick wet against his cheek. His father had never struck him before.

He tried to focus.

"As I said, Adam, this never happened. You will put it from your mind. You will never speak of it. You will never think of it. Do you understand?"

"*Ya*," Adam whispered.

"*Gut*." His father turned with brisk force. "We will bury the man as deep as we can, using our hatchets. We'll also bury the *messer* and my cloak. You will return to the farm and assure your *mamm* that all is well. Then *kumme* back here and bring a spade." His father went on in matter-of-fact tones. "*Ach*, and wash your face; there's blood on it."

Adam murmured his assent, his cheek and mouth throbbing in the cold. He followed his father to a place not far from the dead-eyed trapper and got down on his knees, hacking blindly at the frozen ground with his hatchet, determined to forget . . .

And then he choked on his tears, and Lena knew he had come back to the present.

"The trapper," he moaned, looking at her. "Just a trapper. There was so much blood! *Ach*, I was scared, scared to death. I should have died. I wish I had died."

"*Ach*, no, Adam. No, my love . . ."

He looked at her then, really looked at her, and some semblance of calm seemed to come over him. He reached out and caught at the golden curl with its still-drying tip and rubbed the red paint between his fingertips.

"I had to help bury him . . . put all that blood under the white of the snow somehow. It took hours . . . hours. I have tried to forget . . . I think I've tried . . ."

"Oh, Adam, before the Living *Gott*, it is true that you have been at war all this time. I will not lose you again." She pulled him close to her chest and made soothing sounds in her throat.

He heard her muffled heartbeat and clung to the rhythm, the aliveness of the sound. But then against the ragged edges of his consciousness, something else intruded—he heard a man scream.

Chapter 34

Go back to the house, Lena. Quickly. Send the men for help."

He was back in control. She could see the focus in his golden eyes, intense as a single candle in a dark room.

"*Nee* . . . I will not leave you like this. What is it?"

"Do as I say, *sei se gut*. There is no time. I think it's a mountain lion . . . the one who hunted us. It's got some poor soul . . . I'll go see."

She wanted to protest, to hold him back, but she knew that a rifle would be of much more help. She got to her feet and started to run, turning back only once to look over her shoulder and see Adam headed in the direction of the scream, his hunting knife drawn.

Adam heard the scream come again, strangled, lowering, followed by the primitive growl of a big cat. It did not occur to him to do anything other than go toward the sound. What was a panther compared to the hulking monster of his past . . . and possibly there was a life to be saved. He began to run and soon came upon the leafy copse where the black musculature and seething claws of the big cat covered the figure of a man, now limp and helpless.

Adam drew his knife and hit the back of the cat with all of the savage force that raged like the tide against sharp rocks within the tumult of his mind. But the animal was powerful and sleek, and seemingly only irritated by the blow of the knife as it now turned with full force toward Adam.

He had a sweeping impression of jagged teeth in an ancient primal cry, the feel of a terrible burn in his left leg as the animal struck, and the woodsy, musky scent of the beast itself. Then he glanced to the ground and saw the unmistakable face of his father, head turned, staring at him with gray eyes ablaze.

Suddenly time opened a strange portal and he was no longer himself but his father, slashing at the chest of a bleeding trapper. A lone boy stood by in his mind, watching, sobbing for all that he believed and hoped, all that was lost . . .

Then the cat collapsed upon him and Adam was once again himself, slashing with his knife in powerful strokes until the animal ceased to move.

His fury and anguish were spent. He had killed a preying panther, not a man. He was not his father. He was not bad. He embraced that lone boy inside with all of the wash of emotion that could fill a soul. Then he got to his feet and sheathed his knife.

He went quickly to where his father lay and began to assess the other man's wounds with calm hands. Then he tore off his shirt to make hasty bandages for the areas that seemed to drain with blood.

"Adam."

He lifted his head and met the eyes of his father.

"You . . . killed the cat." There was wonder in his *fater's* tone.

"*Ya*, and you will live yet, I hope." He tightened a bandage, pausing to assess his own thigh. It wasn't bleeding too much. He prepared to lift his father onto his shoulder, feeling a deep peace inside.

"I have wronged you . . . and the Living *Gott*," his father managed with a grunt as Adam swung him upward.

"I forgive you," Adam said simply.

"Do you . . . remember that day?"

"I have always remembered it, *Fater*, but I could not see it clearly until today. I asked for *Gott's* help, and He let me see. His freedom does not cost me . . . I do not have to be that frightened child standing alone anymore. He stands with me, and I stand with myself in Him."

<hr />

Joseph heard the profound words of his son and knew them to be inspired by *Gott*. He closed his eyes against the pain, both inside and out, as he felt Adam do his best to quicken his steps.

"And I would stand with you too, Adam . . . my *sohn*."

<hr />

Adam's eyes swam with tears as he tried to hurry, but the blood soaking his bare back with sticky awareness told him that his father's survival would require fast action and much prayer.

He was greatly relieved when he saw Isaac and Samuel come running. He passed his father into their arms. Adam had a brief look at Lena's face behind the men, frantic and drawn with pain and concern. Her eyes were the last thing he saw as he collapsed to the ground.

Chapter 35

"A stange pair of bedfellows, is what I say," Ruth commented with hands on hips as she finished her ministrations to the two men. Samuel had insisted that they use the master bedroom, and now Joseph and Adam Wyse lay next to each other, well bandaged and topped off with draughts of hard cider.

"*Fater* and *sohn*," Lena murmured from the edge of the bed, near Adam.

"*Ya*," Ellen Wyse said. "But so very different."

"Mebbe not," Ruth declared, reaching to gather some bloodstained cloths. "They was both mumbling about forgiveness and love, both out of their heads, while I saw to them at one point."

"Joseph was?" Ellen asked, clearly amazed.

"Yep . . . and if you think on it—from what I could see of their eyes, they're a match in some ways. Eyes of gold and them what's silverish . . . two things worth the mining for, if you think on it a bit. Now that's a father and son for ya." She caught up a blanket in her arms. "Well, I'd best be tending to the babes. You both stop worryin' now. They'll come through all right. I've tended to animal bites and scratches before, and the trick is to keep any poison from spreading to the blood, keep the wounds clean and clear. We'll do just that."

She started for the door, then glanced at Lena. Clearly the girl wanted to have a few moments with the man of her choosing, even with his father present.

"Uh, Missus Wyse . . . Ellen . . . would you help me reheat the soups? I expect that everyone will be a mite hungry after all the goings-on."

"*Ach*, certainly. Let me do that." Ellen rose, placed a hand on her husband's bandaged wrist for a moment, then followed Ruth out the door.

———◆———

When Ruth and Ellen had gone, Lena hastened to kneel down on the floor next to Adam. She bent her head over his uninjured hand and started to pray, when she felt his fingers move. She looked up to see his golden eyes, fever bright, watching her.

He gave her a lopsided grin when she kissed his hand.

"Going after a panther, alone, with only a knife," she said.

He gestured with his chin toward his father. "And a *gut* thing too."

She squeezed his hand. "Adam . . . *ach*, Adam. I pray now that you will no longer be plagued by bad dreams. What you told me out there . . . such a little boy. I am so sorry."

He squeezed her fingers and nodded. Then she noticed Joseph begin to stir and got to her feet. "I will send the bishop in to you both. He has been waiting to pray over you."

She let go of the strong-boned hand reluctantly, then went to the door, pausing once to turn and drink her fill of him with both her eyes and heart.

———◆———

A heaviness lay on Joseph's chest, the burden of guilt, but tempered now with the knowledge of release. But the silence in which he waited under the bishop's penetrating gaze wore upon him, and he wished the man would simply call for the proper authorities and have done with it.

And then there was Adam . . . lying wounded beside him. Wounded in so many ways, and all because of him.

"I cannot pretend to understand the weight that both of you have carried all of these years," Bishop Mast finally said, easing back in his chair beside the bed. "But I understand the passions that drive men, and I know that sin is sin before the Living God. Not that I am minimizing a murder . . . I suppose, though, Joseph, that there is more that I do not understand."

Joseph felt his heart begin to pound, unsure if he could relate the details again. It had been so painful the first time, but he swallowed and nodded. "What more can I tell you?"

"Tell me about your life growing up."

Joseph stared into the calm, wise eyes of the older man and could not find his voice for a moment. *My life growing up . . .*

"A strange question, perhaps," Adam said.

"Perhaps," the bishop conceded. "But I have found that the intensity that drives most men with earthly desire—passion, lust, even murder— the root of that feeling often lies far back in that person's growing time. It is a curious thing."

Joseph felt the silence of the room hang heavy upon him. *Where can I begin?* He wet his lips. "My father was . . . evil, you might say."

The bishop nodded, and Joseph felt Adam's gaze upon him as he continued. "Evil in frightful ways, but mostly toward my mother. She— she had blond hair, much like Ellen's, long and beautiful. She always seemed very young to me, joyful even, despite my father."

"Does she live yet?" the bishop asked.

Joseph felt a gnawing in his stomach and a racked sensation in his brain, but forced himself to go on. "*Nee.*"

"How did she die?" Adam asked. "You have never said."

Joseph turned his head on the pillow to meet the golden eyes he had once both despised and loved. "He killed her. My father killed her." His voice was thick with tears—strange things to him, and he felt he might not breathe again normally. "She was on the staircase. He struck her, and she fell . . . The banister gave way. I had just come in from fishing, and I saw her fall. I was eleven."

Joseph closed his eyes and felt his son reach a hand over to touch his shoulder. "I am so sorry, *Fater.*"

"As am I," the bishop said.

Joseph opened his eyes; he had nearly forgotten the presence of the other man.

"Such brutality for a child to carry . . . for two children to carry. I tell you both that my heart convicts me. I cannot speak of what you have told me in this room to anyone again. I will not. Joseph Wyse, you have suffered consequences for what you did, even though I understand it better now. And, to be truthful, it is only the Lord who can free you from the memories and loss."

"God is revolutionary," Adam said.

"What's that?" Joseph asked.

"Yes, what did you say?" The bishop leaned forward.

Adam shrugged. "It is something a friend told me. He told me I was chained by the past, and that God is the One to free me. That it is He . . . God, not war, that is revolutionary. I did not fully understand that until now, but, *Fater*, I believe *Gott* can set us both free from the past. I no longer have the desire to lift arms against another. I will let *Gott* do the fighting for us."

Joseph nodded, feeling a peace descend on his soul as he drank in his son's words.

The bishop cleared his throat and blew his nose. "Shall we pray together then?"

Chapter 36

~~~~~~~~~~

I saved it for you, from your vest pocket," Isaac said, handing over the folded and now bloodstained page from the Bible.

Adam smiled his thanks and leaned forward in the chair on the front porch to take it from him.

It was a good two weeks since the panther attack, and the Wyse family had all but taken up residence at the Yoder farm, due to the recovery of the two men. Isaac would go back and forth and do chores with John. Bishop Mast was also staying on, to heal up himself and to perform the wedding ceremonies the next day. And then Isaac would be leaving for a full year or more.

Adam fingered the thin page. "I feel as though I should read it now, for some reason."

Isaac shrugged. "Go ahead, if you feel called. It might mean something more now, with the attack and all."

Adam carefully unfolded the page, so significantly spotted with blood that reminded him of the cross. Then he saw the mark his *bruder* had made with a lead pencil next to a certain verse. He read it aloud. "Zephaniah 3:17. 'The Lord thy God in the midst of thee is mighty; he will save, he will rejoice over thee with joy; he will rest in his love, he will joy over thee with singing.'"

"It is a blessing for you . . . and Lena. And I imagine that before long, I will become an uncle as well. So for your *kinner* . . ."

Isaac drifted off in his speaking, and Adam reached for his hand.

"*Danki, bruder.* I will memorize this blessing and take it to heart. But thank you also for the way that you have understood about Lena. It cannot have been easy."

Isaac grinned. "I will not let you go so easily as to say that it has not been hard, but truly, my heart hungers after the travel with the bishop and the training. I have no time for a wife."

"Then beware, for that is when they tend to find you," Adam warned, and they laughed together, a sound that was becoming more and more natural to Adam's ears.

He looked up as a wagon pulled along the road that led to the house. "We have visitors, it seems. Looks like Caleb King. I wonder if they've heard about *Fater* and the cat? You remember he told us about the meetinghouse site?"

Isaac nodded and rose to his full height. "*Ya.* I will tell *Fater* they are here, though I find them nothing but meddlesome troublemakers."

Adam laughed. "You had better get your bishoplike dignity on about you, *bruder.* Judge not . . ."

Isaac sighed as he made for the door. "'Tis sadly true at that."

It turned out that the crew of men with Caleb King had come to pay their respects to his father and to ask forgiveness of both him and the bishop. It was no small thing to survive a panther attack, and Adam couldn't help but wonder whether their innate superstitions were what really drew them to the house. Surely, they may have thought a man who survived an attack by a mountain lion must be touched by *Gott* . . .

Yet his father was visibly relieved as he limped back into the house. Adam rocked slowly in his chair, letting his head rest back, and tried to start memorizing the verse Isaac had given him. But then his attention was drawn to a prayer of thankfulness as he recalled asking Lena if she would marry him, and he closed his eyes on the sweetness of the memory . . .

She had been sitting beside the bed, as was her wont, and Ruth had insisted that Joseph rise and take some exercise. So they were alone for the first time since the attack. She was reading from her Bible, her lashes downcast, and he thought how truly beautiful she was as she paused to puzzle over a passage, unconsciously biting her lip or tracing the page with a delicate finger. It both soothed him and set his heart pounding to watch her. Then he had reached out to her, and she snapped her full attention to him.

"Adam, what is it? Do you hurt?" She closed the Bible and knelt down next to the bed, taking his hand in hers.

"*Ya* . . . 'tis my heart that hurts, Lena Yoder," he confessed, letting a half smile play about his lips.

"Shall I call for Ruth?"

He laughed. "*Nee*, my love . . . that *gut* woman would not satisfy, I fear."

"Then what is it?"

He grew serious. "Lena, I have never asked you, not formally . . . and now I have it all backward, with you the one, as the *Englisch* say, 'on bended knee.'"

He saw the confusion on her pretty brow and realized he was bumbling things. "Lena, you are the love of my heart, and through you, through the *Gott* who loves us both, I have found freedom. I would share that freedom with you for a lifetime, my dearest. I am asking you to be my wife."

Her pretty lips parted, and he waited, forgetting to breathe, as a look of pure joy suffused the creamy skin of her face.

"*Ach*, Adam . . . *ya*. Yes. I would be so proud."

His eyes had filled with tears as she crept gently forward across his chest to seal her promise with a kiss.

He thought he was dreaming now when he felt her from somewhere behind him, above him, kissing him lazily. His mouth returned the kiss of its own accord, then he blinked his eyes open to see her smiling face upside down as she leaned against the back of his chair.

Lena had been feeding crumbs to the geese that, she had discovered with delight, had a small nesting going under a teaberry bush. They had warned her off loudly, and she smiled, swinging her now-empty basket over her arm. Tomorrow was her wedding day, and she could hardly contain her joy and the thankfulness she felt for Adam's life.

She turned the corner of the house and mounted the steps, looking up to see him drowsing in a chair, his head back, his dark eyelashes thick crescents on the strong bones of his cheeks. She set her basket down and proceeded at a tiptoe, not wanting to wake him—not yet, in any case.

Since his recovery time, Lena had found herself more and more inspired to touch him, kiss him, and to savor the very fact that he was alive. Now she positioned herself behind his chair, noting how the dark strands of his hair clung a bit to his forehead with the heat of the spring day. Then she stretched on tiptoe to find his mouth with her own, gently at first, like a butterfly tiptoeing on a leaf, then with increasing savor when his eyes opened and he stared up at her like she was something from a dream.

"Hello," she said.

He smiled . . . a smile to melt her senses and send her heart racing.

"Hello, I was dreaming of you. Am I still?" He arched his neck for another kiss, and she happily complied.

"I do not know." She giggled like a young girl when she finally drew back to draw breath. "Are you?"

"*Ya . . . ya*, and I would sustain the dream—if you would so comply."

She sighed. "With pleasure."

Chapter 37

Ruth twisted to try to glimpse herself in the small mirror that hung in one of the upstairs rooms where she was trying on her wedding dress with Ellen in attendance.

"How's it look?" she asked doubtfully, feeling a bit like she was going to some fancy masquerade dressed as an Amish lady.

Ellen clapped her gentle hands. "You look beautiful, Ruth—though I know that is not to be the point of our simplicity of dress. But the brown goes so well with your red hair, and the white bit sets it off too. I know that Samuel will be so happy."

Ruth frowned. "I feel a bit like I shouldn't be wearin' this yet—even though I appreciate all of the time sewin' that you put into it."

"Why not?" Ellen asked as she stretched to adjust the prayer covering.

"Well, I'm not really Amish, am I? I don't know your words. I mess up on your ways. I know the bishop said that it would work out, but I'm not a quick study at much in life."

Ellen smiled at her, hugging her a bit. "Everything will be well, Ruth. You will see. And after the way you've taken to mothering Faith as well as saving the lives of both Joseph and Adam . . . you are part of the family. 'Tis simple."

Ruth craned her neck once more at the mirror. "I guess if you think so, but I have the feeling that being Amish is more than dressing plainlike."

"*Ach*, I suppose it is being a person, that's all, with all of the problems and complications that life brings. Being Amish doesn't shield you or protect you from the world—in fact, it is the opposite. You may walk into town in that dress and find that you are stared at for being Plain. Or that people make false assumptions about why you do what you do. But I am glad to give you your first Amish dress, and we will make others together."

Ruth stopped looking in the mirror to turn and catch Ellen up in a firm hold. "Ye're a good . . . *gut* . . . woman, Ellen Wyse. I am proud to call you friend."

They laughed together, then set about adjusting the hemline of the dress properly for the wedding the next day.

Joseph was alone in the keeping room, sitting near the hearth, when Lena came in with a bright smile on her lips. Then he saw her stop when she noticed him, pause, as if uncertain. He realized that she and he had not had any time alone together and wondered now if it was something that she wished. He knew, as part of trying to change in life, that he must set things aright with this beautiful girl who was to become his daughter-in-law.

"Would you sit with me a bit, Lena?" he asked.

"Of—of course. Is there anything I can get you? Some cider perhaps?"

He shook his head. "Please, Lena. Only a moment of your time."

She perched cautiously on the chair near him, and he cleared his throat.

"I will speak quickly. I do not know how much you know or understand of what I have been and done to Adam, but I want you to know that I have begged forgiveness of *Derr Herr* for my behavior. And now I would beg your forgiveness as well, for hurting the one you love."

He watched her visibly wrestling with what to say. "*Herr* Wyse . . ."

"*Fater* . . . if you can, Lena. If not, Joseph will be more than fine."

She shook her head. "*Fater*, of—of course. 'Tis not my place to be asked for forgiveness, but I must tell you that I fear . . . I fear for any *kinner* Adam and I may be blessed with who will live under your roof. I—I know that you beat Adam. I saw, one day when we were young. I would not want that for my sons."

Joseph bowed his head for a moment. "*Ya*, I beat him often, but I give you my solemn word that I am changing, that I will never lift a hand to another child or youth, especially one of my own family. Lena, I can only tell you what Adam told me recently, that *Gott* is revolutionary. He is changing me and the bitterness of my heart."

"God is for you," Lena said slowly.

"I want to believe that."

"If God is for you, then who am I to oppose you? Or to not forgive you? *Gott* forgives me, all the time."

"I have never spoken to you, Lena, of the loss of your mother. I am very sorry. I—I know what it is to lose a mother at a young age."

He felt her study him, weighing his words.

"*Danki* . . . Your son has helped fill that void. I believe that God gives back. He promises to 'make up for the years that the locust has eaten.' And there would be no Adam without you."

Joseph exhaled, feeling as though he had been loosed a bit more from the cords that bound him.

"Thank you, Lena . . . *dochder*, if I may."

She nodded, a slight smile on her lips, then rose to come forward and press a kiss of goodwill against his cheek. Then she left him sitting alone with his thoughts, deeply moved and heartened.

Chapter 38

That evening, the whole of the Yoder and Wyse families were gathered around the hearth with the bishop, eating popcorn and dried apples. They made a merry time of it, and Lena especially enjoyed it when the bishop told tales of his travels. She also realized that she liked to watch the glow in Isaac's eyes as he listened; she was glad to see him happier than he had ever seemed with her.

She listened now as the bishop told of a mountain Amish family, deep in the Alleghenies, where he had found rest and comfort and much humor.

"The *grossmuder* and her granddaughter make a livelihood by crafting homemade items and then selling them twice a year at an *Englisch* fair. It is a tenuous way to live, but they rely fully on the Lord, and the granddaughter has an amazing spirit. She is a bit of a spitfire as well."

"You mean they do art and such?" John asked with interest.

"Hmm? *Ach, ya* . . . all sorts of paintings and decorative household things and broomstick air castles and fine knitting and embroidery too."

Lena watched her brother's face light up with the idea and wondered whether he might take some of his artwork to market one day. The Amish were not traditionally wont to do such things, but if Ruth had anything to say about it, John might be able to make a living painting.

"Well, the granddaughter's a wild one for sure, but a true beauty too. She can shoot a rattlesnake's eye at ten paces and speak Latin table manners as pretty as you please."

"Latin?" Isaac asked.

The bishop waved a hand. "*Ya*. Latin, Greek . . . The *grossmuder* believes in the training of a woman's mind."

"To what purpose?" Isaac queried, and he looked alarmed when Lena gave him a sisterly rap on the knuckles. "What?" he cried as the others laughed.

The bishop went on. "I cannot help but say that it has made the child only a finer person to study, not vain in any way. But you will get to meet them in person, Isaac, and I hope find as much rest there as I have."

"*Ya*, that is my prayer, surely."

Lena realized in the midst of much talk and joking that Adam was gazing at her, a sleepy, warm look that made her want to shake her head at him in reproof. She wished she were sitting closer to him to hold his hand. She was thinking about how she might artfully change positions when an odd sound from the cradle behind her caught her ear. She listened again and heard it, faint but distinctive—it drained the color from her face.

"Listen! *Ach*, please listen," she cried, and the group stilled.

Then the noise came again, a tight, wet cough ending in a terrifying whooping sound. Whooping cough! Lena had heard it before when Abby was two and came down with the disease. Their mother and father had battled day and night for nearly a week to turn the tide of death that almost always accompanied the self-imposed quarantine of the house.

Lena went to peer over the cradle, unsure which babe had coughed, when Ruth bustled her to one side. "'Ere now . . . a bit of the whooping cough, 'tis all. Which one of our pretties is it? Or both, perhaps?"

Lena studied both babies carefully, then realized as the infant's face reddened with the next coughing spasm that it was Faith who struggled to gain her breath.

"There now," Ruth said, scooping up the baby. "Samuel, 'tis Faith."

Lena watched her father come forward, looking suddenly younger and more alert than he had in weeks. "We must fight it, before Mary takes ill as well."

"Likely she already has it," Ruth said.

"*Ach*, what can we do? I have not had young *kinner* in so long," Ellen said, rising from her chair.

"'Twill pass," Ruth soothed to the room at large, even as Faith coughed again against her ample shoulder. "We must make a tent about the cradle with a thin blanket and let her lie there while using steam from a kettle filled with hot water and mint."

Lena stood frozen as she watched the tableau unfold before her—people rushing to gather things at Ruth's request, the bishop bending his head in prayer, and the murmured sounds of comfort as the babe wrestled through another spasm.

"Are you all right, my love?" It was Adam standing at her back, his strong hands on her shoulders.

Lena shook her head. "*Nee*," she said. "I think not."

"What is it? You fear for the babe?"

"*Ya* . . . perhaps. But it is more than that. There are so many here to help, the fear is less. Not like when . . ."

"When your *mamm* died?" he whispered.

She half sobbed, then turned into the shelter of his arms, letting herself be drawn away from the bustle of activity and out onto the darkness of the porch.

The stars lay in a heavy blanket against the shadowy tips of the trees that surrounded the farm against the moonlit sky.

Adam let her sob against him and found loose tendrils of her hair from beneath her prayer covering to twine about his fingers.

"I should go back in," she said after a few minutes.

"Should you?" He turned her gently in his arms until she faced the gloaming of the front yard of the house, the fireflies blinking out a waltzing cascade. "Perhaps, for only a moment, you should look at what is before you. The God who made all of this holds Faith in His capable hands. And Ruth Stone is not a bad angel to have on board either."

He felt her smile through her tears with the tips of his fingers against her face.

"*Ya*, but, Adam . . . sometimes *Gott* says *nee* . . . like with *Mamm*. I miss her so much. I would have been so happy to have her celebrate our wedding day with us."

"I know," he whispered. "But do you think heaven so veiled from this world that she cannot feel our joy through the love of Christ?"

"I have not thought of it that way. And to imagine that there was a time when I was unsure of your faith, of what you really believed. I know by your words that you so love *Gott* and will be a *wunderbarr* spiritual leader in our home."

"*Danki*, Lena. Now come . . . let us go back inside, if you are feeling better."

He escorted her back to the light of the door when Isaac appeared, looking troubled.

"Lena . . . the babe breathes a bit easier, but—but I would speak to my *bruder* alone for a moment if you do not mind."

"Of course . . . please do."

Adam watched her slip indoors, then looked at his brother. "What is the matter, Isaac? Does the babe do as well as you say?"

Isaac stepped farther into the shadows. "It is not that exactly."

"Then what?" Adam felt an anxiety in his spirit for Isaac that he did not know he was capable of—it was amazing how God was allowing him to develop feelings and emotions for a brother he had little known and so little understood while they grew.

"I fear if I tell you that you will think me a bit mad."

Adam reached out and touched his brother's shoulder. "Isaac, tell me."

"Well, when the bishop and I were praying for the babe, it was as if—as if I heard *Gott* speak to me directly. He said very clearly to rise, lay hands on the babe, and bring healing to her in His name. I know it sounds *narrish*, but . . ."

"So did you?"

"What?"

"Did you do it?"

"*Nee* . . . I came out here to ask you what you thought."

Adam sighed. "Isaac, if there's one thing that I understand through the relationship—if you want to call it that—with our father, it's the concept of obedience. When you are told what to do by a greater authority, you do it—or suffer the consequences. *Gott* is clearly the higher authority here, and you should obey. I should think with all of your study that—"

Isaac made a low sound of frustration in the dark. "That's just it—it is study, but no true application in life. And I fear what people in there will think."

"It is not about you," Adam said. "It rests on God. I think you should act."

Lena came to the screen door then, her face haloed by the candlelight within, revealing her anxiety. "*Ach*, Adam, Faith is doing worse. You had better come, please. I'm sorry, Isaac."

"*Nee*," Isaac muttered, brushing past Adam to open the door. "'Tis I who am sorry."

He hurried into the house, and Adam caught Lena's hand to follow.

Chapter 39

R uth heard the dismal rasp for breath and knew a moment of fear. She glanced over the thin blanket that she and Samuel held over the cradle while Ellen fed the steam inside. She could not bear to think what would happen if God should allow the loss of Faith, not when she had come to love and care for her as her own. And what would Samuel feel? He, who had already lost his true wife in the life giving of the child.

Ruth closed her eyes and tried to grasp what Lena had read to her. *"God is for you . . ."* She let the words drift round in her brain, stopping to peer periodically at the little face in the cradle. She was at the end of her nursing abilities; now it really did seem to rest on whether she believed that God was indeed on her side in the matter or not.

Isaac brushed past her in that moment, taking her hands from the blanket and gently edging her aside.

"Please, Ruth," he said. "I must—I must touch the babe."

"But the steam . . . ," she began, then stopped as she saw the intensity of the young man's gaze. Something stilled her words and her hands, and she fell back on her knees. Samuel, likewise, lifted the blanket and sank down to the floor.

She watched as Isaac reached his large hands into the cradle and laid them on the fretful babe. Then she glanced up in surprise when she heard him speak.

"In the name of the Lord Christ, I tell you to be healed and rebuke any illness or harm that threatens you, Faith Yoder."

Then he withdrew. Ruth saw a muscle tense in his face as he watched the baby, clearly expecting something to happen. She, too, looked at the child and, amazingly, saw a lessening in the babe's struggle. She leaned forward and grasped the edge of the cradle, scared that Faith might have ceased to breathe altogether. But as Isaac drew back, Ruth saw normal color suffuse the delicate cheeks, and as she laid a hand on the small chest, she could find no sense of tightness. Indeed, Faith nestled closer to her hand, then dropped into the normal breathing of restful sleep.

Ruth's eyes filled with tears, and she murmured aloud, "God is for you . . ." Samuel moved to slide a hand onto her shoulder.

"What happened?" John asked from the edge of the room where he'd been bustled in the excitement of the room.

Bishop Mast rose from before the fireplace and went to stand over the cradle. "Praise the Lord! *Gott* has healed your sister, John."

Ruth caressed Faith's chest, then accepted her own baby from Ellen's arms. "Thank you, Isaac," she whispered.

"*Ya,*" Samuel said. "How can we ever thank you?"

Ruth looked up to see Isaac's face flush red, and he backed away with hands raised. "*Nee, sei se gut,* this was nothing to do with me. Please give all the praise to the Lord."

Bishop Mast nodded. "The boy speaks aright; all praise to our *Fater* in heaven." He clapped Isaac on the shoulder. "We will have *gut* journeys together, *sohn.* You have the good sense not to garner praise for yourself, and that is a fair start to wisdom."

Ruth watched Isaac murmur a thank-you; he was clearly stunned by what had happened.

But she, as she cuddled Faith close, knew only peace and a deep sense of thankfulness for another way that God had chosen to show that He was indeed "for her."

Late that evening everyone was abed, the trauma with the baby past. Joseph sat alone for a few minutes in the overcrowded house, thinking over the day, when Ellen came to his side.

"You should be abed, my dear," he said as she knelt next to his chair. "'Twill be quite a day tomorrow—one boy leaving, the other marrying. I should imagine that you are a bundle of nerves and would seek solace in sleep."

"I would seek solace with you," she said.

He glanced down at her, at this shy admission, and sighed.

"I know, Ellen, that I have not always been the best of husbands to you. My dealings with Adam, my temper and moodiness . . . There were many times over the years that I might have given you a sound word of praise and never did. You are a wonderful wife and mother. I am sorry for the boys we lost. I've never said that before."

"*Nee*, you have not, but I accept it now and it brings peace to me. I want to say, Joseph, that you seem different since the attack of the animal. I cannot explain it, but I—like it all the same."

He leaned forward and twisted in his chair to cup her face in his hands with gentle fingers. "*Ach*, Ellen, *danki* for seeing a change in me for the better. I hope to continue to change, to improve, in all the ways that the Lord allows. That I might be a blessing and not a curse to you and our new *kinner*."

"Never a curse, Joseph . . . never. I have always loved you. I always will."

He bent and pressed his mouth to her eager one with a great deal of tenderness, kissing her for long minutes, until the fire in the hearth became jewel-like coals.

Chapter 40

Lena rose before dawn, and the day of the weddings began. To her, it passed in a blur of minute details that each seemed something she would never forget: fresh flowers from the field that Abby arranged in mason jars to decorate the downstairs, a hearty search for hairpins to subdue Ruth's red hair in proper Amish fashion, an anxious and hearty cry from Isaac for shoe polish, her own wedding dressing.

At last she stood breathless and ready at the top of the stairsteps. She had brushed her best dark brown dress until it looked nearly new and had ironed and starched her apron and prayer covering until they fell into immaculate folds. A door opened to her left, and John came out, looking stiff and hot in a high collar and Sunday best suit coat.

"You look pretty, Lena," he said.

She smiled, knowing what that kind of remark cost a young boy. Ignoring his gruff expression, she reached to straighten his collar. "And you are very handsome, John Yoder. 'Twill not be long before you too will be—"

He held up a firm hand. "Do not speak of it. I've had tales from Adam and Isaac nearly half the night. I prefer my art and farming . . . There need never be a *mawd* for me."

She laughed, and he offered her a formal arm in the manner of the British. She took it with tender fingertips and they proceeded downstairs.

The keeping room had been mostly cleared of furniture, except for long wood-hewn benches that matched the brightly painted pattern on the floor. It had taken until yesterday for the floor to be finished, and Lena had feared that they might have to marry in the kitchen as she struggled to stop watching the paint dry.

Everyone was gathered in their best dress, and Lena felt a quiver of excitement go down her straight spine as she met Adam's gaze. He wore both a vest and a frock coat of brown, and his breeches were fit in an expert manner, setting off his white hose and dark shoes. She met his eyes and knew a great surge of confidence as the golden eyes gleamed with deep approval of her appearance. She felt encompassed and loved by his look and walked toward him as if in a dream.

They stood side by side, with her father and Ruth opposite, as the bishop performed a rather light and cheerful ceremony. As he reminded them, he and Isaac had to make haste for another wedding he'd been sent word of only that morning.

The sunshine poured in through the windows, and within minutes Lena found herself the wife of Adam Wyse. It all seemed a dream until he caught her in his strong arms and kissed her once and hard. Then he let her go to be bussed by one and all, and she did the same with Ruth and her father.

Then she was in Adam's arms again, and the delights of the food and the day were nothing compared to the surpassing knowledge of his love.

———— • ————

Ruth Yoder . . . The name tasted oddly delicious on her tongue as she tried it out while taking a few moments out of the fun day to nurse

Mary. She had finished and readjusted the odd pins of her new dress when a tentative knock sounded at the door.

"Come in," she called.

Samuel entered smilingly with Abby in tow.

"It seems a certain little girl feels a bit lost in all of the doings of the day. I told her she looked pretty with her starched apron, but I do not seem to be able to satisfy somehow. I think she needs a woman's touch."

Ruth reached up and handed Mary to Samuel, who left, quietly closing the door behind him.

"So, a new woman in the house to stay, Abby, me love? Do ye feel a bit lost over it all?"

"*Ya.*" The little girl nibbled at her thumb, and Ruth struggled not to smile with affection at the sight.

"I would be a mite shook up over things too, if it were me. I suppose one thing ye're thinkin' is that ye might have to call me Mum . . . er, *Mamm*. Am I right?"

Abby looked at her with earnest blue eyes. "*Ach, ya*, Ruth. I want to call you *Mamm*, but I do not feel like I want to do it yet. Is that all right?"

Ruth held out her arms, and Abby came to cuddle on her lap. "It is more than fine, dearie. Ye call me Ruth as long as ye like, and you can tell John to do the same."

Abby hugged her joyfully. "*Ach, danki*, Ruth."

Ruth smiled and knew a feeling of contentment that surpassed any other time in her life—she decided it was joy.

The bishop had pulled up a slight distance ahead so that the family might say their farewells to Isaac. Now the rest had gone inside, leaving Adam alone with his brother.

Adam fooled with the saddle girth of the pack mule and ran his hands over the small bundles of belongings. "Everything seems weather tight. Expect you'll get a lot of rain up in the mountains."

Isaac laughed softly. "Will we be reduced to talking about the weather to say good-bye, Adam?"

Adam raised his head, a smile on his lips. "*Nee*—I will miss you true."

"And I you."

Adam caught his brother's hand in a firm grasp, then pulled him close for a hug. "*Danki* . . . for everything, Isaac."

"I will expect to dawdle a newborn on my lap next year, Adam. Being an uncle suits the dignity of a bishop."

Adam slapped him on the back. "I will give the matter some attention."

Isaac laughed and mounted the mule, leaving Adam to wave him off with the bishop, a curious feeling of loss in his stomach as he muttered a prayer for his brother's welfare.

Chapter 41

Lena took time in the later afternoon to ponder sleeping arrangements on the farm. Of course, Ruth and Samuel would occupy the large bedroom, but if Ellen and Joseph chose to stay on another night, she wasn't sure how all of the couples—she flushed when she recalled that she was now part of the concept of couples—would fit into the various rooms. She supposed that she could simply stay with Abby and postpone her wedding night, but she knew Adam would probably not like the idea.

"Why are you frowning on our wedding day?" Adam asked as he came inside the kitchen door.

She blushed. "No reason. I was thinking about . . . household arrangements."

"Well, as to that line of thought, I asked my *mamm* and *fater* to simply stay on here for one more night. I would, if it please you, take you to our new home for our wedding night. Back to my room."

Something about the last part of his suggestion deepened her blush. To go to his room seemed so—personal. And yet, she was his wife! She pulled at the hem of her apron, clearly flustered.

He laughed. "You can be both shy and bold, Lena Wyse. It is enough to keep a man on his toes and wary at all times."

"Wary?"

"Aye, and that means that I will never grow bored in a life we carve together. My hope is that you will feel the same."

She dropped her apron hem to shyly stretch and kiss his cheek. "I cannot wait to begin—this life carving with you."

He caught her close. "You have wit as well as wisdom, and I fancy you will share many adventures with me through this earthly life."

She would have kissed him again, but her mother-in-law entered the kitchen, then stopped abruptly.

"*Ach*, excuse me—both of you." She made haste to turn, and both Lena and Adam protested.

Adam caught his mother close, and Lena giggled as he hugged both of them tight together. "My two favorite women."

"Adam," his mother scolded with brightened cheeks. "What will Lena think?"

"Lena thinks it is fine," Lena said. "I hope—I hope that the Lord has given me back a new *mamm* in you, Ellen."

"*Ya, ach*, I would love that, Lena."

"See?" Adam laughed. "Family love."

Adam was nervous. He and Lena had taken the wagon and now rode through the quiet trees toward his home. He mentally tried to list all of the things he knew he should do before leading Lena upstairs—feed and water the stock, offer her something from the picnic meal that Ruth had provided, touch her hair and loose its pins.

Lena chattered gaily about this and that. She was nervous too, he could tell. It was silly, he told himself. Once they kissed each other, then all would be well, but kissing was one thing—a far thing—from becoming man and wife.

He sighed aloud without meaning to do so.

"What's wrong, Adam?"

"Nothing."

"*Nee*. You sighed. What is it?"

Now this was fine . . . If he were a different man, he would make some dashing joke and she would smile back with secret happiness. But he knew nothing better to do than to tell the truth.

"Nervous, a bit," he said.

"You mean, am I?"

"*Nee*. I am."

"*Ach*. Me too."

"Don't be." He reached a hand from the reins to clasp her fingers and felt a bit better.

"Why?"

"Hmm?"

"Why should I not be nervous?"

For a moment she sounded like a frightened little girl, and Adam had the jolting awareness that she had lost her mother in a rush. She had, perhaps, had no time to discuss the inner workings of intimacy between a man and wife. The thought terrified him. Perhaps he should have asked his mother to speak with her. But no, that might have been awkward for Lena.

"You should not be nervous because—because it is a perfectly natural thing that happens when two people love each other, and—"

She laughed, and he looked at her sideways. "What?"

"You sound like a mother hen, giving a proper lesson to her brood. I am nervous because I'm thinking of silly things like how I will look in my nightdress. My feet are big, and my freckles stand out in the early morning light, and I have a birthmark inside my left calf that looks like a small continent—"

"All right, all right," he said. "I understand." He could not hear one more of her revealing explanations. He felt like he had just been given a whirlwind introduction to her form that left him feeling breathless and wanting.

"So why are you nervous?"

He looked at her again, hoping she was teasing, but there was complete seriousness in the turquoise depths of her eyes.

"Well . . . I've got to get the chores done, and then . . ."

She clapped her hands lightly. "*Ach, gut*, Adam. Would you mind if I had a bath, then, while you're busy? I know I bathed last night, but it would feel so refreshing after the day."

He ruthlessly pushed aside the images that her suggestion conjured up and nodded. "Of course. I'll hitch up a draft horse and haul the water up from the creek."

"*Nee*." She shook her head. "The creek's fine with me. I will slip down there—I do it all the time at home."

"You do?" he asked in a choked voice.

"Mm-hmm. Sometimes even in the winter. *Fater* thinks the chill water is *gut* for us."

"Oh."

He let his thoughts drift. He knew every inch of the creek bank at home. It would be very easy to slip down a trail and keep a discreet eye on her. He wasn't sure he liked the idea of her bathing outside, but he didn't know how to broach the subject at the moment.

They arrived at the farmhouse and he came around to help her down, letting her linger for a moment in his arms. "You will be careful at the creek, won't you, Lena? There could be snakes . . . or panthers . . ."

"*Ach*, Adam." She laughed and wriggled free of his grasp. "I will be fine."

He stood, watching her go toward the creek bank, already pulling

at the pins around her collar, and he thought in frantic indecision
whether to tend to his pale-skinned wife's safety or see to the stock.
His wife won out.

He waited a few minutes, giving her a chance for privacy, then
slipped along the creek bank, deep in tall, green blueberry bushes, and
glanced up the water. He saw one slender, pale arm and averted his gaze.
Obviously, if she was not screaming, she was not in trouble . . . though
a rattlesnake could strike with swiftness and leave the victim gasping.
He looked again, feeling like a green lad, when her voice drifted across
the dancing water.

"Adam Wyse! Are you spying on me?"

"*Nee*," he answered finally.

She laughed, a light, rippling sound that competed with the music
of the bubbles against the rocks.

"Are you planning on coming in?"

He wet his lips. What did she want him to say? Her voice sounded
calm, inviting . . .

"If you would like."

"*Ach*, I would like. But stay down there, if you do not mind. I
intend to preserve my maidenly dignity for at least another half hour."

He laughed and pulled his coat and vest off. He stripped down
to his breeches and, turning from upstream, sank into the deliciously
chill water, letting himself float while trying to avoid a boyish peeking
at his beloved.

Then her voice came from somewhere near behind him, and he
almost flopped over in the water. "What?"

She laughed. "I said that I am getting out, if you do not mind. I
thought I would warm up a bit inside."

"Right. Sounds *gut*. I will join you shortly."

He heard her gentle splashing away from him and risked one

glance. A moment later he saw her collapse against the muddy bank. She was clad in a light shift and grasping frantically at her lower leg.

"Lena!" He sloshed through the water and saw a snake swimming off in a calm swirl; a rattler, over four feet long, its dull body and thick head cutting easily across the current.

He got to her as she slipped back into the water and scooped her up into his arms.

"You were right," she gasped, managing a tight smile. "Too many snakes."

Chapter 42

Lena seemed to weigh nothing in his arms as he ran with her to the house.

Strangely, the image of an early war flag flashed through Adam's mind. The coiled snake, its rattles exposed. *Don't tread on me* . . . Lena must have had no chance to hear the warning.

If there was one thing he was thankful for at the moment, it was the facts about snakes that his father had beaten into him in an ironic attempt to protect him. Rattlers could climb trees, hang in tall bushes, swim, and would strike in any mood. Their venom did not depend on their size; a smaller snake could be just as poisonous. He thought about putting Lena in the wagon and making the drive back to her home, but he knew that such jolting and time would only spread the poison through her delicate veins.

Adam gained the steps and carried Lena without thinking into the only safe place he had known in the house—his room, his bed. He laid her down gently, swiftly trying to assess if she was having trouble breathing. She didn't struggle, but tears stood out in stark relief against the pallor of her skin. He knew that venom could work in minutes or hours, depending on how much of the stuff was actually injected. Sometimes, if a person was lucky, the bite could be dry, no venom in the wound. The bite mark itself would tell.

"Lena, you must stay warm. I have to remove your shift; it is soaked. Forgive me."

She nodded and moved with restless pain. "Not quite a *gut* start to our wedding night."

He watched her scrunch her eyes closed as he hurriedly stripped off the gown and pulled one of his huge nightshirts over her body. He was quick, impersonal; and she was soon buried beneath the covers.

"I need to look at the bite now, Lena."

"It is my right leg."

"I know . . . but only there? It didn't strike you elsewhere?"

She shook her head.

He raised the blankets and could see the reddened dual puncture marks on the outside of her calf in the light of the sun through the windows. Some slight swelling was already showing. The swelling was a bad sign; it meant that the bite had not been dry and that the poison was beginning to mount in her body.

"You should go for Ruth," Lena said. "She will know the right herbs for a poultice. I cannot seem to remember right now."

Her words struck him like a physical blow, but he kept his voice calm and level. "*Nee*, there's not time enough for that. Do not worry. I know what to do."

Cut and suck . . . cut and suck . . . The phrase ran like broken music through his brain as he turned from the bed. He must clean his sharpest knife.

"I am going to do what you need, sweet, and then we shall enjoy lying in each other's arms." He spoke automatically, turning back to press a kiss on her warm brow. She caught him close, staring up into his eyes.

"Will it hurt, Adam?"

He shook his head. "*Nee*."

Yes . . . yes . . . yes . . . and if I am not fast, then . . .

"I'll be back in a few moments, love. Lie still, will you promise? 'Twill keep the venom from spreading."

"I promise," she said, a fearful look on her face.

"*Gut.*"

He grabbed a small knife from his dresser and raced back down the stairsteps to the kitchen. He plunged the knife into the standing bucket of clean water and grabbed a rough round of soap. He cleaned the blade again and again, then headed back up the steps to his bride.

Lena could not keep her promise to lie still, no matter how hard she tried.

The bite had ceased to burn as intensely as it had, but she felt incredibly restless and her body urged her to walk about—perhaps it would help to settle her stomach.

She slipped off the covers and thought how odd she must look in Adam's nightshirt, though she was having trouble remembering how she had put it on. She began to prowl about the room, Adam's room, and felt a distant thrill of interest to be so close to him.

She moved to his simply carved dresser with its few odds and ends on top. Then she fingered a carved link of chains. It must be the gift from Dale Ellis that Adam had told her about. She admired the smoothness of the wood and felt it strange that her fingertips seemed to tingle with sensation as she stroked the carving.

"Lena! What are you doing?"

She must have jumped in surprise at Adam's frantic tone, but her movements felt soggy and thick. She was in a pile on the floor when he bent over her, lifting her easily against his chest.

"Your eyes, they're so beautiful," she whispered, reaching up to touch him. "But why do you look so sad?"

She felt herself placed on the bed, but the bed became a river raft that seemed to pitch and toss against unseasonable waves. She whimpered, hearing from a long way off. Someone was speaking, demanding her attention. She tried to hoist herself up on her elbows and had the notion that her heart might beat through her chest. Now, how could that be possible?

". . . perfectly still. Do you hear, Lena?"

Adam was at the bottom of the bed, their wedding bed. His dark head was bent intently over her leg. She could feel his damp hair brush against her and it tickled. She almost moved her legs, wondering if he were staring too closely at her birthmark.

"Lena, a quick cut only, 'tis all."

A slashing burn made her cry out, and then she thought she must have fallen off the river raft and tumbled into some strange sea. A sea creature, both delightful and shadowed, like one her father had told her stories of as a little girl, seemed to have found a close bond with her. She felt its kisses on her leg, quick, drawing sucks that came and went, making her shiver in pleasure, and then she drew a deep breath of water and felt herself begin to sink, the water enshrouding her until she fell into a strange sleep.

Adam knew what he had to do. Should even the smallest bit of venom slip down his throat, then he too could become poisoned, and then Lena would be alone in the house. He heard her tightened breath and worked on, carefully sucking from the bleeding wound and spitting the venom into a basin. He had no idea when to stop, and decided after half an hour that he had probably reached all that he could. Yet she was worse.

He covered his face with his hands and prayed, as he had been praying, wondering if he could leave her long enough to fetch Isaac. He had helped the babe. But he could not let her be alone, and his heart echoed what his mind would not—*he could not let her die alone.*

He half sobbed as he rose to empty the basin, then came back to sit beside her on his bed. She was feverish now, lost in incoherent mumblings that he could make little sense of. He thought how young she looked and told himself that the bite was his fault. He had known better; he shouldn't have let her swim.

Dear Gott, help. I will give my life for hers. Help us, please . . .

"Hiya! Hiya there, anybody home?"

Adam nearly fell off the bed when he heard the voice from below. He bundled Lena securely in the covers so she would not fall from the bed, then rose to race downstairs.

"Nutter" Stolzfus stood in the open front doorway.

"Thank *Gott,*" Adam gasped.

"Land of Goshen, *buwe,* whatcha doin' runnin' round in only yer britches—though ye do look a hearty sight. Heard ye got married. I brought you and the missus a wagonload of potatoes. Thought it might start things off nice and simple like."

"Lucas . . . Nutter. Listen, please. Lena lies upstairs. She was bitten by a rattler, and she's getting worse. I need you to go to the Yoders' as fast as you can."

The wizened little man straightened a bit. "A rattler, ye say. Did you cut and suck?"

"*Ya,* but—"

"All right. All right. Calm down now, ole Nutter knows what to do." He pulled an oilskin pouch from beneath his shirt. "Keep this with me always . . . Indian medicine. I traded two wagons full of potatoes to get it. Them rattlers strike hard in the potato fields. Gotta be ready."

Adam shook his head, nearly frantic. "*Nee*, please just go to the Yoders' for me."

But Nutter was already in the kitchen, poking at the low embers in the grate of the fireplace. "Gotta brew a tea, *buwe*. Gotta get it down her throat fast. 'Twill kill the poison. I know you don't believe me, but I know. Seen it work on an Indian bit twice by an eight-footer. Pulled him back from the grave. Don't fret none now."

Adam slowly closed the door and leaned against it. Maybe *Derr Herr* had sent Nutter with a cure. He knew he was willing to try anything. He half stumbled across the room, his eyes filled with tears, and gained the steps once more.

"Come up when it's ready," he called over his shoulder.

He heard Nutter mumble and went back to his room.

Lena had not moved, but he could hear her rasping breath as soon as he entered. He dropped to his knees beside the bed and caught her cold hand close, rubbing it across his face. Was this to be her appointed time to die? It had all happened so quickly. He closed his eyes and rocked his body against the bed, trying to pray but finding that he could not even think to form the words.

Lena was dreaming; she knew it and liked the sensation. It felt safe, like she was cocooned in warmth and her cares were few. She had somehow moved through the water and emerged, everything sparkling about her like crystal glass. Then she climbed to the green grass bank to find herself still clad in the absurd nightshirt. She laughed; it didn't matter. She moved along, breathing in the smells of the mountains in springtime and fresh lilacs. She saw someone ahead of her and knew instinctively that it was her *mamm*. Her feet skimmed the cool grass as she ran, catching up with her mother, whose hair fell glorious and unbound.

"*Mamm?*"

Her mother turned to her and smiled, holding out her arms. Lena hugged her close, never wanting to let go.

"*Ach, Mamm.* It's been so lonely without you, so hard."

A thought occurred to her, like a thousand bursting suns, and she leaned close to her mother. "Adam and I are married, *Mamm.*"

"I know." Her mother's voice was distant, though she stood inches away, and melodic with a music Lena could not name.

"Lena, I must tell you something. I made Adam promise to give you up. He did it for me . . . until he could find a way to be free. He loves you so."

Lena opened her mouth in surprise, wanting to say it was all right, that *Gott* had brought freedom, when something awful began to trickle down her throat, nearly choking her. She held fast to her mother but could not ignore the bitter taste that filled her. The dream was ending, and she didn't want it to. She cried out to her mother, who seemed to disappear before her very eyes as another swallow of the vile liquid filled her, making her turn away, until everything was a palpable fog, cold and gray . . .

"She's a-tastin' it, an' she don't like it none neither. 'Tis a *gut* sign."

Adam felt Nutter tap him on the head where he still knelt.

"Git up now, *buwe*. She's gonna be all right; she's breathin' a mite like a catfish outta water, but she's better. I kin tell."

Adam rose to stare down at his bride. Her color was better, and she surely was fighting the taste of the mixture Nutter kept spooning down her throat. She tossed in irritation, and Adam had to smile faintly as a peace began to steal over him.

He put his hand on Nutter's shoulder. "*Danki, gut* friend."

The old man shook his head. "Had me a bride once meself, ya know? She was hurt when we was working in the deep timber . . . didn't do potatoes then. She died right there in me arms, like the Lord would have it." His weathered hand shook a bit as he got another spoonful down, and then Adam pulled him close to his side for a long moment.

"She'll be awakin' soon and be needin' rest. Then I'm thinkin' that ye'll both git back to the idea of bein' married together, hmm?"

Adam smiled through his tears. "*Ya*, we surely will give it some attention."

Nutter grunted aloud in satisfaction.

Chapter 43

There are two things that come to my mind at this moment," Adam declared as he swung the bedroom door closed and leaned back against it.

It was a week since Lena had been bitten, and once more Adam had arranged for his parents to stay at the Yoders' for the night that he might have time alone with his bride. There had been a great deal of good-natured joking about swimming in the creek as they had driven away, and Adam had literally carried Lena from the wagon to the front door when they arrived. He was taking no chances.

Lena stood, knowing her body was framed by the daylight in her simple shift, and she nervously played with her unbound hair. "What are the two things?" she whispered, thinking he would woo her somehow with words, and her bare toes curled against the floorboards at the prospect.

"Let's see." He half closed his eyes as if struggling to remember, and she shivered in anticipation. "Well, a *gut* friend told me once that it is God, not man nor war, who is revolutionary."

"That—is true," she murmured, surprised at the bent of his words.

He smiled at her then, a rich smile that made her think of melting toffee, and his eyes glowed golden bright. "You think perhaps I have grown my *bruder's* tendency of thought, to speak of God at a time like this?" he asked.

She shook her head.

"*Gut.*" He pushed away from the door and walked toward her. He touched his fingers to the throb of her pulse at her neck, and she leaned into his hand. "I know that God is revolutionary because of the second thing that comes to mind," he whispered, reaching to rub a thumb across her cheeks.

"Wh-what?" she gasped.

"A certain maid told me once that 'a first kiss is forever.' Do you recall?" He took her in his arms, and she put her hands across the breadth of his tanned chest.

"I remember."

He bent to press his mouth to the shoulder of her gown, only pulling away when she shivered from the sensation of his kiss. "*Gut.* Very good," he whispered. "Well, God is revolutionary because that first kiss was forever, is forever, and will be forever." He punctuated his words with his lips, and she had to grasp his shoulders to remain upright.

Then he swept her up into his arms and held her, nuzzling at the base of her throat.

"Adam, I have something to tell you."

She watched him lift his head, his eyes suddenly alert as he eased her to the floor.

"The bite, it pains you? Is—is this too much after you've been so ill? I can—"

She put her fingers to his lips. "*Nee*, Adam. Listen." She reached to stroke his hair. "When I was ill, *Gott* gave me a dream. I—I know it may sound strange, but I saw my *mamm*. She told me of your promise to her—to let me go."

He stared down at her. "*Ya*. 'Tis true, but no one knew. Only *Gott*, so it must be true that He gave you this truth."

She stretched on tiptoe to kiss the damp hollow of his neck. "*Ach*, Adam. Thank you for your promise. But tell me true, have you found freedom?"

He drew her closer, gazing down at her with passion and happiness shining in his eyes.

"*Ya*, Lena. Freedom through *Gott*, through forgiveness, through love." He ran his hand down her back.

"Lena," he said. "I would this day that you remember . . . that you take everything I have . . . all of me. I am somehow whole now, but I know not how except by God's grace. I offer myself to you." He held her. The silence of the room caught and held the breath and life of them and kept secret watch over their embrace.

Later she ran her fingers through his dark hair and kissed him until she noticed that the daylight had begun to fade outside the window.

"Look," she whispered. "'Tis our wedding night."

He laughed in appreciation. "And what of our wedding afternoon?"

"That was spent in the arms of love," she said, and closed her eyes once more.

Reading Group Guide

1. What similarities and differences did you find between the colonial culture of the Amish and current renditions of the Amish? Consider community, priorities, faith, etc.

2. How does the past keep Adam from having an abundant life? What in your own past limits you?

3. Ruth begins to cling to the verse regarding "God being for her." How do you feel this truth works out in your own life with God?

4. How do you feel about the Amish dissident stance, their refusal to "bear arms," and how does this relate to the biblical idea of not "sparing the rod," as Joseph does?

5. Joseph is a character driven by fear. How does that fear play out in the poor choices he makes on a daily basis? When has fear caused you to make a poor choice?

6. How does Lena and Adam's relationship ultimately become strengthened by challenges to their union?

7. What is wrong with Isaac's perception of God and faith? In what way does he have a "religion" but not a relationship with God?

8. What is the role of the panther or mountain lion in the book? What does the animal symbolize?

9. How does Dale's ready acceptance of Adam remind you of a time when you have found an immediate connection with someone?

10. Dale gives Adam a chain as a reminder of the burdens he might give to God. What chains hold you prisoner in your life that you struggle to give to God?

11. How does Lena's faith change and grow throughout the novel?

12. Samuel wants the best for Lena, but his desire to keep her safe leads him to give her poor advice. What was this advice? Has this ever happened to you with someone who loves you a great deal?

13. What are your thoughts on "bundling"? How would this tradition work or not work in today's culture?

14. How does the title of the novel represent a duality in meaning? What are its different layers?

15. How does John mirror Adam in terms of frustration and searching for truth?

16. God sends Ruth into Abby's life as a comfort after her mother's death. How has God comforted you during grief?

Acknowledgments

Thank you deeply to the following people who made *Arms of Love* a reality: Marie and Gilbert Stout, Gilbert V. and David Stout, Bud Gyurina, Donna and Charles Long, Ruth and Faith Brickley, Asa Brickley, Natalie Hannemann, Natasha Kern, the staff and company of the Hershey Cocoa Beanery, the staff and doctors of Geisinger Medical Center's Heart Institute, Kimberly Evans, John Evans, Sara Falis, Melissa Cherry, Brenda and Bruce Lott, Becky Monds, Allen Arnold, and the entire TN team. Thank you to my Amish and English readers with a very special shout-out to Dr. Steven Nolt who answered endless questions with extreme patience and his amazing expertise of Amish culture. And lastly, thank you to these unique and wonderfully loving vessels of God's love to me—Elizabeth Wiseman, my Ward, Scott Long II, Christin Ivey, Donna Boudakian, Grant and Grace Long, my companion writer's dog, Sophy, and my hero, comrade in arms, and heart's desire—Scott Long Sr. Thank you all.

A Novel Bible Study
on *The Arms of Love*
written by the author

The following is a four-week Bible study on the novel you have just read. It can be done alone or with a reading/Bible study group. The goal of the study is to enrich your reading experience with biblical application to your everyday life.

Week One—The Past

Then Moses said to the LORD, "Please, Lord, I have never been eloquent, neither recently nor in time past, nor since You have spoken to Your servant; for I am slow of speech and slow of tongue." (Exodus 4:10–11 NASB)

Day One: Does the Past Hold You?

Author's Insight: The creation of the characters of Adam and Joseph Wyse is a study of the way in which the past can grab hold of the present and future and taint them with troublesome memories, disturbing sins, or unspoken but ever-present omissions of truth. The past can hold you and restrain you from having the abundant life that God desires for you. For us, time is linear—we cannot travel backward and fix things—but time is not linear for God. He can own your past, reshape it, and use it for good in your life today. If you've watched one of those "value of antiques" TV shows, you may have seen this scenario: A man comes in with a cabinet from the 1700s, but he tells the appraiser with pride that he "redid" the piece: buffed out the scratches, repainted it, and so on. The appraiser shakes his head sadly and tells him that had he not redone the cabinet, it would have been worth a hundred times as much! The past is like your old cabinet, your old self—God wants it with an appraiser's eye, with all the dents and flaws. He alone can redo your past, and He waits to do so.

Novel Question: Can you identify with Adam in any of his struggles with the past? List these points from the novel.

_____

_____

_____

Next, consider how the concept of surrendering the past to God might alter or does alter Adam's words at these points. How would the scenes play out differently with more love and truth in dealing with the past?

_____

_____

_____

Who or what situations in your own life do you avoid because confronting them would mean facing the past?

_____

Prayer: Dear Lord, please bring to mind the people I need to forgive through You for the past. Let me list them or their initials here. Search my heart and reveal situations in my life that would benefit from letting go of the past's hold on me.

_____

Day Two: Past Failures

Author's Insight: I know from my own battles with the past that those times and situations can sometimes produce nightmares, so it was not difficult to write Adam's struggles with his dreams. He also refers to times he's tried to pray and has been met with darkness. He feels like he's a failure in his faith at times. Samuel even blames him and holds him accountable for a past he cannot consciously recall. Adam is a perfect example of how we can use acceptance, God's acceptance, to encompass the things we count as past failures in our lives—the "I should haves" or "I wish now that I wouldn't haves." We don't know how God can work out those past issues to shape us more like His

Son, to bring us greater strength, and to teach us to live out our deeper resources of love and compassion.

Novel Question: How does Lena's regret over not finding a midwife to help her mother make her feel?

_____

_____

Circle the life areas in which you feel a sense of past failure.

Family   Honesty
Children   Patience
Friends   Kindness
Spiritual life   Judgment
Personal integrity   Work

Next, list three specifics of the areas circled above that you wish to pray about to release these past perceptions of failure.

_____

_____

_____

Prayer: Help me, dear Lord, with these areas (times or people) where I believe that I have failed or that someone has failed me. Help me to see a new and greater purpose in these experiences as I allow You to work through them in my life.

Day Three: Neither Now, nor in Times Past

Author's Insight: *I could not do it then, so I cannot do it now.* Whatever your "it" of failed attempts is, you can know that you're not alone. We all judge the present and future by past attempts. Adam and Lena might have continued to gauge their relationship on past attempts and found themselves without any future together at all. But I wanted to write that conflict, that struggle over things not working before, to show that God can turn any situation around. I mean that—*any.* There is no mess, no sin, no brokenness too great for the cross. Christ's sacrifice would have been made if yours was the only human life He would save from eternal judgment. He would have died for you alone; He died for you alone. The evil of the world would have you believe that who you were in the past, what you were capable of, is all that you will ever be. God says that "He is doing a new thing." Try again and rest in that assurance, and then keep trying. You will find that the past fades in the light of faith.

Novel Question: How does Adam persist in his love for Lena despite past failures?

_____

_____

_____

What could you not do in the past that you can do or face now?

_____

_____

What do you want to accomplish or believe now that past experiences would tell you that you will not be able to do?

_____

_____

_____

Prayer: Dear Lord, help me to understand the past as practice for a new now and a growing future. Take my past inabilities and transform them for Your glory so that I might see how I progress each day in You.

Day Four: Pleading with the Lord about the Past

Author's Insight: When Dale is leaving, Adam tells him that he has prayed and pleaded with the Lord about the past but he's basically gotten nothing back in response. He's still trapped, still wounded, still chained. Dale says something interesting—that Adam does not pray "aright." I deliberately did not have Adam reject this revelation because he so earnestly wants to be free, but without Dale's insight, he doesn't recognize the link between his relationship with his father and the past. Some might ask, "But why does the responsibility for the past sin fall on Adam? Why is he the victim?" And maybe on a deeper level, "Why are there victims of the past, Lord? Why am I one of them?"

Novel Question: How might this story have ended very differently if Adam had not found the courage to pray about the past with his father in mind?

_____

_____

_____

Whom do you truthfully feel like you have to pray for or about in regard to your past? How difficult is this?

_____

_____

_____

How is this difficulty lessened when we remember that we are "in Him" or comforted and held by God?

_____

_____

_____

Are you angry at God about the past?

_____

_____

_____

Prayer: In You, oh Lord, all things are possible. Help me to surrender the times that I feel like a victim of someone or some situation of the past. Help me to admit to You when I am angry with You about the past and to know that You understand. Transform the wounds of my past into a dynamic future for You.

Day Five: The Past Is His

Author's Insight: On the previous day's study, I touched a bit on the reality of being angry at God for the past. It is not easy to get past that anger and He knows this, but it is possible. I know because I've had to do it—to move from railing and crying to walking in companionship with God through trials. My hope is that the reader will take away a sense that Adam's past belongs to God. I wrote it so the past is not even primarily Adam's to own, though he battles this concept. In our lives, God holds our past, present, and eternity in His loving arms. What we perceive as bad, difficult, or unfair at the moment might have long-lasting and overarching effects for good in our lives.

Novel Question: How does God's ownership of the past reveal itself through Ruth's story?

_____

_____

_____

Whom do you believe your past belongs to? Is it difficult to believe that the past belongs to God?

_____

_____

_____

What steps can you learn from Ruth in choosing the truth that God wants to take control of your past for a better today?

_____

_____

_____

Prayer: Dear God, even Christ had to choose to make decisions about what belonged to You and to acknowledge this truth before others while He walked the earth. Help me to learn from your Word how to go about making these similar choices in my own life and to accept that my past belongs to You.

Week Two—God Is for You

"For, behold, I am for you, and I will turn to you, and you will be cultivated and sown." (Ezekiel 36:9 NASB)

Day One: Take a Closer Look

Author's Insight: "For, behold . . ." I chose this scripture as the key one of the novel for a number of reasons—one of which is its command to "look . . . look closer." The "for" also can mean "Because of what came before," so it might read "Because of what came before, look closer . . ." We have trouble with looking closer at situations that disturb or bother us, and consequently, we have difficulty looking closer at the heart of the Living God. We forget that it is He who allows everything to happen to us and for a reason. It is because we are hurt, angry, or do not understand that we do not behold, or it is because we cannot look closer without the recollection of intense pain, like those who struggle with post-traumatic stress disorder. Both Adam and Joseph are tormented by the pain of the past, pain that they try to look closer at but cannot. They each must wait on God's timing. And for each of us, there is a time when God commands, "For, behold . . ."

Novel Question: What are some issues that Lena refuses to look closer at or to behold? How do these issues affect her decisions?

_____

_____

_____

Search your heart. What is it that God is asking you to behold right now in your life that you are resisting?

_____

_____

What do you fear will happen if you do behold this issue or event?

_____

How have you seen God conquer fear, turmoil, and trouble in the past? How might He work to do the same if you take the risk of looking closer at something?

_____

_____

_____

How does John's introspection, or childlike view, make him more willing to examine difficult situations?

_____

_____

_____

How can you be more "childlike" in your faith and willingness to behold?

_____

Prayer: Oh Lord, give me the trusting heart of a child, a child who does not know pain or fear, so that I might be willing to look more closely at my life—my past, present, and future. Help me to remember that all is in Your hands and that You can work out "all things for good for those who know and love You and are called according to Your purpose."

Day Two: "I Am for You"

Author's Insight: Jesus talks about the fact that "there is no greater love than this—that a man lay down his life for a friend" (see John 15:13). When you really think about what He is saying and meditate on it, you realize that He did that—He died on the cross for *you*. You might say, "My past is too bad, and what I'm doing now—well, He would not approve." But the truth is that all the sins you've ever sinned, all that you will sin, were covered in the overwhelming victory cry of the cross, when God shouted throughout all time—"I am for you!" In the character of Ruth Stone, I wanted to create someone who would struggle to hear this cry, who would not believe that it actually meant something for her life—which seemed so miserable and lost. I wanted Ruth to be what we all feel at times—far from the victory and God's word of promise that He truly is for us and loves us more than we can ever fathom.

Novel Question: When have you felt like Ruth Stone as she trudged along that dirt road, seemingly alone, until Adam rode up to her? Did you have trouble feeling like God was for you at this time? Why or why not?

_____

_____

_____

In this world, it is hard to find someone, anyone, who is truly "for us." What are the emotions you have experienced in dealing with people when you have discovered that they were not truly for you as you thought? Have you been hurt, disappointed, bruised in spirit, and so on?

_____

_____

Circle the areas of your life where you have felt that someone or something was not truly "for you."

Work
Family
Friendships
Marriage/romantic relationships
Parenting
God

Explain your answers.

_____

_____

Now list the areas of your life where you have seen God at work or in your favor, being for you, even if only for a moment.

_____

_____

How does God's idea of being "for you" differ from human ideas of love, friendship, or support?

_____

_____

Prayer: Dear Father, thank You that You root for me, that You stand by me, that You died for me. Help me to see You in those situations that I find are impossible in my life because someone is against me. Help me to know and remember that You are greater than all of my worries, doubts, and wounds.

Day Three: "I Will Turn to You"

Author's Insight: When a child cries, parents will usually stop what they are doing and turn to assess the situation—to see what the child needs or wants. How much more does our heavenly Father turn to us when we cry out to Him? This idea of turning is played out within the novel. I deliberately used the words "turned to" or "turned from" in many situations between Adam and Lena in order to capture the difficulties of working out a loving relationship in a fallen world. It is very, very important to remember that the evil of this world wants us to believe that God has turned His face from us when we have troubles. But the truth is that God is ever more present when we struggle—we simply cannot see Him always, but we can rest assured that if He promises to turn to us, to hear us when we cry or hurt, He will do so—because God cannot lie!

Novel Question: Mary Yoder asks Adam to turn from the one he loves for a time. How difficult is it for him to keep this promise? Why? How does God intervene in Adam's story as to how he keeps the promise?

_____

_____

_____

Spend three minutes of quiet time thinking of God being for you and turning to you. Think about Him as the voice of a thunderous crowd, cheering you on, rooting for you. Think of Him as a loving Father, who loves despite all of what we are or have done, who is turning to you right now—reaching out, taking you in His arms, holding you close.

How difficult was it for you to be still with the above thoughts of God? Why?

_____

_____

What does it look like to you when God "turns to you"?

_____

_____

Prayer: Oh Father, You have said in Your Word that I should call You Dad or Daddy, that I should come into Your presence knowing that You are thrilled to see me—even if I have done wrong. You love me, not because of who I am but because of who You are. Please let me feel You turning to me this day.

Day Four: "You Will Be Cultivated"

Author's Insight: The Yoder family cultivates their garden and orchard in preparation for growth and harvest. Similarly, God cultivates us in preparation. Cultivation, in its truest sense, involves turning over hardened ground, breaking through to new soil, scraping and marking the dirt to prepare for the seeds to come. It does not sound easy or pleasant for a garden—how much less pleasant does it seem for us? Who wants to face God as the Gardener cultivating our lives? We, in truth, would much rather stay as we are—we don't want to be raked and harrowed. We are scared of what that process might mean if we turn our lives or a situation over to God—what is He going to do? How much is it going to hurt? But cultivation as preparation is necessary for new hope and new growth, and we can trust the nail-scarred hands of the Great Gardener.

Novel Question: Pick one of your favorite characters from the novel and consider how God cultivates their life and growth.

_____

_____

Draw a map of your daily life as if it were a garden. What are your crops of concern? Your responsibilities? Your thorns? Where is there hardened ground that needs to be worked?

Consider your struggles or "thorns" or even your hardened soil from the above map. What is keeping you from letting God cultivate these areas? Confess this to God and ask Him for strength and a true desire to have the soil of your life worked.

_____

_____

_____

Prayer: Dear Jesus, it is no mistake that Mary thought You to be the gardener of the cemetery when You had first risen from the grave and defeated death for us all. She saw You as what You are: the Gardener of Grace, the One who uses nail-scarred, gentle carpenter's hands to hold me up as You work in these areas of my life that I surrender now to You. Please cultivate me in preparation for healthy growth and the receiving of more of Your abundant love.

Day Five: "You Will Be Sown"

Author's Insight: Lena sows her garden with care and forethought. She considers how best to lay out the crops and works in ways to add new seeds. The Bible says that "we are God's field." He works and labors over each of our individual lives as a master gardener plans and perfects his work. But we are not simply a "for show" garden or a garden that looks good on the outside but has serious blight in the heart of the plant. No, God wants us to be healthy down to our roots. So He cultivates and then He promises that we will be "sown." We will have new seeds planted and nurtured in us, seeds that have the potential to change our lives, to give us more abundance and hope—seeds of strength to move forward into the Gardener's hands.

Novel Question: When Lena prays while kneeling in the mulch, she wrestles to surrender the seeds of anger in her as an offering to the Lord and He helps her. When have you prayed to God about a "seed" of something in your life, be it good or bad, and heard His response?

_____

_____

One of the most important things to remember in this idea of sowing is that God is not the only one at work in your life. There is an enemy of our souls who also seeks to sow seeds in our minds and hearts. He is called the Deceiver and the Accuser. What are some "bad seeds" that are sown in your mind or heart right now? Anger? Hatred? Jealousy?

_____

_____

Now take a minute and turn these bad seeds over to the One who owns the garden of your life, who paid for it with His blood, who redeemed it for His glory. Confess these seeds to Him and ask Him to deliver you again and again when these ideas and thoughts might seek to take root in your life.

What are some good seeds that God is sowing in your life right now?

Prayer: Dear Lord, Master Gardener of my life, help me to prepare to be sown for Your glory. Root out all seeds of sin from my life; help me to grow in Your grace, Your idea of love. Help me to be sown beyond all my limitations and expectations.

Week Three—God's Arms of Love

"The eternal God is a dwelling place, and underneath are the everlasting arms." (Deuteronomy 33:27 NASB)

Day One: The Eternal God

Author's Insight: One of the things that most of the characters in this novel wrestle with, in one way or another, is time. Whether it's the past, worries about the future, or making decisions in the present, time influences life. This is true for most of us. We wish we hadn't done something in the past, want something to change in the present, or perhaps have fears or concerns about the future. We live in linear time, but God does not. For God, all of time is an open story, so He understands our lives in the context of a whole, not a part of time. This allows Him, from His eternal perspective, to do what is best for us. God is without ending or beginning. His eternal gaze is graced by power that we cannot comprehend, but He is constantly working things out in our lives for the good, for His glory.

Novel Question: How does time influence Adam's struggles in the story?

_____

_____

_____

What time in your life do you wish you could change?

_____

_____

Pray for one minute, asking God to access the time you listed above and to bring about change related to this time.

What do you fear about the future?

_____

_____

How can you surrender these fears to the eternal God?

_____

_____

Prayer: Eternal God, you know all about me—even before You "knit me together in my mother's womb." You know the choices I have made; You know where I am now and where I will go. Please let me grasp just one moment of Your eternity, one sense of Your power over time.

Day Two: A Dwelling Place

Author's Insight: For Adam and for Joseph, the concept of home is not a pleasant one. For many of us, whether now or in our childhood, it is the same story—home does not or did not mean *security* or *love*. Maybe it was a place of stress, abuse, or neglect. Maybe you close the door on the place where you sleep and wish everything outside that door would disappear. God understands our need for a dwelling place, a true home. God promises that we can find that home in Him and that because of His eternal nature, it is an eternal home—one of endless love, support, and genuine caring. A place to dwell means a place to linger, to stay, to be comfortable in who you are and to know that you are accepted. God offers this dwelling place based on the cross, not on what you do. Deuteronomy 33:27 offers hope that you always have a place to dwell, to abide, to lay your head down in the power and presence of the Living God.

Novel Question: What is home like for Isaac? Why does he have such a deep attachment to animals?

_____

_____

_____

What was your childhood home like?

_____

_____

_____

Do you feel that you have a true dwelling place of peace in your life?

_____

How does this verse give you hope of a dwelling place beyond the earthly walls, past or present, of a house?

_____

_____

_____

Prayer: Dear Eternal God, thank You for loving me, for offering me a dwelling place, a place to live in abundance on this earth, even in the midst of troubles. Help me to spend more time with You, talking to You and discovering the wonders of the dwelling place that You have made for me.

Day Three: The Underneath Part

Author's Insight: For Adam, what lies underneath the functioning of his days is the part of his life that is most important. It gnaws at him, draws him, and confuses him badly. All of us carry "an underneath part" in our lives. We all have secrets, sins, and hurts that form an interior of our lives that we often try to avoid—much like we'd rather see the top of a cliff than be looking up at its precarious underside. Yet there is deep value to what is underneath—God might say that this is where our souls are hidden, where "who we really are" plays out in a day, where the secrets of our hearts beat. God also says that what is underneath Him is His everlasting arms. I love this image—just imagine God's arms underneath all of your hidden self, holding you, surrounding you, loving you. God is more than willing to encompass all of our underneath parts if only we will allow Him to do so.

Novel Question: Lena is very impulsive and young as a character. I wanted her growth to occur at glacier speed—the way our own growth usually happens. How does Lena learn, even to a small degree, that what lies underneath, in both herself and others, is what truly matters?

_____

_____

_____

What lies "underneath" in your own life? What do you not like to talk or think about?

_____

_____

_____

Now consider the underneath supports that gird your life, giving you strength and encouragement. List these.

_____

_____

_____

What role do you allow God to play in your underneath life?

_____

_____

Prayer: Dear Father, Your underneath, what You have for me that is hidden, is that which is good, which supports a dwelling place in You. Help me, in times of trouble, to realize that You have control of what lies underneath and of all that is seen. Be glorified in my life for Your Son's sake.

Day Four: The Everlasting

Author's Insight: It is sad to reach the point where you feel that "nothing lasts forever." Lena must face this in the loss of her mother as she knew her on earth. We often feel like this when we are tired, discouraged, and feel beaten by life. But God speaks of things being "everlasting." His Word is one of these absolutes. His Word, the Bible, does not change, and more than that, His Word promises that "Jesus is the same—yesterday, today, and forever" (see Hebrews 13:8). This can offer us great hope when we feel like "God surely wouldn't understand." Jesus, God, understands. He knows, from both our vantage point and His vantage point as King, who we are in Him. Nothing is impossible for the everlasting God. Allow Him to show you the depth of His power as you walk through these limited days on earth.

Novel Question: What values or things are everlasting in the novel?

_____

_____

_____

What do you believe to be true and everlasting in your own life?

_____

_____

_____

There is a difference between never-ending and everlasting. Sometimes when we are in pain, we think that it will last forever. God promises us something different. What seemingly "never-ending" situation can you surrender to God?

_____

_____

_____

Prayer: Oh Everlasting God, help me, with my limited vision, to trust what You are doing in my life as being for Your glory. If I hurt, help me to see an end to the suffering, an end to my grief, to my pain—in this lifetime. Thank You for who You are and that You are ever mindful of me and Your everlasting plan and purpose for my life.

Day Five: God's Arms

Author's Insight: Perhaps you have had the gift of being held by strong arms. Perhaps you yearn for this now. God's arms are strong—the arms of a king, the arms of a carpenter, the arms that stretched willingly against the wood of a cross for you. Perhaps you feel at times that your arms are asked to handle and carry more than you can manage—like Lena felt following her mother's death. But God promises that He has you in this earthly life, that He "hems you in, before and behind" (see Psalm 139:5). He surrounds you with His arms and gives you the protection of the ultimate warrior. This doesn't mean that you will not have troubles in the world, but God has overcome this world and stretches His arms out to you at this very moment—waiting and willing.

Novel Question: Pick a character who is overwhelmed and then comforted by the unseen but all-powerful arms of God. How does God hold this character close in His arms?

_____

_____

Arms can be defensive or sheltering, bold or gentle, warring or kind. What kinds of arms have you experienced in your own life? Who or what has held you or held you away?

_____

_____

_____

We associate strength with musculature in arms, yet many a thin arm has done mighty a task. It is no easy task, for example, to surrender, to yield. What have you had to yield to in your life with God's blessing?

_____

_____

_____

Make a list of all those whom you long for God to hold in His arms, to feel His strength and protection. Put your name at the top of the list.

_____

_____

_____

Prayer: Dear Lord, I surrender the above names to Your everlasting arms, to Your power and might, to do with as You see fit. Work in these lives, Father, and thank You for the opportunity to be an example of Your loving arms in my own life—with both friends and those who hurt me.

Week Four—Freedom

He has sent me to bind up the brokenhearted, to proclaim . . .
freedom to prisoners. (Isaiah 61:1 NASB)

Day One: Christ Was Sent for You—the Brokenhearted

Author's Insight: *Arms of Love* is not a bright and happy novel; it was never meant to be. It was meant to capture the way that God works through our times of brokenness to bring about amazing transformation and healing potential. Jesus was sent by the Father for this very reason, to help you when you are brokenhearted. And although you may not feel this way now, everyone will experience a broken heart sometime in this earthly life. But the fact that the Father loves so much as to foresee this brokenness and to offer healing should give us pause when we would rather do anything but be broken. Everyone is scared to suffer a broken heart, but it is not the end—only the beginning, or Christ's mission would be incomplete. There is more to come in your life.

Novel Question: Name the brokenhearted in this story.

_____

_____

_____

What (or who) has broken your heart? Or what do you feel will break it?

_____

_____

_____

Imagine talking with Jesus personally. Ask Him about the brokenness or fears listed above. How does He respond to you?

_____

_____

_____

If you could not think of what He would say, read the Psalms for three minutes—any of them that you like. Do you find any mention of brokenness in God's Word?

_____

_____

_____

What have you learned from being brokenhearted that you would not have learned any other way?

_____

_____

_____

Prayer: Dear Lord, thank You for this brokenness in my life, because I know You have planned for my healing. Thank You for what You are doing through these times. Help me to release all fear, worry, grief, and anger to You and to know that this brokenness will draw me closer to You if I allow it.

Day Two: The "Binding Up" Process

Author's Insight: I have often said that "God is the best surgeon; He just sometimes chooses to operate without anesthesia." It's a quote that gets me through the rough times in life, and sometimes, repairing a wound and binding it up hurts more than the original wound itself. To a large extent, this is what PTSD is all about. People "make it through a trauma" but then have to deal with the harsh reality of it later in life. It seems unfair to have to continually relive a suffering, or to have something haunt you again and again. But God has a solution in Christ "to bind up the brokenhearted."

Novel Question: How does this story work to explain that being healed and transformed is not always an easy or painless process?

_____

_____

_____

"Binding up" is a relatively old-time expression when it comes to medicine. It involves things like resetting bones, closing wounds, and enduring the process—all without the benefit of modern-day painkillers. When have you felt pain in the healing process, either physically, spiritually, or emotionally?

_____

_____

_____

Now consider Christ as the One who is wrapping the wound in your life. How can concentrating on His nail-scarred hands lessen some of the pain of the process?

_____

_____

_____

What needs "binding up" in your life—healing by the One who was sent for just such a purpose?

_____

_____

_____

Prayer: Dear Jesus, You know what it is to be wounded, to suffer. You loved me enough to come for such a time as this, to bind up my broken heart. Help me to surrender this time and pain to Your loving hands and to trust that all You do is for good as You work and bind.

Day Three: The King's Proclamation

Author's Insight: Part of the backdrop to *Arms of Love* is the war and a very distant king. This king made proclamations that were unfair, taxation in particular. However, Jesus, who will come again as King, says that He makes a proclamation written in eternity, one that is more than fair, more than hope, and more than we can ever hope to understand. His proclamation is one of personal freedom, bought and paid for at His cost. There is no price or tax involved here—He offers freedom and eternal life with Him as a gift. This proclamation, like that of an earthly king, is meant to resonate throughout the land, but unlike an earthly king's statement, Christ's proclamation resonates throughout eternity. His is an everlasting gospel, good news, of peace. Have you heard what the King has to say?

Novel Question: What does God proclaim to the characters throughout this story?

_____

_____

_____

What have you heard God proclaim in your own life?

_____

_____

_____

What do you long to hear Him proclaim?

_____

_____

_____

How can you proclaim, or tell others, even without words, about the good news of Jesus Christ?

_____

_____

Prayer: Dear Lord, make a proclamation in my life that rings so loud and clear that I cannot help but hear it and understand. Proclaim Your freedom, Your justice, Your eternalness through my days and even in what I do not say or do not understand.

Day Four: To Be a Prisoner

Author's Insight: Many things hold the characters in this novel captive; I wrote it this way to model our own lives. Whether it be financial, emotional, social, or something else, we are all prisoners to something. Sometimes it's even in loving too much so that we do not allow God room to work—like with Samuel Yoder. But Christ wants us to be held captive by no one or nothing. He understands the degrading conditions, the negative self-talk, the abject loneliness of being a prisoner. He knows the power of sin because He was the One to overcome it. The enemy would deeply like us to remain prisoners all our days on this earth, never knowing or understanding freedom in Christ. The movie *Braveheart* sums it all up in one great quote—"Every man dies, but not every man truly lives." We don't live an abundant life because we are prisoners, but there is a Way out . . .

Novel Question: Which character's personal "prison" bothered you the most and why?

_____

_____

Jesus commands us to minister to those in prison. Do you know where your local jail is? What is your attitude about those imprisoned there?

_____

_____

_____

What holds you prisoner, even in a small way?

_____

_____

Practice saying to yourself, "I am free in Christ in this situation."

Prayer: Dear King Jesus, You promise freedom. Let me feel it. Teach me to walk in Your ways of freedom, to not listen to gossip or lies, to not give in to anger or hate. Help me not to be a prisoner any longer to habits or to thoughts or actions, because You have set me free.

Day Five: True Freedom

Author's Insight: Each of the characters in the book gets a small taste of true freedom—that freedom found in God. I wanted Adam to struggle on a lot of fronts about being free—his promise, the war, his passion, his love—because we all struggle to have true freedom. God wants us to know that true freedom comes with accountability and wisdom, responsibility and trust—as a gift through His Son. It is not a political freedom or one framed by earthly hands, but rather a freedom won by the nail-scarred hands of the cross. These hands know that true freedom comes at a cost that you never could have paid alone—that's why He did it for you.

Novel Question: When does Adam experience true freedom in the story? Why?

_____

In what ways do you long to be free in your own life?

_____

Remembering that "all things are possible through Christ," how can you gain more freedom in the areas listed above?

_____

What freedom do you sometimes take for granted or neglect?

_____

When have you experienced the knowledge of true freedom?

_____

Prayer: Dear Lord, You are the source of true freedom. You give and You take away, but You are good. Thank You in advance for the ways that You will work in my life to bring me true freedom. Thank You for the cross.